MW01123966

Santa Claus Is Dead

A novel by Jason Twede

Text copyright © 2006 by Jason Twede
Illustrations copyright © 2006 by Missy Ames
Cover design by Benjamin Midget
All rights reserved.

No part of this publication may be reproduced, stored in a re-
trieval system, or transmitted in any form or by any means, electronic, mechanical, photocopying, recording, or otherwise without
written permission.

Summary: A detective and penguin solve the murder of Santa
Claus and save a young girl falsely accused of the crime

for Brennan

Santa Claus
Is Dead

Dear Santa,

Last Christmas I asked for only one thing. I wanted my sister Jenny to get better so she could play with me again. Jenny didn't get better. What I got instead was a doll. Jenny died last month from cancer.

Please do not send me anything this year. All I want is my sister back, and it doesn't look like you can give me that.

Susie Thompson

DECEMBER 22

Chapter One

Susie Thompson stared at the ceiling. Her eyes were red, the skin around them rubbed raw. Spending the night at Santa's house had not been what she had hoped for.

The house had been what she expected: gingerbread walls, a roof covered with snow like frosting, kitschy ornaments hanging from every plant within a two-mile radius. Every room seemed to have a fireplace, and every fireplace was always lit.

A nice fire hazard, Susie thought. Officer Barnes, who did safety presentations in Susie's school back in Colorado, would never have approved.

"I don't approve either," Susie said. Nobody was around to hear.

She sat up in her bed and looked out the window. A faint glow appeared on the horizon, drifting horizontally past the fir trees in Santa's backyard.

Maybe that meant it was morning. It was hard to tell—the sun never rose during the North Pole winter. Except the reddish glow that barely rose above the distant mountains and circled the horizon, the sky was always dark, the stars always shone, and the moonlight always glimmered off the snow.

While the house had been as expected, Santa had definitely not. Nor had his wife. The cookies Mrs. Claus had brought to Susie several hours ago still sat on the nightstand, and the cup of milk still lay on the floor where Susie had knocked it over after Mrs. Claus had left the room. The milk had long since dried, and the carpet was crusty.

How could Santa marry a woman like that?

Susie knew the answer already. She could still see Mrs. Claus in her tight, red, satin nightgown bringing in milk and cookies to her room. Susie had blushed when Mrs. Claus had bent over to set them down on the nightstand. It was obvious why Santa had married her. Susie had watched enough television to know that rich and powerful men always either had a girl like Mrs. Claus or wanted one.

Who would have thought that Santa would be such a fat, greedy prat—a pathetic old man getting his kicks with a girl half his age; a self-indulgent capitalist manipulating his way to wealth, wealth, and more wealth?

Susie had once believed in Santa. It was just over a year ago that she had written her first letter to him—a desperate plea for him to somehow make her sister better. But the cancer had killed Jenny anyway.

Even after everything else that had happened in the year since—her family's bankruptcy, moving to a new school, her parents' impending divorce—she still had hope after Santa answered her second letter and invited her to visit him at the North Pole. He wanted to change Christmas, he had written. The world had changed and its children needed something different than hoards of toys. He asked Susie to come and help him make the change, to use her memories of her sister to make things better, to find a way to prevent other children from suffering as much as Susie and her sister had.

Now Susie wished she had never come. Santa's words at the Village Council meeting the day before kept echoing in her mind. *Think of the untapped wealth that would come to the North Pole if we simply redirect our efforts into the health and human services field,* Santa had said. *Think of the wealth.*

Susie pressed a hand to her forehead. *How dare he? How dare he use her sister!*

It would have been better to find out that Santa did not exist. To discover that the dream was just a dream would have been better than to discover that the dream was a lie.

Suddenly, a blaring siren screamed from the yard outside. Red and blue lights swirled in the trees and snow outside and on the walls and ceiling inside Susie's room. Voices and yelling interrupted the silence. The front door to the estate opened. Footsteps pounded through the halls.

Susie's bedroom door burst open. Shattered gingerbread ricocheted off the walls and on her face. Men in dark green uniforms ran into her room, grabbing and yanking her head back with a pull of her hair. She kicked and swung her arms at them.

"What are you doing?" she screamed.

The uniformed men grabbed her nightgown and dragged her out of bed. Before she even reached the floor, she was pulled to her feet and led out the bedroom door. The man holding her upper arm squeezed it as he pushed her through the other uniformed men. Her hair caught on something.

Susie cried out again: "What are you doing? Why are you hurting me?"

She stumbled down the stairs, but the tight grip on her arm yanked her back to her feet.

Mrs. Claus stood at the bottom of the stairs behind several other men, also wearing dark green uniforms. Her blonde hair bounced on her satin-clad shoulders. Her eyes were wide, her mouth was tense, and her entire body was shaking. An officer pulled a chair to her and helped her sit down. She would not look at him.

Susie yelled at her, asked her to do something, but Mrs. Claus just sat there, shaking yet frozen. Her hand rose to her lips.

The men shoved Susie out the front door and an icy wind blasted into her face. Her body started shaking, too. Tiny specks of ice and snow pelted against her. She stumbled again after stepping on a patch of ice on the front porch.

"What are you doing to me?" Susie yelled again. "What's going on?"

The officers ignored her and shoved her toward a police car. She dug her bare feet into the snow and gravel. The officers dragged her, and the gravel dug into her feet.

A man picked Susie up while two others held her arms and feet in place. A car door was opened, and Susie was shoved inside. She kicked out a foot and held the car door open.

"Tell me what is going on, right now," Susie said.

"You're under arrest," an officer replied. Another grabbed her foot and pushed it back in the car.

"For what?" Susie asked.

"For murder."

The door slammed shut.

CHAPTER TWO

JOHNNY ICEBERG, 22-year veteran detective with the North Pole Police Department, shouldered his way through the crowd pushing against the barricade tape. His trench coat snagged on several cameras, and his feet kept getting tangled in power cables. Flashbulbs flickered left and right. His eyes, used to the winter's perpetual night, squinted. *I wish it was summer*, he thought.

He broke through a mass of elvish cameramen and polar bears stringing microphone cables back and forth. Just ahead, a circle of people, elves, animals, and even a couple of snowmen stared at the ground in front of them. Most had taken off their hats, and two others had dropped their cameras in the snow. Johnny peered through the crowd and his fears were confirmed. He ran his hands back through his slightly graying hair and blew out a long breath. There, in the middle of the crowd, was a large man in a red suit face down in the snow.

A penguin wearing a trench coat and a black brimmed hat waddled up from behind a clutch of trees.

"This is bad, Johnny," the penguin said. "This is really bad."

"Why are these reporters screwing with a crime scene, Paul?" Johnny asked the penguin.

"This media circus is the least of our problems right now," Paul said.

"What's the situation?"

"Hard to tell the details, but the reports are correct. Santa Claus is dead."

Johnny bunched up his mouth. "Get these people out of here," he told Paul.

Paul turned to the crowd. "Everyone, move out," he said. Nobody did anything. Paul gritted his bill, muttered something about respect and penguins and preferential treatment for those over three feet tall, and waddled up to the nearest reporter team. He grabbed a camera, one of the big ones that could only be carried by snowmen, walruses, and polar bears, threw it into the snow, and climbed on top of it. He held his flippers to his mouth and made an impromptu megaphone out of them.

"Whatever you're doing, stop it right now, turn around, and listen to the penguin!" Paul shouted.

The entire crowd silenced. One of the photographers, an elf propped up on snowshoed stilts to get above the crowd, got tangled up with a seal and fell to the ground. A snowman standing nearby laughed. The elf jumped to his feet and started accusing the snowman of pushing him. The animosity between elves and snowmen was well known. A few of the elf's coworkers, both human, had to calm him down and pull him away.

"This is a crime scene," Paul said. "I need everyone out of here and behind the yellow tape, *now!*"

An arctic fox interviewing a couple of elves shook her head, but trudged back toward her car anyway. Her human cameraman picked up the equipment and followed. A team of huskies pulled the snack sled back behind the yellow tape, and most of the media followed. A few did not budge.

Paul waddled up to a human, craned his head upward, and looked the man in the face.

"Get out," Paul said.

"I don't listen to anyone whose face can't even reach my butt," the man, a rookie reporter for channel 17, said.

"Yeah, bug off shorty!" another man, a photographer for *The*

Northern Lights, said. "Who do you think you are, anyway?"

Paul grabbed the nearest branch, broke it from the evergreen tree, and swung it at both men's knees. The first limped away, but the second just flinched while holding his ground. Paul grabbed the photographer's ear, yanked him down to his knees, and shoved his badge into the man's face. The letters NPPD stood out prominently on his shield-shaped badge.

"North Pole Police Department, that's who I am!" Paul said. "You wanna take this downtown?"

Johnny walked over, knelt down, and looked the rookie reporter in the eye.

"Rule number one when dealing with the cops," Johnny said.

"Don't mess with the penguin," a polar bear finished the phrase from behind Johnny's back.

The reporter struggled back to his feet and trudged away. The photographer looked menacingly at Paul as he stood. Paul took a quick step towards the man as though he were going to tackle him. The man's eyes opened wide in fright as he tripped over himself and fell back in the snow.

"Morning, Steve," Johnny said to the polar bear, who was wearing a sweater that highlighted the latest tour of Tainted Nog, a local rock band. "I'll give you an exclusive a couple hours before we do a press conference."

"You better, Johnny," Steve smiled, his white canines glistening in the moonlight. "You still owe me for the fruitcake fiasco." Steve started lumbering away.

"Hey, Steve," Johnny called out. "What's with the sweater? You're not cold, are you?"

Steve rolled his eyes. "No. Some human just got put into upper management. He decided that *animal nudity conflicts with the traditional values our viewers hold dear*."

"Management," Johnny said. He shook his head.

"No kidding," Steve said. He continued on his way.

Johnny ran a hand through his hair and turned back to Paul.

"You didn't have to assault them," Johnny said.

"It got the job done," Paul said. "I don't have time to negotiate with rumor-spreading half-wits."

Johnny looked around. *Man, I wish I were home*, he thought while knowing it was not true. *What would I do at home, anyway?* The place had been lonely the past nine years. He wondered what his daughter was doing right then. Last he had heard she was in Europe somewhere.

Johnny broke himself from his reverie. The scene was barren except for the trees, the snow, and the body. Behind a hill, the red glow from the never-rising winter sun inched across the horizon.

"It's kind of peaceful," Johnny said.

"Except for the dead guy," Paul said. "A pretty significant dead guy."

"I don't think I've ever been out here before," Johnny said. "Not in the winter, anyway."

Johnny walked up to the body, behind a large snowdrift littered with dozens of tracks meandering all over. Ice and snow, stirred up by the wind, was scattered across Santa's red coat. Johnny pulled off his glove and winced as his bare hand felt the chill air. He pulled a latex glove on in its place. He searched though the coat. There was a small spot of blood but no open wounds. One leg looked twisted backwards.

"Any idea what killed him?" Johnny asked.

"No," said Paul. "There's nothing obvious. We'll have to wait for the autopsy report."

"Who's doing it?" Johnny asked. "It had better not be that elf at North Polar Regional that did it on the Murdock case."

"Masterson's having our lab do it."

"What?" Johnny asked.

"I don't get it either," Paul said. "Maybe you can call Sara in a few hours and ask her why he's having her do it. It'll give you a reason to talk to her."

Johnny glared at Paul.

"Thanks, Johnny," Paul said as he chuckled smugly. "I needed a good laugh."

Johnny scowled. His social life was nonexistent—he spent most evenings watching reruns of *Northern Exposure* or *The Adventures of*

Yukon Joe. Even though he had developed a friendship with Sara Albright, a lab technician at NPPD, and sometimes wanted it to become something more, he had never had the resolve to pursue it. He found it rather annoying that Paul knew all of this.

"How about we focus on what we're supposed to be doing?" Johnny said.

"Fine," Paul said. "It's just hard to believe that—" Paul looked over at Santa's body. A rush of dejection stopped him mid-sentence. He shook his head and changed the subject. "So how'd you manage to land this case, Johnny?"

"Masterson likes having a good reputation among the officers," Johnny said, "and we all know that's going to be the first thing to disappear the minute he tries to actually solve something himself."

"So he puts someone on the case with a reputation in the toilet?" Paul said.

"It makes the public happy," Johnny replied.

Paul smiled. Nine years ago the North Pole had experienced its first murder. Johnny Iceberg had solved the case, albeit by somewhat suspect means. Since then, Johnny had become more well-known at the NPPD for his tendency to break rules—including a rather notorious incident in which Johnny deliberately ran a snowmobile into a polar bear suspected of drunk driving.

But the public's memory of the North Pole's only murder investigation was long, and Johnny was still the most celebrated officer at the NPPD. Even though Police Chief Masterson and the rest of the department had no respect for Johnny, the public would demand that Johnny be put on the case anyway.

Johnny scratched his nose. It was starting to freeze up.

"Santa's body isn't going to tell us anything for a while," Johnny said. "What *have* we found out?"

"I've got the reports from the first officers on the scene," Paul waved a pink notepad in the air.

"Go for it," Johnny said.

"You're not going to like it," Paul said.

"Why not?"

"The same reason I don't like it," Paul said. "Looks like some elf

15

found the body about three hours ago—at four or four-thirty—said there was one set of tracks that led to Santa's body. Nothing else."

Johnny stooped down among the dozens of footprints littered through the snow and flicked the dirt and pine needles out of a few tracks.

"I know," Paul said. "The whole scene's jacked up. Nobody thought about investigating the tracks till after everybody stomped through the scene. We don't even know if they were human or elvish or anything."

Johnny stood up and turned back to Paul. "Did anyone bring the donuts, yet?" he asked.

Paul threw the notepad into the snow. "Are you even listening to me?"

"I want a donut. Where are they?"

Paul threw a pencil into the snow near the notepad. He nodded toward several uniformed officers standing near one of the police cars. As Johnny approached, one of the officers held a brown box in his hand while the rest munched on the donuts. Johnny looked in the box, fingered several donuts, and scowled as the other officers looked at him curiously.

"Where's the blueberry?" Johnny asked.

"Sorry, Iceberg," one of the officers said. "The early cop gets the blueberry donut. Maybe if you had showed up on time you would have gotten one. Have a chocolate."

Johnny stared at the officer and smacked the box out of his hand. The donuts tumbled to the ground, raspberry jelly and vanilla pudding oozing into the snow. Johnny took his foot and systematically ground each donut into a slushy glop.

"What's wrong with you, Iceberg?" an officer asked. "You're stepping on the donuts!"

Johnny took the donut from the officer's mouth and threw it toward the body and the mess of footprints surrounding it.

"So now you're watching where people step?" Johnny demanded. "Why couldn't you have done that three hours ago! Now we've lost the only clue we have to Santa's killer!"

"Since when did you start caring about protocol, Iceberg?"

"Like that polar bear you 'accidentally' ran over?"

Johnny stepped into the officer's face. "I do whatever I feel like as long as I bring down the bad guys."

"And we can't?"

"You tell me how letting everyone destroy a crime scene helps you catch the bad guy, Jones, and I'll let you shove your gut with donuts to your heart's content."

The officer frowned at Johnny.

"I'm not Jones—he is," the officer pointed to the one next to him.

Johnny took a step toward him and moved within an inch of the officer's face. Johnny scowled. He looked at the officer standing just to the side, the one who was apparently Jones.

"I can't tell any of you apart," Johnny said.

"I'm an elf, and Jones is a walrus!" the officer said.

Johnny looked back and forth between them again.

"You're wearing the same hat," Johnny said.

The walrus's whiskers started quivering, his eyes narrowed, and he started scooting toward Johnny menacingly. The elvish officer shook his head and said something about one-shot wonders. Johnny grabbed the collar of the walrus's uniform and pulled the whiskered nose up to his.

"Get out of here, all of you," Johnny said. "You've already screwed up my investigation enough."

Paul, who had come up from behind, started pulling Johnny away from the walrus. Johnny yanked himself free of Paul's flippers, kicked one last donut, and walked with Paul back toward the body.

"You're going to pay for those donuts," an officer called after them. "And I don't go back to work until I get one."

A gust of wind rose from beyond the forest. Johnny pulled his hood around his head and shivered. A forensics team had just arrived and was prepping the body for transportation. Paul shouted some orders to the team, but Johnny did not bother listening.

"What was that all about?" Paul asked, referring to Johnny's scuffle over the donuts.

"They screwed up the crime scene," Johnny said.

"You know, everything would be a lot easier if you tried to work with people instead of throwing a fit," Paul said. He was holding the notepad and pencil again. "They might actually want to help us out if you did."

"Right. Just like you worked with the media two seconds ago?" Johnny said.

"There's a difference," Paul said. "Officers can help us. Reporters just get in our way and start riots."

"You watch too many movies," Johnny said. "There are plenty of reporters that'll help you out if you help them. Those two you assaulted might have something you want in the future, and now they're not going to give it to you."

"I got a call from Masterson," Paul said, changing the subject, "while you were busy smashing donuts."

"I don't care about Masterson," Johnny said. "I want to talk to this elf they found on the scene. Where is he?"

"He's not here. Jones let him go after getting a statement."

Johnny froze. After a moment, he shrugged and shook his head. Paul was talking again, but Johnny didn't want to hear it. He trudged away from his partner, feeling disgusted with the entire morning.

"I guess it makes sense," he said to himself. "If you're going to screw up the crime scene you might as well dismiss the only witness, too."

Paul struggled through the snow until he reached Johnny.

"Johnny, I said I got a call from Masterson," Paul said again.

"I heard you the first time."

"He ordered them to let the elf go. He said that we've already got someone in custody for the murder."

"Based on what?" Johnny asked. "We don't have evidence against anyone yet. Who authorized the arrest?"

"Masterson."

"Wait just one minute," Johnny said curtly. "Masterson assigned me to the case. Why would he do that if he's already arrested somebody?"

"I don't know."

"Who's the suspect?"

"Will you quit yelling at me?" Paul demanded. "I don't know that either. All Masterson told me is to wrap up our investigation here, and that we won't be allowed access to the suspect."

Johnny yanked the notepad from Paul and started flipping through the information. There was writing on only two pages—and it was just as Paul had described earlier. The elf's name had been written down at least: Mitchell. Employee in Santa's Workshop—Wheeled Toys Division.

"You want to go find the elf?" Paul asked.

"Why would we do that if there's already a suspect in custody," Johnny said sarcastically. "If Masterson says they have the killer, then I'm *sure* they have the right guy." Johnny's voice became serious again: "Of course I want to talk to the elf."

"I hate to break it to you," Paul said, "but I'm afraid we're just clean-up on this one. They just want us to take statements and build a case against this guy they already have in custody, and if that's our assignment, then so be it."

Paul was probably right, and that made Johnny even angrier. It would be just like Masterson to put Johnny just close enough to the action to get him excited and then not let him do a thing.

"Fine," Johnny said. "We'll go back to the station and only go find this elf if something comes up. I have some things to take care of, anyway."

"Like what?" Paul asked skeptically.

"Sure you want me to tell you?" Johnny said. "I'd hate you to be liable for what I do."

Paul shook his head. "If you want to disobey a direct order from the police chief, then that's your choice. This better not come back and bite me in the butt."

Paul waddled back toward the media and the other officers. Before following, Johnny took one last look at the body. He wondered if he should be feeling anything. He had believed in Santa once. He should probably feel something.

Johnny shrugged and pulled his coat around himself more tightly. Maybe he had seen too much over the past twenty-two years: the political games played by Santa, the Mayor of the North Pole, and the Village Council; Santa's remarriage; the pollution spewing from the toy factories.

I wonder what will happen to Christmas this year, Johnny thought. Santa never had any children. He supposed the responsibilities of running Christmas would be turned over to Mrs. Claus. Johnny laughed at that. The idea of Mrs. Claus taking over Christmas was going to go over with people like a lead balloon. It was not that she was a woman. It was more that she was *a woman*.

For once, Johnny was glad he didn't have any children to worry about. His daughter had grown out of the Santa thing a long time ago—at least Johnny assumed she had. He had not talked to her since she had left nine years ago.

A sudden gale whipped specks of ice into Johnny's face. He closed his eyes and walked back toward the car.

CHAPTER THREE

JOHNNY STOOD by the door to holding room four. A sign, taped to the door, reminded potential suspects not to worry because "*Christmas at the North Pole Penitentiary is celebrated with a home-made turkey dinner for all inmates, as well a slice of pecan pie person-ally baked by Mrs. Claus*" and that Christmas presents "*are carefully rewrapped after being searched.*" Johnny looked up and down the hall. Seeing nobody else around, he opened the door and walked into the room.

Sitting at a table in the middle of the room was a girl in a drab, blue jumpsuit. Her sandy blonde hair was pulled back into a pony-tail. She scowled at Johnny as he entered. Johnny paused mid-stride and stared at her, a puzzled look on his face. He quietly shut the door behind him. He walked to the security camera, unplugged it, and sat down across from the girl.

"Good morning," Johnny said.

The girl did not move. Her hands were cuffed and her feet were shackled.

"You're the one who was arrested at Santa's house this morn-ing?" Johnny asked.

"Just so you know, I think you cops up here at the North Pole are a bunch of idiots and I'm not telling you anything, and you might as well leave and save yourself the trouble of asking me questions because I'm not going to answer them and—just leave me alone," the girl said.

"Nice to meet you, too," Johnny said. "My name's Iceberg. Johnny Iceberg. I'm a detective and I'm leading the investigation that got you arrested."

Susie glared at him.

"Did anyone tell you why you were arrested?"

"They said I killed somebody."

"Did they say who?"

"I thought you were in charge," the girl said.

Nobody has told her anything, Johnny realized. Susie brushed a hair away from her face awkwardly. Her cuffs had a couple of Christmas tree stickers on them. Apparently they made somebody feel better about arresting a little girl.

"Can you tell me," Johnny said cautiously, "why anyone would suspect that you murdered Santa Claus?"

Susie's eyes widened at the question. Her face became pale, her hands started shaking, and she slowly shook her head.

"Santa Claus?" Susie whispered.

Johnny nodded. "His body was found in the forest at about four in the morning."

Susie took a deep breath. Her face relaxed and her eyes became fierce again.

"Why don't you tell me why you think I did it," she said sarcastically.

"Look," Johnny said. "I *don't* think you did it. I haven't seen one scrap of evidence that says you did. As far as I'm concerned, whoever arrested you doesn't have a clue about what he is doing. I mean who arrests a ten-year-old girl for killing Santa Claus?"

"I'm eleven," the girl said. "Almost twelve."

"Like I said, you're a little girl—"

"I am *not* a little girl."

"What's your name?" Johnny pried. "Where are you from?"

"Why? Don't you know already? Are you sure you're in charge here?"

"I thought I was," Johnny said, "but somebody's been doing a fine job of screwing things up behind my back."

"Sounds like your problem, not mine."

"*Santa's beard!*" Johnny swore. "Are you always this difficult, or only with people who are trying to help you?"

The girl glared at Johnny. "My name is Susie Thompson, from the United States. And I don't appreciate you swearing."

"What, do they teach North Pole slang in the United States now? How did you know I swore?"

"It was obvious."

This girl's a smart cookie, Johnny thought. She reminded Johnny of his daughter, only his daughter wasn't eleven anymore. She may have been when she and her mother had left nine years ago. Johnny wasn't sure. *Oh quit thinking about it*, Johnny chided himself. Christmastime always made him depressed.

Johnny shook his head and looked at Susie. She was looking at him funny.

"Susie," Johnny said, glad that he was able to at least get her name out of her. "I don't think you killed Santa Claus," he told her again.

"You don't?" Susie seemed surprised.

"No, I don't. But obviously somebody does, or else you wouldn't be in here. I want to help you get out of here, but in order to do that I need you to help me. Now, let me ask you again. Can you tell me why someone would suspect you of murdering Santa Claus?"

Susie looked away from Johnny and toward one of the walls. A poster with Santa wearing Bermuda shorts and playing a ukulele was taped to the wall. Susie bit her bottom lip and turned to look at Johnny again. After a long pause, she spoke.

"I don't know. They–they didn't tell me anything. They just threw me in the car and told me I was being arrested for murder and drove here and made me change into these clothes and put handcuffs on me and brought me here and shoved me in the chair and left me here."

"Has anyone come to question you yet?" Johnny asked.

Susie shook her head.

"Have they appointed you an attorney?"

Susie shook her head again. *So much for due process,* Johnny thought.

"Look, Susie, I know it must be hard for a little gi—" Johnny caught himself as he saw Susie's eyes narrow, "for you, being locked in here without knowing why, but let's be honest here. You were in Santa's house. I know you're going to tell me that doesn't matter, and I'm inclined to believe that, but to a lot of people, that's going to look suspicious. How about you start by telling me what you were doing there."

Susie said nothing and stared at Johnny, biting her lip again. Finally, she nodded.

Santa Claus had invited Susie to the North Pole from her home in the United States. After he had given her the grand tour of the North Pole, he brought her to a meeting with the North Pole Village Council in which Santa proposed to change Christmas. He wanted to shut down the toy factories and start cancer research institutions, charitable foundations, and non-profit welfare programs that would operate in countries throughout the world. Susie was delighted. The Village Council, however, did not like the proposal. The mayor started talking about civil unrest and how people don't like change, and all the elves' representative seemed to think about was how many elves would lose their jobs if the factories closed. The other two on the council, the snowman and the reindeer, didn't say anything.

"And then Santa changed everything he was saying," Susie said. "He started talking about how much more money his plan would bring to the North Pole—even more than the *'gross national product of the United States'*. I couldn't believe it. All he wanted was more money and he was using me and my sister to get it. He didn't care about curing diseases and helping poor people! He only cared about helping himself. I guess he's just as greedy as everyone else on that stupid council. Have you seen his house? Have you seen his wife?"

Everyone at the North Pole had seen Santa's house. It sat on a hill on the far end of town, where everyone in town could see the giant gingerbread walls coated with gumdrops and licorice. And it would have been impossible not to have seen Mrs. Claus after all the front-page features in the tabloids during the months preceding the wedding two years ago.

Johnny thought about what Susie had said about Santa wanting to change Christmas. If that were true, the list of people who would want to kill Santa would be endless. All the elves would be displaced from their jobs at the toy factory. The economy would take a definite dip, and that always spelled disaster for those in politics.

Johnny could not help but think about the members of the Village Council. There was Morgan, the President of the Elvish Labor Union, whose abrasive personality had caused several well-publicized tense negotiating sessions between him and Santa.

There was Frosty, who would not have any particular problem with Santa other than the fact that Christmas had displaced the snowmen, the indigenous people of the North Pole, from their native lands.

The animals, who were semi-indigenous to the North Pole, were notoriously peaceful folk, easy for everyone to get along with, which always made Johnny wonder why Paul was so difficult. Dasher, the animals' representative on the Village Council, would have no apparent reason to harm Santa, especially considering he was on of the most respected members of Santa's reindeer team.

Finally, there was Mayor Georg Wassail. His election as Mayor had always been suspect. Rumors of bribery and election fraud still plagued him—as did rumors of the infamous Three-Antler Squeeze, a controversial play that won the Romping Reindeer the North Pole Hockey Championship five years ago, a team of which Mayor Wassail was part owner. But Mayor Wassail's tongue was every bit as sweet as he was not, and he quite deftly talked his way out of that controversy. In fact, he had even talked his way into reelection three years ago. It was public knowledge that Mayor Wassail hated Santa Claus. Santa was Head Claus, the political figurehead of the North Pole and equivalent to the Queen of England. Mayor Wassail despised the fact that Santa was in power as a monarch and did not have to worry about elections and public sentiment.

Susie had just armed Johnny with several valuable pieces of information. "Thank you, Susie," Johnny said. He stood up. "You have helped me a lot."

"You still don't think I did it?" Susie asked.

"No. But now I know why a whole lot of other people may have wanted to," Johnny walked to the door and stopped. He turned around. "So why did Santa invite you up instead of some other kid?"

Susie was about to say something pointed when Paul opened the door behind Johnny.

"Johnny, you've got to get out—" Paul stopped when he saw Susie. "Never mind. I thought you were with the suspect. Who's the little girl?"

"She *is* the suspect," Johnny said before Susie could yell at Paul for calling her little.

Paul looked dumbfounded. It took him a moment before he could speak.

"Then you need to get out of here," Paul said. "They're coming to transfer her to the Diamond Maker."

"The what?" Susie asked.

"The North Pole Penitentiary," Johnny explained.

Due to the recent success of a group of community activist sea lions, the Village Council had adopted a resolution to change the focus of the penitentiary to rehabilitation. In truth, little had changed in its operations. Whenever people asked how the new rehabilitation plan was helping the inmates, they were told that by the time they were done, the amount of pressure exerted on the inmates would make diamonds out of all the coal Santa had given them over the years.

"One minute," Johnny told Paul. "Just go back to the main office and clean out your files or something."

Paul shook his head and left before he got in trouble, too.

Johnny turned to Susie. "Do you have an alibi?"

"A what?"

"Santa probably died sometime between midnight and four this morning. Is there anyone who can give us proof that you were somewhere else during that time?"

"Mrs. Claus. She brought some milk and cookies to my room last night, trying to act like she was nice and that she cared about me."

"Good," Johnny opened the door and looked out into the hallway.

"So are you going to help me?" Susie asked.

"Do you promise that you didn't kill Santa Claus?"

"Are you deaf?" Susie asked. "What do you think I've been saying the past five minutes?"

"I know what you said," Johnny looked her in the eye. "But do you promise?"

"Yes. I promise. He was a fake, and I couldn't stand him, and I'm not really sad that he's dead, but I never killed anyone. I've never hurt anyone."

"I'll get you out, then," Johnny said. "I promise."

Johnny stepped out of the room and closed the door. The hall was still empty. He quickly walked away from the holding room and back to the main office. Just as he reached it, he remembered. *I didn't hook the security camera back up.* Johnny grimaced. Although there wouldn't be any evidence pinning it specifically on Johnny, Masterson would know that *someone* had been in the holding room against his wishes.

The office was filled with desks, officers of all kind, and seven giant plastic Christmas trees—each one a different color. The orange tree was made out of neon lights. The officer nearest to it, a moose wearing a green Santa hat that clashed badly with his uniform, was squinting while reading over some paperwork.

In the far corner, right next to Johnny's desk, Paul sat in his. He was shoving a stack of papers back onto the pile of trash on Johnny's desk. Johnny walked over and sat down. After a moment of silence, Paul spoke.

"That girl is seriously the suspect?" Paul whispered.

"Ridiculous, isn't it? Santa invited her up here from the U.S. The next thing she knows, she's being dragged away in handcuffs."

"Did she do it?"

"Paul—she's eleven!"

"So? You said she was from the States. We've all heard about kids down there taking guns to school and going on rampages. So she's an eleven-year-old girl, but—"

"She promised that she didn't do it."

"So does everybody that gets pulled in here."

"She's a kid. Promises still mean something to her."

"If you think that, it's been way too long since you've dealt with a kid."

Johnny looked away without responding.

"How about we follow up on that elf?" Paul said.

Johnny raised his eyebrows. "I thought you wanted to do clean-up work for Masterson, since they already have a suspect."

"Look at it this way," Paul said. "If this girl really did it, then talking to the elf will back up her arrest. That will make Masterson happy. If you're right, and she didn't do it, then talking to the elf will help us find the right suspect. That will make you happy. Either way, we've got to talk to this elf."

Johnny nodded his head. He found it no coincidence that it had been an elf who had found Santa's body when the elves also would be the hardest hit by Santa's proposed Christmas change.

"We'll check out the elf right after I talk to Masterson," Johnny said.

"Wait," Paul said. "Talk to Masterson about what?"

The conversation was interrupted by two officers, both elves, escorting Susie through the office in shackles. Nobody in the office said anything, but everyone watched her walk to the front door.

"Nice work guys," Johnny said loudly. Everyone turned and looked at him. "What did you arrest her for, mistaking all of you for lawn ornaments?"

Most officers ignored Johnny and went back to their work. Someone let out a sarcastic *ooh, nice one Johnny*. One elf looked like he wanted to say something back but did not. Johnny caught Susie's eye through the chaos of paper work and Christmas decorations and nodded to her. She nodded back, a curious look on her face, and walked out the door.

"So, what did you want to talk to Masterson about?" Paul

asked.

"He's got to let Susie out," Johnny said. "The whole thing is crazy. You saw how wrong that looked, a little girl being treated like a felon. As soon as the media hears about this, it's going to look really bad," Johnny paused. "And I promised her I would get her out."

"Hold on there, Johnny," Paul said, grabbing Johnny's arm to stop him. "I agree that the idea of an eleven-year-old girl killing Santa is odd, and I agree that she needs to be let go if she's innocent, but going to Masterson is not what we need to do right now. He didn't like you when you were his partner and he likes you even less now—"

"It's not my fault that we didn't get along as partners," Johnny cut in. "I was paid to show him how to be a good cop. If he wants to blame me because he missed that lesson, that's his problem."

"Your personal quarrel aside," Paul said, annoyed at having to hear this tirade from Johnny as he had so many times before, "as soon as you talk to him he'll know you disobeyed orders, and he'll throw us off the case. The best way to get this girl out is to find out who really did it, and the fastest way to do that is to follow up on our leads right now."

Johnny hated it when Paul made sense.

CHAPTER FOUR
—Santa's Workshop, 10:37 AM

Santa's Workshop was a series of immense warehouses. Each building's exterior was completely covered with color-coded paint. The buildings were located behind the Drifting Knoll in the industrial district on the outskirts of the city. They had been built during the mid-1800's—during the reign of Timothy Clause, when the industrial revolution finally spread past Greenland. In fact, only Timothy Claus's now infamous mental instability could explain the exterior of the Wheeled Toys Division—pastel blue, mauve zigzags, and a twenty-foot high orange stripe that circled the entire building just above the ground floor windows.

Johnny and Paul stepped out of their patrol car in the front parking lot. Johnny pulled a watch from his coat pocket. Paul put on his trench coat and straightened his hat.

"You'd think that the North Pole would be the one place in the world that has enough snow plows to keep the roads clear." Johnny slammed the car door shut. "It's past ten-thirty."

"I know what time it is," Paul said. "You kept pointing it out in the car."

They walked toward the entrance to the factory. The entrance had two doors. The first was painted green and had a shining red light bulb for a doorknob. It came up to Johnny's waist. The second, a bulging red oval that was nearly as wide as it was tall, was covered in small twinkling lights and reached nearly seven feet high.

Paul whistled as Johnny stood in front of the second door. "Santa was one big dude," Paul said. He went through the smaller door, and Johnny walked through the larger one.

The factory was a madhouse. Elves ran everywhere, some carrying completed cars and others toting bags of wheels, axles, and windshields. A pile of wagons nearly reached the ceiling, and a pile of cars filled an entire corner of the factory.

A giant paper-mache statue of Santa Claus stood in the center of the factory, his hand stretched out and his eyes looking stern. Across its large belly someone had painted the words: "*The world is counting on you.*" "Have a Holly Jolly Christmas" blared over the intercom and mixed with the clanging, shouting, scraping, and whirring sounds of the factory.

A large, officious-looking elf approached Johnny and Paul. His name tag, shaped like a small present, said "*Mundango—Manager.*"

"Can I help you?" Mundango yelled over the noise.

Johnny flashed his badge. "We need to speak with Mitchell," Johnny yelled back.

"Who?" Mundango asked.

"Mitchell."

"Who?"

Johnny swore. He hated pronouncing elf names. There were hundreds of ways to pronounce every single name, and only the elves themselves seemed to be able to master the nuances of their pronunciations. To make matters worse, the different pronunciations meant that the elves did not need last names to help tell one person apart from another. In fact, they only utilized two letters of the alphabet to start their names, L for females and M for males.

Fed up with trying to say the name, Johnny showed Mundango Mitchell's name written on his pad of paper.

"Oh, Mitchell," Mundango said, giving the name a slight accent at the end. "You know, he's rather busy right now. Is this important?"

"Just get him," Paul shouted.

The elf huffed, nostrils flaring and ears jiggling. He scuttled away, muttering something about the plight of elves.

"This place is crazy," Paul said, taking off his trench coat. "I've never been inside before."

"It's something," Johnny said, his voice giving away his impatience. A nearby row of elves hurriedly attached wheels to a tricycle. Their supervisor yelled at them to do it over again. Several scowled. No one looked happy.

Mundango returned. A second elf, carrying a handful of tools, followed close behind. Mundango tried to say something, but Johnny cut him off.

"Are you Mitchell?" Johnny shouted at the second elf.

"Y–y–yes," the elf stammered. His uniform, which had once been obviously red and green, had several bleach stains on the shirt and pants.

"We need to ask you some questions," Paul said.

"Just one minute," Mundango said. "You can't pull one of my employees off his job. We have less than two days to meet our quotas for Christmas, and you don't even want to know how far behind we are!"

"We need to borrow an office," Johnny told Mundango.

"No. Wheeled Toys is *not* going to be the last to complete their orders this year. Everyone here vowed that Christmas would be cancelled before we did that again."

"Well, you just might be in luck."

Johnny slapped Mitchell's shoulder, "You want to tell your boss, or should I?"

Mitchell cowered and dropped a screwdriver. Mundango looked puzzled.

"You didn't get another DUI, did you?" Mundango asked Mitchell. "Do you know how backlogged we'll get with you off the line?"

"Get me an office," Johnny commanded.

"Tell me what's going on," Mundango demanded.

Paul grabbed Mundango's shirt collar and lifted him off the floor. "We need an office, a table and three chairs, *now*!" Paul threw Mundango back, and Mundango stumbled into a couple of elves carrying a large engine. Bolts and screws clattered to the floor and rolled all over the factory.

Mundango cowered and pointed to an office in the corner. He scurried off before either Johnny or Paul could say anything else.

Johnny grabbed Mitchell by the arm and pulled him toward the office. Paul followed. They passed a group of elves slamming toy trains into a wall, testing their durability. They checked their conditions after each impact, as well as the state of the crash-test action figures inside.

Johnny opened the office door and shoved Mitchell inside. A few stools and empty boxes lay strewn about. The walls were bare. Three large windows looking back into the factory were on one side. A small surveillance camera was mounted in an upper corner.

"Have a seat," Johnny said.

Paul pushed a chair into Mitchell's legs, forcing the elf to sit down hard. His hands were shaking.

Johnny closed the door and pulled up a stool while Paul set up a table that had been knocked over. Mitchell's eyes followed every movement Paul made.

"Relax," Johnny said. "He's just a penguin."

Paul smiled. Mitchell continued shaking and nervously played with his fingers.

"Look," Johnny said, "you know why we're here. You found Santa's body last night. You claimed there was a single set of footprints leading to the body and nothing else."

Mitchell nodded.

"Was that set of tracks yours?" Paul asked.

"No," Mitchell said.

"Then there must have been two sets of tracks, right?" Johnny asked.

"Well, I didn't—I wasn't counting my own," Mitchell said.

"So you lied to the other officers."

"Look, what are you implying?" Mitchell stood up and shouted. He waved his hands around in desperation. "You think I killed Santa Claus?"

"Did you?" Paul asked.

"No!" Beads of sweat had formed on his brow.

"Then how do you know he was killed?" Paul asked. "How do you know he didn't just keel over all by himself?"

"I don't know!" Mitchell shouted. "I just assumed he was, well … killed. I mean who goes wandering around in the forest at four in the morning?"

Johnny and Paul let the question echo against the concrete walls.

"Well, that's just the million dollar question, isn't it?" Johnny said. "Why don't you tell us about yourself—help us understand the kind of person who goes wandering around the forest at four in the morning."

"I–I was coming home from work."

"That's awfully late to be coming home from work," Paul said.

"They're working us fourteen hours a day! It's insane."

"The factory opens at six," Johnny said. "That means you get off at about 8:30 at night. That gives you six more hours to account for."

"Care to do some explaining?" Paul asked.

Mitchell let out a deep sigh and pressed his forehead into his hands. "Look," he said, "all this stays between us, okay?"

Johnny and Paul looked at each other. Paul nodded his head slightly and narrowed his eyes. Johnny walked to the windows and shut the blinds. He walked to the surveillance camera and yanked out the transmission cable.

Johnny walked back to his chair, smiling tensely at Mitchell the entire time, while Paul rolled up his sleeves and dramatically cracked his flippers. Mitchell tried to shrink down even further into his stool.

"Okay, Mitchell," Johnny said, "from here on out nobody else will have any idea what's going on in here."

Paul smiled at Mitchell and leaned in a bit closer. "Spill the beans, elf," Paul said.

"You promise you won't tell … my wife?" Mitchell whispered the last two words.

"You're looking at least twenty-five years behind bars if you don't start being straight with us," Paul said.

"Okay, okay," Mitchell said, "But if you run this past my wife, I'm denying it all."

Johnny and Paul sat silently and stared at Mitchell. Paul cracked his flippers again, and Johnny straightened the papers in his file.

"I was at a bar," Mitchell said. "The One-Horse Open Sleigh."

"The one on Snow Street," Johnny said.

Mitchell nodded. "I had a drink."

"One drink in four hours?"

"Maybe I had a couple. Please don't tell my wife," Mitchell pleaded. "She thinks I've been dry for the past year."

"What time did you leave the bar?" Johnny asked.

"About three o'clock."

"And then you decided to take a stroll through the forest and stumbled on to Santa's body?"

"I didn't do anything wrong. I just pulled out my cell phone and called 911."

"And that's everything that happened?" Johnny asked.

"That's it."

"Well, Mitchell," Johnny said, "let's hope your story checks out, because your track record of honesty isn't too good with us right now."

"You aren't going to tell my wife, are you?" Mitchell asked.

Johnny stared at Mitchell. "You can leave now, Mitchell. There's a batch of tricycles that need your attention."

Mitchell stood up and hurried toward the door.

"Oh, and Mitchell," Johnny added, "don't leave town any time soon."

CHAPTER FIVE

SUSIE SAT on the floor of her cell, her back against the cold wall. She had been transported to a maximum-security facility. Eight armed guards had escorted her from the police station to the armored van that transferred her. Another nine guards had escorted her from the van and into the prison.

For the few minutes she had been outside, she tried to figure out how long it had been since she was arrested, but the sky looked the same as it always did—dark, filled with stars, a faint reddish glow along the horizon. She had no idea what time the officers had taken her from Santa's house, and she had no idea how long she had been stuck in that room at the police station.

What am I going to do? she thought.

She ran her hand along the bare, concrete floor and shivered. She had asked a guard for a blanket, but nobody had brought her one. The only thing they had brought was a black-and-white striped jumpsuit to replace the blue one she had been given at the police station. At least they had the decency to let her change in the bathroom, even if they did have a female officer, an elf, stand guard outside Susie's stall. The officer's eyes were barely higher than the bottom of the stall door, making Susie feel uncomfortable as she had changed.

The weather up here must make everyone insane, she thought.

No, she amended, *not everyone*. There was that one cop, Ice Cube or whatever his name was. He had seemed nice, though she wondered when he was going to get her out. He *had* promised.

But then again, the prison guard had promised to bring her a blanket. Santa had promised that he would do everything he could to prevent other children from losing their sisters. Her mother had promised that Jenny wouldn't die. Adults were always promising things.

Susie looked at the prisoners in the other cells. Across the hallway was a large polar bear with grungy teeth and scars all over his face. Every now and then he would grab the bars to his cell and try to shake them apart.

In the cell right next to her sat an elf with a shaved head and a crazed look in his eyes. He also had black and white striped clothing on. He hobbled around his cell, muttering incomprehensibly to himself. Every so often he would take his hands and quickly flip his pointy ears. On more than one occasion he had asked Susie if he could flip her ears. Susie had turned her back to him and did the best she could to ignore him.

The main door to the maximum-security area opened and a guard escorted in a man in a dark suit. The suited man's light brown hair was slicked back, his face was clean-shaven, his eyes were dark and intense. Glints of light reflected off his polished shoes. The creepy elf in the cell next to Susie's finally looked away from her to smile at the suited man.

"Well, look who's come to visit!" the elf said in an excited voice. "You have any cookies for me, Chief? Maybe a glass of milk?"

"Keep it down!" the guard yelled as he banged the elf's cell bars with his nightstick.

The suited man ignored the elf. He stopped in front of Susie's cell and looked at her for a few moments. His face had no expression.

"Hello, Miss Thompson," he said briskly. "My name is Chief Tom Masterson. I'm in charge of all the police officers here at the North Pole. Are they treating you well?"

Susie didn't know how to respond. The creepy elf laughed and shouted at Masterson: "They treat us great! Why don't you spend the night? We have an open cell."

The elf pointed to the empty cell next to the polar bear. Masterson, ignoring the elf, nodded at Susie's cell, and the guard opened the door.

"Are you letting me go?" Susie asked as she quickly stood up.

"No. We just need to have a little chat." He turned to the guard and motioned for him to bring her along.

The guard stepped in the cell and reached for Susie, but she pulled away.

"Don't touch me," she said defiantly.

The guard hesitated and looked at the Chief. Masterson nodded.

Masterson led Susie out of the maximum-security area and the guard followed dutifully behind her. They then passed by several rows of cells, most of which were filled, and through a narrow hallway until they reached a small room. Masterson entered, Susie followed, and the guard closed the door behind them.

There was a small table in the middle of the room with a chair on each side. Masterson invited Susie to take a seat. She kept standing. Without reacting, Masterson sat down and looked at her. The guard stood by the door.

"I want to tell you what's going on, so there are no surprises," Masterson said calmly. "You are being charged with the murder of Santa Claus—"

"But I didn't kill him! I'm supposed to be let out of here," Susie pleaded. "Didn't that detective tell you?"

"Oh?" Masterson asked, leaning in and staring Susie straight in the eye. "Which detective would that be?"

"The tall, skinny one with the penguin. I think his name was Ice Cube."

"I'm sorry, Susie, but nobody has any intention of letting you go," Masterson said, his voice sounding as if he had already known who the detective had been. "Detective *Iceberg* is about as dependable as a walrus in a three-legged race. I wouldn't count on anything he told you. He makes a lot of promises he can't keep."

Susie looked devastated. It was one more broken promise to add to her list.

"Now that *that's* cleared up—" Masterson straightened his suit coat, "because you are only eleven you are not going to be tried as an adult. Under North Pole law, the maximum sentence you could receive is fifteen years without the possibility of parole."

"Lucky me," Susie muttered.

Masterson ignored her and continued: "The United States has been informed of the situation, and they have asked that we extradite you."

"Extra what?"

"Extradite. They want us to send you back to your home in Colorado so you can go on trial there."

Susie's eyes brightened and a trace of a smile appeared on her face.

"So, when am I leaving?" she asked.

"You're not," Masterson said. "We have informed the U.S. that we will be keeping you right here."

"You're what? You can't keep me here! Send me home!"

"Perhaps you haven't caught the gravity of the allegations against you," Masterson said in a slightly demeaning tone. "This isn't just another homicide. This is regicide. You killed Santa Claus. He was North Pole royalty. You aren't going anywhere."

"I didn't kill him," Susie said weakly. "I didn't kill anyone."

"We have evidence against you, Susie. Did you not threaten to kill Santa Claus yesterday evening?"

"No," Susie said.

"Let me refresh your memory." Masterson pulled out a notepad, flipped through several pages, and then started reading: "According to Mayor Wassail, you looked Santa Claus straight in the eye and said, 'I hate you! I wish you were dead.'"

Susie's face turned red. She had forgotten that she had said that.

"You have made a lot of mistakes, Susie," Masterson said. "It was a bad idea to threaten Santa in the first place, it was a worse idea to do it in the village council chambers where our most prominent citizens could hear you, and it was even worse that you have just lied about it."

"It wasn't a threat," Susie cried. "I was just mad at him."

"We have also found the stash of cyanide in your suitcase," Masterson said. "At this moment, my lab technicians are making sure that cyanide was the cause of Santa Claus's death."

Susie was crying. She didn't even know what cyanide was.

"I just wanted you to know what was going on," Masterson said. "I try to be fair."

Masterson stood and the guard opened the door.

"It's not true! I didn't kill Santa!"

"That's for the judge to decide, not me," Masterson said.

Susie didn't know what to say. This police chief obviously did not care that she had not done the crime.

"I'll be in touch," Masterson said. Then he was gone.

CHAPTER SIX

PAUL WAS angry. He had wanted to drive straight to the One-Horse Open Sleigh to check out Mitchell's story. However, before even starting the car, Johnny had called Sara in the lab and learned that Sara had discovered a few things from the autopsy. Paul told Johnny that he was letting a pretty face get in the way of the investigation. Johnny told Paul to cram it. Since Paul was too short to operate the gas and brake pedals, they always ended up doing what Johnny wanted to do.

As they entered the lab, their eyes immediately focused on the tall, round body lying on the table and beneath a white sheet. A tall slender woman with red-brown hair sat on a chair next to the table, looking perplexed.

"Is this a bad time, Sara?" Johnny asked.

"No, I'm just—I've never done an autopsy before," Sara answered.

"So why hasn't anyone called in someone from the hospital?" Paul asked.

"Masterson's orders," Sara said. "My undergrad degree was in veterinary science. He said that was good enough."

"Veterinary science, eh?" Johnny asked, still irritated about the argument from the car. "That's convenient because Paul has something stuck up his—"

"So have you even started the autopsy?" Paul cut off Johnny, also still irritated.

"Yes, I've started," Sara said defensively. "I may not have finished it yet, and I may not be doing a great job, but I can still tell when I've found something you should know about."

"Calm down," Johnny told Sara. "Penguins tend to act irritable when everything is just fine. What is it we should know about?"

"Come and look."

Johnny pulled a stool up to the table for Paul, who snatched it away and climbed on it. He brushed aside a couple scales hanging at eye level. One scale contained a large wad of grey matter that smelled like sour milk and bile.

"Sorry about the scales," Sara said. "We just don't have the right equipment. I had to send Limphus to Yule-Mart. She got the produce scales there—which was no small feat for her, being an elf and all." Her face turned slightly red, and she started speaking more quickly. "I know it looks like we're in the dark ages. I just don't have enough petri dishes to hold his stomach contents!"

Neither Paul nor Johnny could think of any way to respond. They simply looked at the scales and nodded while Sara fidgeted with the body. The silence thickened, making everyone feel even more awkward.

"Well … uh," Johnny finally said, "don't forget to write down how much everything weighs."

Sara let out a laugh and shook her head. "I guess there's no reason to try to look intelligent when I'm around you two," she said.

"So, what have you found, Sara?" Paul asked.

"Look." Sara pulled the white sheet down. Both Johnny and Paul shivered. It was one thing to know that Santa Claus was dead, but it was something else entirely to see the cold, pale body lying on the table below them.

"As you can see, there are no stab wounds," Sara said. "No punctures of any kind—except where I cut open his stomach. It's the same all over the body."

"Is that blood?" Paul asked, pointing at Santa's chest.

"Yes. Some of it is his, but not all of it. We don't know whose. It doesn't match any samples in our database. We found a lot of hair, too."

"Do you know whose?" Johnny asked.

"Well, we know Dasher, and Dancer, and Prancer, and Vixen —" Sara's voice trailed off.

"Right," said Paul. "Flight practices and pre-lift off protocols."

"We were already planning a trip down to the training grounds," Johnny said.

Paul looked at Johnny questioningly. "We were?" he mouthed the question.

Johnny ignored Paul. "Any other hair?" Johnny asked Sara.

"Several long blonde strands."

"Mrs. Claus," Paul said.

"A few that belong to an elf—Mitchell according to the database."

Johnny and Paul looked at each other. Paul was irritated.

"The One-Horse Open Sleigh," Paul said. "I told you we need to go there."

"We will," Johnny said. "I never said we wouldn't."

"I think I'm missing something," Sara said.

"We've met Mitchell," Paul said. "We had a nice chat, and I think we're going to have another one pretty soon."

"There's one more hair sample from the body," Sara said, sensing some tension between Paul and Johnny and wanting to steer clear of it. "Again we don't have an I.D., but the DNA matches the unidentified blood."

"So we need to find this mystery guy," Johnny said.

"There's a couple more things," Sara said. She pointed out dozens of bruises scattered all over the body. They were all large—a few grotesquely so.

"He looks pretty bad," Paul said.

Sara nodded. "The X-rays showed multiple fractures: broken ribs, broken arm, broken collar bone."

"Like he was beat up," Johnny said.

"Like he was *really* beat up," Sara said. "Whatever happened, it wasn't quick, and it wasn't clean."

Johnny grimaced. He had heard that cops in big cities—New York, Sao Paulo, Mexico City—got used to these kinds of things. But the North Pole was small. It's total population, including elves, humans, snowmen, and animals, barely topped 30,000. They just didn't have a lot of violent crimes. It was tough for Johnny to focus on the body and the evidence.

"And one more thing," Sara said. She held up a baggie filled with black powder.

"Probably soot," Paul said, "from the yoga instructor's place."

"What yoga instructor?" Johnny asked.

"Santa's yoga instructor," Paul said. Johnny looked puzzled and shook his head. "It's how Santa gets down the chimneys. He takes yoga lessons—and they get more intense as it gets closer to Christmas. Didn't you read the file, Johnny? It was all in there."

"I read the headings," Johnny said. "I didn't need to read it because you already had. It would be a waste of investigation time and brainpower."

"You have no idea that you just insulted me, do you?" Paul said. Johnny ignored him.

"Anyway," Paul said, "the soot must've come from the practice chimney he used at the facilities."

"Sounds possible," Sara said, "but I'll do an analysis to verify it."

"Thanks, Sara," Johnny said as he and Paul started to leave. "You've helped a lot. You're—uh—really good with scales."

"Before you go … " Sara tore off a small sheet of paper and scribbled a phone number on it. "I've heard that Masterson's not very happy with the of two you."

"Why?" Johnny asked. Paul's face tensed up with anger.

"I don't know," Sara said. "I've just been hearing things. Be careful."

"We will."

Once they reached the garage, Paul blew up:

"So, now Masterson's mad at us! I told you to follow the rules," Paul yelled. "And I told you it would come back and bite my butt if you didn't. You may not care whether the Chief likes you or not, but

I don't want to be in his doghouse. I don't want to do traffic duty for the rest of my career."

"We'll be fine," Johnny said.

"Right," Paul said angrily. They walked the rest of the way to their patrol car in silence.

"By the way," Paul said as he opened his car door, "you could really use some flirting lessons. That was one of the worst demonstrations of a man talking to a pretty woman that I have ever seen."

"Oh, give it up," Johnny said. "I'm not interested in her or anyone else."

"Yeah, and my feet aren't webbed," Paul said. "Let's just go to The One-Horse Open Sleigh, shall we?"

"Change of plans," Johnny said. "We're going to the Reindeer Training Grounds."

"What? Why?"

"Because I'm the one driving and that's where I want to go."

No wonder your wife and daughter left you, Paul thought as he grudgingly followed Johnny to the car.

CHAPTER SEVEN
−Reindeer Training Grounds, 12:28 PM

"Historical marker *ahead*," Paul had read from a green highway sign as he and Johnny approached the Reindeer Training Grounds. Now, as Johnny pulled their car into the parking lot at the Training Grounds, they could see it—a fifty-foot high ice sculpture of Santa, one arm gesturing majestically toward the sky and another placed resolutely on the shoulder of Rudolph, a giant red spotlight embedded into the nose.

A plaque at the base of the sculpture read "*On December 24, 1964, Santa Claus placed Rudolph at the head of his reindeer team. Prior to Rudolph's position on the reindeer team, some conditions necessitated the cancellation of the annual Christmas flight, the most recent of which had occurred in 1939.*"

"I wonder what the other reindeer think about that," Paul said, as he and Johnny walked past the monument.

"I wonder what *Rudolph* thinks," Johnny said. "I don't think I'd like a fifty-foot replica of myself sitting outside my house."

"Neither would your neighbors," Paul said. "Even the six-foot version of you isn't very attractive. Now, if it was a fifty-foot ice sculpture of Mrs. Claus—depending on what her outfit was like—maybe they'd go for that."

The area surrounding the training grounds was beautiful. Hun-

dreds of white and black spruce trees surrounded the area, breaking
only for a large clearing, about the size of four hockey rinks, where
Santa and his sleigh could take off from. The clearing was boxed off
with a low, log fence, and there was a barn-like structure made out
of metal at one end of the clearing. The roof reflected the stars from
the dark, constant pre-dawn sky of the North Pole.

As they neared the building, Paul took a deep breath, then let it
out with a vibrant "Ahhh."

"Nothing like a good breath of fresh air, eh Johnny?"

"Smells like manure to me," Johnny said.

"Ah, what's the matter, Johnny?" Paul said patronizingly. "Holiday blues?"

Johnny said nothing in response.

"So, you think they're even here?" Paul asked.

"Smells like it," Johnny said. He opened a door to the building
and stepped inside.

Inside, they were shocked to see a gold-plated gas fireplace, a
52" plasma TV, a large chandelier hanging from the center of the
vaulted ceiling, and three reindeer sipping lattés while lounging
about on Italian leather furniture. Another two reindeer were
shooting pool in the corner.

"Can I help you?" came a voice from behind them.

They turned around and saw one of the reindeer. Which one,
they could not tell.

"Yes," Johnny said. "We need to talk to Rudolph."

"Rudolph?" the reindeer said, his legs stiffening and nostrils
flaring slightly. "Why?"

Johnny pulled out his badge. "He's the top venison around here,
right?"

The reindeer looked extremely insulted. He reluctantly led
them through the immaculate stable. His hooves made no sound as
they walked across the plush red carpet. Three reindeer eyed them
curiously from their recliners, while the two reindeer playing pool
whispered something.

They arrived at a large wooden door with Rudolph's name engraved on a gold plate mounted to the door. The reindeer knocked

lightly with his hoof.

The door opened abruptly. A reindeer, slightly shorter than the one who had escorted them, stood there with a curious look on his face.

"What is it, Vixen?" Rudolph asked shortly.

"We're with the NPPD," Johnny said, edging in and flashing his badge. "We need to ask you a few questions about Santa Claus."

Rudolph gave Vixen an odd look but quickly changed his expression as he turned to look at Johnny and Paul. "Sure. Come in."

The walls were plastered with magazine covers and newspaper clippings of Rudolph. A gold trophy, complete with silver antlers coming out the sides, sat on a shelf behind Rudolph's desk. Johnny squinted to read what was written on it but could not tell. A Dutch porcelain plate, with a windmill and candy cane blades painted on, hung on the wall. Rudolph shut the door and motioned for Johnny and Paul to sit down.

"Boy, am I glad you guys are here," Rudolph said, looking antsy. He sat down behind his cherry-wood desk. "Do we have clearance to go?"

"Clearance?" Johnny asked. "What are you talking about? We're here about Santa Claus."

"Yes, I know all about the Santa situation," Rudolph said somberly. "We got a call from your department this morning informing us of the tragic news. I asked them if we still had clearance to go for Christmas Eve."

"Why wouldn't you?" Johnny said.

"Oh, it's one of those bureaucratic things, you know. An obscure provision in the Christmas Bylaws."

"And what provision is that?" Paul asked.

"It has to do with the Claus succession. If the person who stands in line to become the Head Claus is the one who kills the sitting Head Claus, then the next person in line after the killer takes Santa's place."

"So what you're saying," Johnny said, "is if Mrs. Claus was the one who killed Santa, she wouldn't be able to take Santa's place as Head Claus."

"That's correct," Rudolph said.

"So who is the next in line after Mrs. Claus?" Paul asked.

"That's the thing," Rudolph said. "No one knows. I think Santa has some distant relatives somewhere in Norway, but Mrs. Claus is the only possible successor who would know how to perform the job."

"So if I follow this right," Johnny said, "if Mrs. Claus is the one who killed Santa, then the Christmas flight is essentially off this year."

"That's right," Rudolph said.

"Do you think that Mrs. Claus killed her husband?" Paul asked.

"Of course not!" Rudolph said.

"Then why bring it up?" Paul asked.

"Because I know enough about police work to know that she would have to be a suspect," Rudolph said. "And I want it to be clear to you that I know she couldn't have killed him."

"How do you *know* that?" Johnny asked. Rudolph looked flustered. His nose turned bright red. It was a moment before he answered.

"I hope you're not serious. Mrs. Claus is the most decent person I have ever known. Even Santa acted like he felt sorry for me at the beginning, but from the first day I met Mrs. Claus nearly three years ago she has never treated me as anything but a true leader of the team."

Paul gave Johnny a quick roll of his eyes. Rudolph didn't seem to notice and went on:

"But like I said, I know that unless you catch your guy soon, Mrs. Claus won't be cleared in time to take over the flight. Worthless bureaucracy's going to ruin Christmas."

"Well, Rudolph," Johnny said carefully, "what would you say if I told you that we already have a suspect in custody?"

A look of relief passed over Rudolph's face, and his nose lit up again. Paul looked at Johnny again, this time a bit angry. Why was Johnny was giving Rudolph all the facts about their investigation?

"So we have clearance to go, then?" Rudolph said excitedly.

"How would we know?" Paul said curtly before Johnny could

say anything else he should keep confidential. "We don't have anything to do with the Christmas launch. Call the mayor or a judge or whoever oversees the succession."

"But before you do," Johnny said, "we need to ask you some questions about Santa."

"Why?" Rudolph said. "I thought you said you had the guy who killed him."

"What would you say if I told you that we think the suspect in custody didn't actually do it?" Johnny asked.

Paul eyed Johnny angrily again.

"Somebody else?" Rudolph asked, getting flustered again. "Like who?"

"We thought maybe you could tell us," Johnny said. "You are the *true leader of the team*. We figured you would know all kinds of things that nobody else would know."

"Me? Why would I know anything about the murder?" Rudolph said. "Santa's never done a bad thing to anyone. I think if you've got someone in custody, they're probably the person you're looking for. I can't imagine that many people didn't love Santa Claus."

"What would you say if I told you the person in custody is a—"

"That's enough, Johnny!" Paul said through his gritted beak. He turned and gave a forced smile to Rudolph. "Do you think the other reindeer would know of anyone who wanted to do Santa in?"

Rudolph snorted disdainfully. "I don't think so," he said. "I was the closest to Santa. He told me everything that was going on. I can't imagine the other reindeer would know anything I didn't already know about."

"What about Dasher?" Paul asked.

Rudolph's nose got bright red. "What about him?"

"Dasher's on the North Pole Village Council, right?" Johnny said. "Since Mayor Wassail was elected they've had all sorts of closed door meetings. Don't you think Dasher might know one or two things you don't know about?"

"You can ask him if you want," Rudolph said, sounding put off, "but I doubt he knows anything. To tell you the truth, I think he is secretly enjoying the fact that Santa's not around. He's just living up his last year before retirement."

"This is Dasher's last year?" Johnny asked. "I haven't heard anything about that."

"That's because he hasn't done much," Rudolph said. "Sometimes I don't think anyone on the team, besides me, actually works around here. You saw them out there. Watching TV, shooting pool. They think they don't have to practice because Santa is dead and Christmas isn't going to happen. I don't think they even know the Christmas Bylaws. That's why Santa put me in charge here. I care about Christmas."

"It sounds like you reindeer have some problems of your own going on," Johnny said.

"You could say that," Rudolph said. "With Santa gone, things are just like they were before 1964. Suddenly 'Blush-nose' is scrawled all over the bathroom stalls. Suddenly there aren't enough cards for me to join a poker game. Suddenly there aren't enough sticks for me to play pool. They suddenly don't let me join in their little reindeer games again. Now that Santa's gone, it's back to ostracizing Rudolph!"

"Okay, then," Paul said, growing weary of Rudolph's tirade. "If you can think of anything that you think we should know, give us a call."

After Rudolph escorted them out of his office and closed his door, Paul confronted Johnny.

"What was all that?" Paul asked Johnny angrily in a loud whisper.

"What was what?" Johnny asked.

"Jack Frost, Johnny," Paul swore. "Since when is it okay to give the facts of an investigation out to a civilian? That's confidential, and giving it out can blow a whole case."

"Come on, Paul, you give a little, you get a little. He gave us some good information."

"Like what?"

"That all these other reindeer aren't too sad to see Santa gone," Johnny said.

"We could've got that information out of him without you giving him every detail about the case!"

"What's he going to do with that information? The department's going to make a statement by the end of the day, and everyone will know what I just told him, anyway."

"You're the guys investigating Santa's death, right?" a reindeer interrupted them. Both Paul and Johnny flinched with surprise and immediately cut off their argument.

"May I speak with you for a minute?" the reindeer asked.

"Who are you?" Johnny said, not being able to tell any of the reindeer apart.

"Dasher."

"Okay, Dasher," Johnny said. "What did you need to talk to us about?"

"I just wanted to make sure that *Rudolph*," Dasher spat the name, "didn't give you the wrong impression."

"About what?" Paul asked.

"About who calls the shots around here," Dasher said.

"And who does call the shots around here, Dasher?" Johnny asked.

"I do," Dasher said. "But Rudolph seems to think he's in charge."

"He does ride at the front of the team, doesn't he?" Johnny said.

"Only because he has a spotlight for a nose," Dasher said. "The rest of us have been here much longer than he has. Just because his birth defect pulled us out of a tough spot forty years ago doesn't mean that he has some mandate to run the team. I have seniority on the team, and I'd appreciate it if all correspondence with any of the reindeer goes through me."

"I'll keep that in mind," Johnny said. "Did you have anything important to tell us about Santa, or did you just want to assert your authority?"

Dasher huffed and glared at Johnny. "You had best watch how you proceed with this case, detective. Not everyone wants Santa's killer caught."

"You know, Dasher, we'd like to have a chat with you about that," Paul said. "Do you have an office where we can talk?"

"Privately," Johnny added.

Dasher shook his head. "I don't think you're ready to hear anything I have to say." He glanced over to Rudolph's door. "Not until I can be sure who you will and won't repeat it to."

Dasher tried to walk away, but Johnny grabbed his collar and yanked the reindeer's head back around.

"What are you talking about?" Johnny demanded.

"Don't break any rules to get to me," Dasher warned, pushing Johnny's arm away with an antler. "I'll make sure the right people find out." Johnny let go, and Dasher disappeared down the hall.

"Santa's Beard!" Paul said. "Do you think you could have handled that any worse?"

Johnny bunched his mouth and said nothing.

❄   ❄   ❄

Outside the stable, the icy North Pole wind had picked up. As they passed by the monument, Paul, who had calmed down, shook his head.

"Somehow I don't think Rudolph minds having that thing out here," Paul said.

"And I doubt the rest of them like it one bit," Johnny said.

"No kidding," Paul said. "It sounded like an episode of *Frozen Love* in there. I'm amazed Santa got a single flight off the ground with that drama-fest going on."

"It's ridiculous," Johnny said. "If they could get along they might figure out how to get the flight off—with or without Mrs. Claus."

"Just like we might be able to solve this case if you would stop trying to break every rule and procedure," Paul said. Johnny just grunted, so Paul changed the subject: "Dasher seemed pretty adamant about being in charge."

"I can see why," said Johnny. "Would you want to follow Rudolph?"

"Who'd have thought that Rudolph was a brown-noser at heart?" Paul said. "'*I don't think they've even read the bylaws.*' He would be worse to put up with than you are."

"And I don't know if Dasher's any better," Johnny said. "I'll carry on my correspondence with whoever I feel like." Johnny looked thoughtful. "Paul, figure out how we can get Dasher to talk to us. He could tell us a lot more about that council meeting yesterday—and we need to find out what else he could tell us."

"Why am I in charge of figuring out how to talk to him?" Paul asked.

"Because I'm busy figuring out how to handle our next stop," Johnny said.

"The One-Horse Open Sleigh, I hope," Paul said.

"Nope," Johnny smirked. "We need to visit Mrs. Claus."

"Why? So we can check out Susie's alibi?" Paul said, frustrated. "We went through this on the way over here. Until we have an actual culprit to pin this on in her place, an alibi isn't going to do us any good."

"I'm not going over there to talk to Mrs. Claus about an alibi," Johnny said.

"Then what are you going to do, interrogate her?" Paul asked sarcastically.

Johnny grinned.

CHAPTER EIGHT

JOHNNY AND Paul walked up the candy cane lined path to the Claus home. The entire area was still and quiet—the only sound came from a beaver nibbling on a gingerbread shingle. The lights strung around the firs and spruces were still turned on. A sign posted in the yard informed them that Tusk Brothers Yard Affects, LLC had installed the polymerized frosting on the roof of the Claus Estate, *"ensuring a Christmassy look and smell year round."* A light could be seen coming from inside the front room.

Paul thought the situation was just a little too cliché—aside from lousy soap operas how often did beautiful young women really marry rich old men so that they could kill them and take over the fortune? Wasn't the whole point of these kinds of marriages the fact that the old guy was going to die soon, anyway? Wouldn't Mrs. Claus have just inherited everything without a drop of suspicion if she had simply waited a few more years?

Johnny, of course, wouldn't listen. Maybe she wanted to take over before everything was changed, maybe Santa was blowing the fortune betting on curling matches, maybe she had been a spoiled rich brat prior to the marriage and just *couldn't* wait any longer before taking over. Besides, Johnny had told Paul cryptically, maybe they would find something else to help them out while they were there.

Johnny knocked on the door, just below the holly wreath. Nobody answered. He knocked again, but again, no answer.

"That's odd," Johnny said.

"Hardly," Paul said. "Her husband died this morning. She's probably taking care of funeral arrangements."

"Maybe," Johnny said. He turned around and looked at the house again. The light in the front room was now off.

"Did you see that?" Johnny asked.

"See what?"

"The light. It was on, but now it's off. She's home."

"So what're you going to do, kick down her front door and talk to her?" Paul said. "We don't have anything on her other than a *possible* motive, and it's a stereotyped motive at that. If she doesn't want to talk to us, she doesn't have to until we have a real case against her."

"I need to get in there," Johnny said. "She's hiding something from us."

"Get of it, Johnny." Paul said. "We should be either at the One-Horse Open Sleigh following up real leads or back at the station digging up real evidence against Mrs. Claus."

Johnny said nothing. He looked around the yard as if probing for spies, and, finding nothing, peered down the side of the house. He pulled a candy cane from his pocket and put one end in his mouth.

"What're you doing?"

"I'm going to look around," Johnny said.

"You're going to snoop around the house?" Paul asked in disbelief. "Masterson will fire you."

"It's not like I'm breaking and entering," Johnny said. "Unless I have to," he added, smiling tightly.

"It's called trespassing, Johnny, and it's stupid. Whatever you find won't be admissible in court, and it's just bad police work."

"It's police work like this that solved the Murdock case nine years ago," Johnny said.

"Don't pull that one on me." Paul was angry. "Every time you want to break the rules, you pull out the Murdock card. You're lucky you ended up catching the guy, or they would've had your badge in a heart beat."

"It wasn't luck, it was instinct. And my instinct tells me there's something in this house that we need in order to solve this case."

"You don't have a warrant!" Paul said, waving his flippers in the air in frustration.

"After I get some dirt on her, then I'll get the warrant."

"You're putting the sled in front of the dog team. You know just as much as I do that that will never fly," Paul said. He turned away and kicked at the crusty snow. "I don't know why I'm even having this conversation with you—you already know everything I'm saying."

Johnny crept along the side of the house, checking out the walls and windows as he went, and made his way toward the back gate.

"So you're just going to break the window and climb in?" Paul asked, following Johnny.

"I'm going to open the window and climb in."

"What if it's locked?"

"Then I'll pick the lock."

"What if Mrs. Claus hears you?"

"She won't."

"How do you know?"

"Because you're going to be my lookout."

"Lookout?" Paul said. "What am I supposed to do, quack like a duck if I see someone?"

"Why don't you just act like a penguin?" Johnny stopped, a quizzical expression on his face. "What kind of sound does a penguin make anyway, Paul?"

"Oh, shut up, Johnny." Paul turned away, disgusted, and headed back toward the car parked in the driveway.

"Great," Johnny said. "If you see Mrs. Claus coming, shout 'Oh, shut up, Johnny' and I'll get out as fast as I can."

"No, Johnny. You're on your own on this one." Paul opened the car door.

"Where are you going?" Johnny demanded.

"I'm going to do some *real* police work."

"And since when could you reach the gas pedal?"

Paul gritted his bill and slammed the door shut. He began walking down the road towards town. Well, Johnny thought, if Paul was expecting Johnny to go with him, he was sorely mistaken. Snooping would be easier without a penguin tagging along, anyway.

Johnny edged around the side of the house, careful to keep himself out of view of any windows in case Mrs. Claus was watching. Thankfully, the pine trees and perpetually dark sky made it rather easy for him.

Johnny actually had little interest in interrogating Mrs. Claus. She would just give them some alibi and maybe back up Susie's—which would require more time spent trying to determine their validity. No matter what she said, she wouldn't be able to add much to their investigation that wouldn't just end up giving them a lot more work to do and a lot more dead ends. Johnny hated dead ends.

Johnny had had something else in mind for some time: the Naughty List.

Nobody knew exactly how Santa put together the Naughty List, but common knowledge was that it was based on one's actions, words, and *thoughts*—including premeditating murder, Johnny assumed. If Susie's name was not on the List it would be enough to create reasonable doubt of her guilt, and she could be set free.

There was, however, the possibility that Susie's name was on that List. In that case, Johnny didn't know what he would do. According to North Pole legend, the List only contained names—not descriptions of what everyone had done to get their names on the List.

But Johnny was positive Susie's name was not on it. There was something about her—something behind her fierceness that told Johnny she was a good kid. She was so much like Johnny's daughter, Emily, had been: feisty, idealistic, and good.

Johnny and Emily had parted on bad terms. She had been ten or eleven at the time and had let both Johnny and her mother, Tara, know exactly how much the divorce was hurting her. But she had always blamed Johnny more. She had constantly lectured him about drinking too much, about spending all his time at work, about ignoring her even when he was home. Johnny laughed sadly at the memory. Just like Susie, Emily had never been afraid to speak her mind.

Now, nine years after Emily had disappeared with her mother into a plane headed to Montana, Johnny realized his daughter had always been right. The divorce was his fault. No matter how much he tried to excuse himself, he had had enough time to realize the truth. He had wrecked Emily's life. He wanted to call her, to apologize, but he could never bring himself to do it. Every now and then he would stare at the phone, wanting to call her, but he had never worked up the resolve to actually pick up the receiver and dial.

Johnny shook his head and let the memories fade away. There was another girl who needed him right now.

He edged around the Claus home, peeking into each window. Inside one was a room with a large red bed and bright green wallpaper. In a second was a room with a red miniskirt and matching vest hanging next to a washer and dryer. Johnny had always wondered what kind of woman wore a miniskirt in the North Pole—especially during the winter. But neither Santa nor the tabloids had ever objected to her attire.

Inside the third window sat a large oak desk in the middle of the room, facing a closed door. A posh leather chair sat behind the desk, and another was next to the door. The floor was littered with opened envelopes and letters, a large pile of which also sat on the desk next to an inkwell, quill, and two large scrolls.

This was it: Santa's office.

Johnny tried to open the window, but, as he had expected, it was locked from the inside. He pried it open just enough to slide his hand inside and pick the lock with the now sharpened candy cane he had been sucking on. He lifted the window slowly and grimaced at the loud squeak the hinges made. After rubbing them down with a handful of snow, he lifted the window again—this time without any noise—and climbed into the office.

A dark fireplace was in a corner. If it had been lit and the lights had been turned on the room would have been quite cozy. As it was, it was simply dark and cold.

After quietly locking the door, he walked to the desk, knocked several letters off the pile, and picked up the two scrolls. The first had the word "*Nice*" embroidered across the top in shiny green lettering; the second said "*Naughty*" in large black letters. Johnny smiled smugly and stuck the Naughty List in his coat pocket.

Just as he laid the other scroll back on the desk, two shadows from outside crossed the room. Reflexively, Johnny ducked out of sight and crouched beneath the window. He heard footsteps crunching in the snow.

"… Mayor tell you what he wanted?" a voice said in a hushed tone.

"Apparently the lovely Mrs. Claus has some dirt on him that he wants us to recover."

"What type of—"

A slammed door from inside the house, followed by the clatter of something falling to the floor and breaking, jolted Johnny's attention from the conversation outside. He could see somebody's shadow beneath the door, and the doorknob started rattling.

Jack Frost! Johnny swore silently as he dove into the chair nook beneath the desk. He desperately hoped whoever was outside wasn't near the window—although he was well covered from the front of the desk, anyone would be able to see him from behind.

The lock on the door clicked, and the door creaked open. Johnny pressed his head to the ground and peered from under the desk. All he could see was a pair of long, slender legs, supported by a pair of sparkling white open-toed pumps with six-inch heels. Mrs. Claus.

Whatever she was doing, she was obviously agitated. Johnny could hear her rustling through papers frantically as she walked back and forth feverishly. Dozens of letters and envelopes fell off the desk and to the floor. A soft clang—Johnny guessed it was the inkwell getting knocked over—echoed in the room.

The Naughty List! Johnny thought. It was still in his coat pocket. He had no idea whether she would notice it missing.

A loud thump came from outside. Mrs. Claus took a step toward the still open window and stopped. Johnny's entire body tensed up as he watched her foot and leg, just inches away from him. A snowflake was tattooed on the ankle and her toenails were painted bright red.

With a sudden turn, Mrs. Claus rushed away from the window and out of the room. She slammed the door behind her.

Johnny suddenly let out his breath. He hadn't even realized he had been holding it. He crawled out from under the desk and pressed himself against the wall beneath the window. There was no sound coming from outside. Whoever had been there was gone.

Carefully, he climbed out the window and, after checking for any signs of the two men, crept back to the patrol car at the front of the house. Cursing the noise the engine made, Johnny backed out and drove away.

He smiled. He had the Naughty List.

❄   ❄   ❄

Susie watched as the guard, a human, came to her cell. His hair was disheveled and his pants looked like they may have fit fifteen years ago. What did he want? Were they just going to accuse her of killing Santa Claus again? She was getting sick of it.

The guard walked past a sign that read "*All inmates are automatically placed on the Naughty List. Santa's coal delivery will arrive Christmas morning at 8:30 a.m.*"

Who cares? Susie thought. *I wouldn't get what I wanted from Santa anyway.*

The guard extended his hand through the bars, something shiny pinched between his fingers. Susie read his name tag and laughed—the first time she had done so in almost a day. Chip Larson just did not sound like a cop name.

"Here you go," the guard said tartly, cutting off Susie's laughter.

"Oooh, Money," said the creepy elf in the next cell over.

"What's this for?" Susie asked, suspicious.

"Your one phone call. Call whoever you want."

Susie took the shiny metal piece from the guard's hand. It was a coin, about the size of a quarter. One side had the number 25 on it, the other a snowflake.

"Use it wisely," the guard said.

"If I was wise, I wouldn't have come here in the first place."

"Most kids would kill for the chance to meet Santa Claus," the guard snapped.

"Why, *Chip*?" Susie shot back, not ready to take flack from this guard. "So they could roll around in the mud with a greedy pig?"

"Watch your tongue, you little brat!" the guard smacked his nightstick against her cell bars. "Santa spent his entire life doing good for this world—and he may have been the best Claus since Nicholas. I'm sorry that I don't find it amusing that you've killed him."

"All he did was give out toys. You call that great?"

The guard's expression changed. When he spoke again, his voice was suddenly very quiet: "When my dad ran off with an elf and left my mom with nothing, that toy meant everything to me," he said. Susie could not quite tell, but it looked like the guard's eyes were tearing up.

"What's the matter, *Chip*?" the elf smirked from inside his cell. "Little girl hurt your feelings?"

"Shut up." The guard banged on the cell bars with his nightstick as he wiped his eyes. The elf jumped around like a monkey, shouting more taunts, but the guard ignored him and walked away.

Susie turned around. She stood on her bed and looked out her barred window. She felt strange, guilty almost. *I didn't mean to make him cry*, she thought. She had never once in her life made an adult cry. Adults never cared enough. They didn't cry.

But there was the guard, crying over the death of Santa Claus. How could the memory of a single toy have such a strong effect on that guard? How could it possibly have made Santa so important to him? Whatever it was, there was nothing Santa had done for her to make her feel the same way.

But still, Susie thought, *I guess Santa had helped some people*.

She didn't want to think about it anymore. She looked out her barred window and stared at the black sky with the faint light on the horizon. She had no clue what time it was. The sky never changed, and now that she thought about it, she didn't much care what time it was, either.

She looked at the coin with the snowflake. One call. Who would she call? Her parents? She didn't want to talk to them. They were too busy getting divorced and fighting over who got which DVD's. They probably didn't even realize she was gone. The Ice Cube guy and his penguin friend? She didn't know their number. Besides, why waste her time? That chief had said that it had just been another promise that wouldn't be kept. Who else was there?

Susie looked at the coin, spun it in her hand a couple times, and threw it out the window as far as she could.

Chapter Nine
—The One-Horse Open Sleigh, 2:57 PM

PAUL WALKED up to the One-Horse Open Sleigh, breathing heavily. Between his penguin legs and a monster snowdrift on 34th Street, it was a miracle he had made it to the bar in just over an hour. *If only my legs were a bit longer*, Paul thought ruefully, wishing for probably the first time in his life that he wasn't quite so penguinish. Or, he added, *if Johnny hadn't been such a jerk they could have come in the patrol car and worked to solve the case together, like partners are supposed to do.*

After he caught his breath, Paul walked to the front door. It was locked. He knocked, but nobody answered. He tried peering though a window, but the glass was so foggy that he couldn't see into the building at all. He pounded on the door one last time, hard enough to jar a wad of snow that had collected on the door.

As the snow fell, Paul could see a sign that had been covered up: "*Holiday Hours: 5:00 p.m. to 5:00 a.m. through Christmas. Sorry for the inconvenience.*"

Well isn't that just swell, Paul thought.

He backed away from the door and kicked at the snow in frustration. The last thing he wanted was to spend extra time doing police work during the Christmas season. His children often asked him to spend more time with them—going to their school plays, going to their curling matches—and Paul did the best he could. He never took on extra duty, no matter how much overtime Masterson offered. But Paul never felt that he did enough.

But he always made sure he spent extra time with his family during the Christmas season. During the week before the holiday he had always tried to leave work each day early in the afternoon, and he had *always* taken Christmas Eve off.

Paul had known when Masterson first put him on the Santa case that everything would be too hectic for an easy week. He and Johnny would have to do everything they could to get it done before the Christmas Eve lift-off. Paul knew that taking his usual time off would be pretty much impossible, but what put Paul in a *really* bad mood was the amount of time being wasted because Johnny insisted on chasing a bunch of non-existent leads. If Johnny had just driven over here they could have moved on to talk to the yoga instructor and then come back to the bar when it opened. Now Paul had to decide whether to wait for another two hours for the bar to open or to spend another hour walking to the Frozen Yoga.

He supposed he could call someone at the department to pick him up and drive him to the yoga facility, but he didn't like asking for a chauffeur. Besides, the dispatch would just ask where Johnny was and why Paul wasn't with him. Paul didn't feel like getting into that. He was mad enough without verbalizing the whole situation.

He could call Sara. Even if she asked, Paul wouldn't have to explain everything to her.

Paul pulled out his phone, but before he even started dialing a burly man appeared from behind a storage shed.

"Paul!" the man said in a gruff voice. "It's been a long time."

"Good to see you, Jim," Paul said, smiling at the bartender. "How's business going?"

"Pretty good," Jim replied. He walked up to the door and opened it. "I just renovated the interior. You should come in for a drink and check the place out. I know I don't open for another two hours, but I can make an exception for an old friend."

"You know I gave up drinking when I got married, Jim," Paul

said. "Besides, I doubt it would go over well back at the department if I got smashed while on duty. But I wouldn't mind having a seat and checking the place out."

"I gotcha," Jim said. "Well, I just happen to have some fish and chips cooking in the kitchen, and I know you were always a sucker for 'em. You didn't give those up when you got married, did you?"

Paul laughed. "I didn't marry a mountain goat. Allison likes fish and chips just as much as the next penguin."

Inside, Paul was amazed at how good the place looked. Back when Johnny and he were drinking partners rather than police partners, the place had been a hole in the wall—sticky beer all over the floor and benches with slivers. The only things that had brought Paul and Johnny inside were the cheap Sea Lion's brew and the famous fish and chips.

Now the place looked quite welcoming. The booths along the far wall had been carved into replicas of famous Claus sleighs: Nicholas Claus's white original, Santa's current one, Cassio Claus's legendary purple one with studded emeralds. The long counter had been sanded down, polished, and engraved with the names of famous patrons, including the Abominable Snowman. The oak tables set throughout the room looked new, although one had a broken leg. Giant murals of happy customers—human, elvish, animal, and snowman—dressed in lederhosen and giving rousing toasts with overflowing mugs of ale filled the walls. Ceiling fans with hanging lights now replaced the single bulbs that had once been in their place. Perhaps the most impressive change, in Paul's opinion, was the odor. It did not smell like vomit anymore.

"Impressive, Jim," Paul said as he climbed a barstool like a ladder and sat down.

"Thanks," Jim said. "Let me go grab you those fish and chips."

Jim ran back to the kitchen. Paul leaned on the counter and wondered what Jim's clientele must be like now. The place just didn't look like a grubby little place for cops to hang out after hours anymore. Before his marriage, Paul had come here almost every night after work—so had both Johnny and Masterson, back when they had been partners. Johnny would always sit by Paul, and gripe

DECEMBER 22 ❄ 2:57 PM

about Masterson, who would find several of his friends and, no doubt, gripe to them about Johnny.

But then Paul got married. Sometimes he missed drinking with the guys—there was nothing quite like a bunch of woozy cops hitting on the bar maids and watching curling matches—but in the end it was okay. There was also nothing quite like taking his kids out to a frozen pond and teaching them how to hit a slap shot.

It was too bad Johnny's life had not gone the same way. Even though Johnny blamed the partying and drinking for killing his marriage, that wasn't what did it. Tara had always been a little wild too, and she could put up with a little drinking from her husband. Besides, Johnny had never been an alcoholic; he had been a workaholic. Back then he usually worked an extra 20 to 25 hours every week. Now Johnny never took extra shifts, he never went drinking, and he never got together with friends. It was as if Johnny was trying to undo what he had done to his family. But now there was nobody for him to go home to. There was nobody there to thank him for coming home on time. Paul knew it ate Johnny up inside, that he desperately missed his daughter, but they never talked about it.

Jim returned from the kitchen with a large plate of fish and chips. He set the plate down on the counter.

"Dig in," Jim said.

Paul grabbed a big piece of deep-fried cod and nibbled it down. It had been too long since he had eaten here.

"So," Jim said, "what brings you out to my place after so many years? You investigating last night's fight?"

"What fight?" Paul asked.

"Some oddball started picking a fight with a bunch of elves last night. They broke one of my good tables," Jim said, pointing to the broken table in the corner, "not to mention all the mugs they busted. The guy ran off before I could throw him out."

"Was the guy a regular?" Paul asked.

"Never seen him before," Jim replied.

"I can look into that for you later, send over a composite artist and the like. But right now, there's actually another crime I'm investigating."

"What crime is that?"

Paul hesitated before he answered. He didn't like to release information about a case. But this wasn't information about a case—it was just stating that there was a case.

"The murder of Santa Claus," Paul said.

"You're kidding!" Jim said. "Someone offed Santa?"

"Afraid so."

"Wow," Jim said, still taking in the news. "I don't know what I could tell you about that."

"Do you recognize this elf?" Paul asked, pulling a picture of Mitchell out of his coat pocket.

"Mitchell?" Jim said. "Of course I recognize him. He's in here 'bout every night."

"Was he here last night?"

"Sure was," Jim said. "He was involved in that fight."

"Really?" Paul asked, curious. "You know what started the fight?"

"Haven't a clue," Jim said. "I figured it was just a couple of drunks fighting over a girl or something."

"Drunks?" Paul asked, remembering Mitchell's claims about having only one drink.

"Well, Mitchell's a bit of a binge drinker," Jim said. "Must've had at least eight drinks last night."

"Eight, eh? You sure it was that many?"

"Yeah. He and his group of elf friends come in here every night after work, complaining about their jobs."

"So these elves aren't too happy with their boss."

"Not at all," Jim said, then paused a moment. "Hold on there. Are you thinking that Mitchell killed The Claus?"

"Mitchell *was* the one who found the body coming home from here last night. Let's just say that he has been less than straightforward with us."

"Well, I can tell you this," Jim said. "Mitchell may hate his job, but he didn't kill Santa."

"What makes you say that?"

"First off, Mitchell's not that kind of elf. He's all talk when he's had a few drinks, but nothing more. Besides, he was so drunk when I threw him out last night, I don't think he could have killed Santa if he wanted to. I'm surprised he made it past the curb."

"So Mitchell was pretty wasted last night."

"Sure was," Jim replied. "I told him he needed to go home, go be with his wife."

"What time was it when you kicked him out?"

"Around three-thirty."

"Is he always here that late?"

"Yup."

"These elf friends of his," Paul asked, "any of them capable of killing Santa?"

"That I don't know," Jim said. "Like I said, these elves complain about their wages and how much time they have to work. I don't know any of them as well as I know Mitchell. I'd hate to say they were capable, but then I'd also hate to say that they weren't and be wrong."

Paul nodded. "Do they come in every night?"

"Most nights, yeah."

"Let me know if you notice anything suspicious with that crowd."

"Sure thing," Jim said. "By the way, where's Johnny? Last I heard, you two were partners?"

"We're still partners," Paul said bitterly. "He's just too busy to investigate the case, it seems."

"Too bad," Jim said. "I would have liked to talk to him again. It's been a long, long time."

Jim went back in the kitchen, and Paul ate another piece of fish. He pulled out his cell phone and called Sara at the department. She said she would be over in a few minutes.

Why do you keep hiding the truth, Mitchell? Paul asked silently. During the interview at the Workshop, the little elf had seemed almost desperate for him and Johnny to believe his story. Was it really nothing more than trying to hide a drinking habit?

Paul needed to have another chat with the elf, right after he visited Santa's yoga instructor. Paul ate a chip and waited for Sara.

CHAPTER TEN
—FROZEN YOGA, 4:34 PM

WHAT A *ridiculous name for a place*, Paul thought.

Sara had just dropped him off. Paul watched her drive away and shook his head. Who knew that a woman who spent all day with petri dishes could be so entertaining? Paul made a mental note to remember her ridiculous story about a walrus, six displaced hamsters, and a PH analyzer—his two boys would get a real kick out of it. It had certainly made the ride much more enjoyable than a typical one with Johnny. It was sometimes annoying to spend so much time with a depressed and depressing guy.

Sara had, of course, asked where Johnny was. Thinking it best to keep his argument with Johnny to himself, Paul had simply told her that he was checking out Mrs. Claus. That drew out a small groan from Sara, who had then suddenly became quiet. After a moment she had continued with the walrus story as if nothing else had been said.

Paul often wondered if anything was *ever* going to happen between Sara and Johnny. They obviously liked each other. But Sara, it seemed, thought of herself as little more than a science geek, and Johnny had turned himself into a social recluse. It made Paul wonder if his own relatively happy life was something extraordinary.

Oh well, Paul thought. *I have other things to worry about right now.*

He turned around and looked through the large, glass windows of the front of the Frozen Yoga building. There was not much to look at on the inside. It was all one big room with a wooden floor. There were mats along some of the walls. At the far end of the room was a large fireplace with a fiber-optic Christmas tree spinning beside it.

Paul opened the door and walked inside. A tall, lean man dressed in a one-piece spandex jumpsuit was sitting in lotus position on one of the mats, his eyes closed. Paul coughed loudly, and the man jolted upright. His hair had been waxed out to the sides and looked like giant furry elf ears.

"May I help you?" the man said, flustered.

Paul flashed his badge. "NPPD. Are you Santa's yoga instructor?"

"Yes," the man said. "Why do you ask?"

"I'm investigating a crime."

"Is this about Santa's murder?"

Paul looked shocked. "How'd you know about that?"

"It's been all over the news. How wouldn't I have heard about it?"

Paul had almost forgotten about the herd of reporters that had been at the crime scene. Jim must have not caught the news before Paul had shown up at the One-Horse Open Sleigh. *Trust the media to step in and mess things up.*

"Yes, that would be it," Paul said.

"Well, I don't know what happened to him," the man said. "I was absolutely shocked when I heard the news on the radio this morning. I almost choked on my tofu-cane."

"Santa's been training here lately, right?"

"Sort of."

"What do you mean 'sort of'?"

"Santa's not the most diligent person when it comes to exercise," the yoga instructor said. "He's missed his last three appoints, two if you don't count today. I guess I shouldn't include it in the bill given his … current status."

71

"When was the last time you saw Santa?"

"December 17th, at 3:58 p.m."

Paul gave the yoga instructor an odd look.

"When he finished his appoint last Thursday—I always have clients out two minutes before the hour."

"You notice anything strange at that time?" Paul asked. "Did he mention anyone who might want to hurt him?"

"No," the man said, reflecting back. "Santa never mentioned anything to me. He was always too out of breath to say anything."

"Is this the chimney he practiced with?" Paul asked, pointing to the fireplace on the opposite side of the room.

"Yeah."

"Mind if I check it out?"

"Go right ahead."

Paul walked over to the chimney. The yoga instructor followed on his heels. The chimney was bare except for a stocking on the mantle that had the words "*Lotus Bunny*" written on it. There was no log in the chimney. In fact, the chimney looked quite clean.

"Who's Lotus Bunny?" Paul asked.

"That would be me," the man said.

"That your legal name?"

"That's just what my friends call me," the man said. "My real name is Kiplan."

Even better, Paul thought.

"Is the chimney always this clean, Kiplan?" Paul asked. "Looks like it's never been used."

"It's been used," Kiplan said, "but it's always this clean. It's not a working fireplace. We only use it for Santa's exercises."

"So you never light a log in there, fill the chimney with smoke?" Paul asked. "You know, make it more realistic?"

"Heavens no!" Kiplan said. "If we actually lit fires in this fireplace, Santa would get his cute red exercise suit all dirty every time he did a practice run."

"That would be a travesty."

"Why are you so concerned about my fireplace?"

Paul was about to change the subject when Johnny came running in the front door. *What is he doing here?* Paul had expected he would meet up with him back at the station.

"Paul!" Johnny said. "You've got to come with me!"

"I'm in the middle of something, Johnny," Paul said sternly.

"It can wait. This is important."

"And investigating Santa's death isn't?"

"Just get out here!"

Paul was going to protest, but Kiplan did not need to hear all of this. Paul gave Kiplan his number and told him to call if he could think of anything. Paul then stormed out the door with Johnny.

"What's so important it couldn't wait, huh?" Paul said angrily, standing on the sidewalk outside. "You catch a peek of Mrs. Claus?"

"Check this out," Johnny said, pulling a scroll from his coat.

Paul stared at the scroll. "That isn't—"

"Santa's Naughty List," Johnny finished the sentence for Paul. "And guess what I found? Susie—"

"*Jack Frost*, Johnny! You stole Santa's Naughty List? If Masterson finds out about this, he'll have your badge so fast that—"

"Paul," Johnny cut him off, "just shut up about Masterson and proper procedures for once in your life. Look at the list! Susie's name is not on it. That alone should be enough to get her released. And look at what else I found on the—"

Before Johnny could unroll the scroll, a gunshot rang out and a bullet shattered a window just behind them. From inside the building, Kiplan shrieked and whimpered something about disrupting the harmonic energy of his yoga studio. Paul and Johnny ran and ducked behind Johnny's car. Just down the street, near the Gingerbread Dude's Fine Guitars, a bald man was running down the sidewalk. Johnny took off after him. Paul followed, doing his best to keep up despite the snowdrifts and his short webbed feet.

The bald man dodged through people as he ran down the streets of North Pole Village. Johnny was right behind him. If there were not so many people around, he would have just pulled his gun and shot the guy. Johnny jumped over some elves and almost ran into a caribou as he chased the man. The Christmas lights draped between the lampposts were a rainbow blur as he sped past them.

The bald man cut left down a side street, knocking over the cart of a chestnut vendor. The vendor, a walrus in an apron, cursed at the man. Johnny ran by and stumbled through the chestnuts strewn across the sidewalk.

The road was dark, an alley in North Pole Village's downtown that the sidewalk plows had shoveled excess snow into. The bald man was nowhere in sight. Johnny drew his gun, climbed over the piles of snow, and searched the crevasses in the walls, behind a dumpster, and around a stash of frozen boxes.

As Johnny reached the back of the alley, searching behind a door listlessly swinging back and forth, the dumpster lid flew open behind him. He turned around with his gun, but before he could face the dumpster, two gunshots rang out.

He looked down at himself. He was fine. The bald man slumped over the rim of the dumpster, holding his bleeding shoulder as more blood trickled down his leg from a shot in his thigh. His gun had fallen to the ground. Paul stood at the entry to the alley, gun pointed at the man.

"Nice shot," Johnny said.

Paul holstered his gun and waddled through the heaps of snow. He picked up the bald man's gun with a stray piece of newspaper. Johnny pulled the man off the dumpster and cuffed him. He moaned as Johnny pulled his right arm behind his back. Johnny ignored him. Without any concern for the bald man's pain, Johnny and Paul dragged him back to the patrol car sitting outside the Frozen Yoga.

❄   ❄   ❄

As Johnny shoved the man in the back of the patrol car, Paul opened his door.

"Don't get in yet," Johnny told Paul. "The list. You have to see it."

"I'm not sure I want to know anything more about it, Johnny," Paul said. "I don't want to lose my badge just because you feel compelled to do illegal stuff."

"Just shut up for one minute, Paul," Johnny said. He shoved the list in front of Paul's face. Near the end of the scroll, which had been compiled alphabetically, the name "Chad Tyler" was circled in heavy red ink.

"That was on the list when you found it?" Paul asked.

"Yep," Johnny said.

"Are there any other names circled like this?"

"No," Johnny said. "I looked through the entire scroll—that's the only one."

"What about other lists—Naughty and Nice from past years?"

"I didn't have a chance to check," Johnny said. "I didn't even look at this one until I had gotten away from the Claus house."

"Why?"

Johnny told Paul about the men he heard outside, as well as Mrs. Claus's frantic entrance and exit from Santa's study. After hearing the entire story, Paul stood quietly.

"I don't like this," Paul finally said. "There's something big going on right under our noses."

"I know," Johnny said.

"This doesn't really change anything, though," Paul said. "You still got the list illegally—it won't be admissible in court."

"Who cares, Paul?" Johnny said. "This list isn't enough to convict anybody. But it may be pointing us in the right direction—just like the conversation I overheard. Now we have two new leads: Mayor Wassail and this Chad Tyler. And maybe Mrs. Claus, given how odd she was acting. We can't worry about 'legally obtained evidence' until we know who to go after in the first place."

Paul shook his head and got in the car. "I'm not going to waste my time arguing with you," he said.

As Johnny drove back to the police station, Paul tried to get a few answers from the bald gunman in the back seat. *Who are you? Why were you stalking us? Why did you attack us? Who are you working for?* The suspect wouldn't talk. He just looked at Paul and smiled cynically. Finally, when the man spat, Paul quit.

"We'll just go over this again at the station," Paul said. "I promise it will be much less pleasant for you the longer you hold out."

Paul turned around and switched the heater off.

Johnny turned it back on. Paul turned it off again.

"Knock it off," Johnny said, turning it back on again.

"It's an oven in here," Paul said, flipping it off.

"Are you kidding? It's freezing!"

"Then wear a coat."

"I *am* wearing a coat!"

"Then you should be fine."

"Look," Johnny said, "just because evolution gave you natural insulation—"

Paul had reached over to turn it off again, but Johnny grabbed his partner's flipper and shoved it into the dashboard. The radio suddenly turned on and blared the wail of heavy metal guitars and a man shrieking off-key: *"I've got a sack of coal, 'cause I've got no self-control."*

"You listen to Frostbite?" Paul asked.

Johnny changed the channel.

"We're live at the North Pole Police Station where Police Chief Tom Masterson is about to make an announcement," a reporter said.

"At four-thirty this morning," Masterson started off with no introduction, "Santa Claus was found dead in the Evergreen Forest. The cause of death has been determined to be cyanide poisoning.

"We have a suspect in custody: an eleven-year-old girl from the United States named Susie Thompson. The United States has requested her return, but their request has been denied. Miss Thompson will face trial here at the North Pole.

"No other details will be released at this time. Thank you." Masterson's voice was followed by the traditional yammer of reporters blurting out additional questions. After it became clear there would be no additional comments from Masterson, the station cut back to the studio, where talk-show host Rulon Nogger was opining various conspiracy theories to explain Santa's death.

Paul switched the radio off and scratched his head. Johnny's hands gripped the steering wheel, his face bunching up in anger.

"What does he think he's doing?" Johnny yelled.

"A press conference," Paul said, knowing a literal answer would annoy his partner.

"He's not supposed to release the names of suspected minors. Every cop knows that."

"Like you follow the rules to the T," Paul said. "Besides, this isn't your normal, everyday case. Santa was Head Claus. Masterson's probably been pounded with questions all day long."

"What about the poison?" Johnny said. "Why is he talking about evidence and test results that we—the detectives assigned to the case—have never even heard of? He's keeping us in the dark, that arrogant—"

Johnny looked back and saw the bald man with a big smirk on his face. Johnny slammed on his brakes and the man's head flew forward, smacking the bars that separated the front and back. The man scowled at Johnny and he accelerated again.

"I don't like it either," Paul said. "I don't like all this stuff going on behind our backs, but it's sure looking like I was right: we're probably just clean-up on this case."

"And so you're just going to do what Masterson wants?" Johnny accused Paul.

"I said that that's what they want us to do," Paul snapped back, "not that I'm just going to lay down and take it—"

Johnny slammed on the brakes and screeched the car to a stop. He had only noticed the snowman crossing the road and the traffic officer, an elf whose name Johnny had either forgotten or never bothered to learn, at the last second. The bald man in the back of the car smacked his head on the bars again. The snowman outside scowled as he walked by, just inches away from the front of the car. Johnny stared at him. You didn't see them in town that often—they tended to stay out in Snowman's Land.

Why don't they just put stoplights in? Johnny thought. There wasn't a single one in the entire North Pole. It was a waste of police resources, sending officers out to direct traffic at every intersection. It drove Johnny crazy, especially when he was assigned traffic duty.

The elf officer motioned them forward and Johnny accelerated again.

"So, what do you think we should do?" Johnny asked.

Paul pressed a button on the dashboard and a soundproof window rose behind the two front seats.

"We can conduct our own investigation behind their backs just as easily as they can do it to us," Paul said. "We just have to make sure that we do a *better job than they do*." Paul pointed at the Naughty List. "That means our evidence and our procedure has to be *legal*. That means we work with what Masterson gives us so that we don't get reassigned."

Johnny ignored Paul's accusatory tone. "I don't work with someone who goes behind my back."

CHAPTER ELEVEN

WHEN THEY got to the station, Paul booked the bald gunman and filled out a weapon discharge report. Despite the size difference between him and the gunman, Paul knew how to turn the man's injured arm just right to make him think twice about struggling. Johnny went straight to Masterson's office. Officers peeked their heads up from their work as Johnny stormed through the station.

Johnny reached Masterson's door, threw it open, and went inside. The door slammed behind him.

"Detective Iceberg," the police chief said, coat over his arm. "I was just leaving, but I'm glad you're here. I've been meaning to talk to—"

"What's this thing about poison?" Johnny cut him off. "Did you plan on telling me about that, or were you just hiding it to sabotage our investigation until you could jump in and save the day when we couldn't solve the case?"

"I'm doing nothing of the sort," Masterson said calmly.

"Oh, come on," Johnny said. "Where's all this 'evidence' you mentioned during the press conference? Give it to me."

"Miss Thompson threatened to kill him during a Village Council meeting just a few hours before he was killed—"

"That's bull," Johnny cut him off again. "She already told me about the council meeting, and she mentioned nothing of the sort."

"And I had explicitly ordered you to stay away from her, Iceberg." Masterson stood up and glared at Johnny. "Since you obviously don't listen to what I say anyway, I see no compelling reason to go through the rest of the evidence against her. You may leave, detective," Masterson waved Johnny out of the office.

"Don't change the subject," Johnny yelled at the chief. "I said that she never threatened him."

"And criminals never lie, do they, *Johnny?*"

"She's not a criminal," Johnny said. He hated it when Masterson used his first name.

"Look, *Johnny*," Masterson said, calming himself and sitting down, "it bothers me just as much as it bothers you that we've arrested an eleven-year-old girl for murdering Santa Claus. Jack Frost, it bothers everyone in the department. But that's just how it is."

"What about the cyanide?" Johnny said, picking up a picture from Masterson's desk. "I want to see the toxicology report on that and the evidence you have linking the poison to Susie."

"No."

"No?" Johnny said. "You can't conceal evidence from me. I'm the lead detective on this case!"

"The case is already solved," Masterson said, standing up again and taking the picture from Johnny's hands. "The girl will be tried and convicted within a year. I'm taking you and Paul off the case as of right now."

"You're *what?*"

"You and Paul have been reassigned to traffic duty tomorrow at True North Plaza. The Mayor will be giving a speech, and it will be congested."

Johnny just stood there, in shock.

"That will be all, detective," Masterson said. "You don't need to write a report on your findings. Just report for traffic duty tomorrow at eight."

Johnny couldn't believe it. *Traffic duty?* Out of desperation, Johnny pulled the Naughty List from his coat pocket and stretched it out on Masterson's desk.

"You see this?" Johnny said. "Susie couldn't possibly have killed Santa without premeditation. Don't you think plotting murder is bad enough to get you on this list? Her name's not here. But this is," Johnny pointed out the circled name.

"Where did you get that?" Masterson asked.

"That's not important. What's important is—"

"Did Mrs. Claus give that to you?"

"Quit avoiding the point, *chief*. Susie Thompson's name isn't here. Santa circled somebody else who is listed. This case isn't remotely solved yet. This list, by itself, is enough to get Susie released on bail."

"You stole it, didn't you?" Masterson said tersely. "I can't admit stolen evidence. Can't you follow the rules just once, Johnny?"

"Will you quit talking about rules and orders," Johnny demanded. "We're trying to catch a killer, and this may point us in the right direction. At the very least it creates some doubt about pinning everything on Susie. Once we know who really did it, then we can get all the evidence we need."

"Your logic escapes me," Masterson said. "The only thing this list does is prove to me that you are an insubordinate detective and that I cannot trust you with a significant case like this. Your behavior is completely unacceptable. I am suspending you without pay for five days."

"You're what?"

"You breached protocol on the most important case we have ever investigated," Masterson said, taking the Naughty List and putting it in his desk. "If you are not out of this building within thirty minutes I will have you arrested. I have already reprimanded and suspended you, Iceberg. Don't push it—my only other option is to fire you."

"But—"

"I said don't push your luck, detective," Masterson cut him off. "Get over it. Susie Thompson is *not* your daughter. Mindless devotion to her isn't going to undo everything you did to screw up your family, and it won't bring Emily back. Now get out, or I will fire you."

Johnny stared menacingly at Masterson. The Police Chief matched his glare. Johnny finally broke away and left the room in a flurry, again slamming the door behind him.

As Johnny walked out of Masterson's office, Paul was there waiting.

"What's going on, Johnny?"

Johnny kicked a chair as he walked down the hall and threw his fist against the wall.

"He's not letting her go, is he?" Paul asked.

"We're off the case," Johnny said. "And he suspended me."

Paul shook his head. "What did you say to him?"

"I told him he's concealing evidence."

"And he suspended you for that?"

"He suspended me for breaking into Mrs. Claus's house."

"How'd he find out about that?"

"I showed him the list. He wouldn't listen to anything I said about it."

Smooth, Paul thought. "Well, that puts us in a bind, doesn't it?" he said. "So if we're off the case where did he reassign us? Or where did he reassign me, since you've been suspended."

"Traffic duty."

"Ouch," Paul said. "At least your suspension will get you out of *that*."

Johnny did not find Paul's comment funny.

"Don't you even care that we've been pulled off the case?" Johnny asked.

"We were never really on the case, Johnny." Paul looked up and down the hall to see if anyone could overhear him. Finding nobody, he lowered his voice: "Look, I'm going down to question that guy that shot at us. We both know he has something to do with this whole mess, and I can interrogate him without being on the Santa case.

"Like I told you, I have a hard time believing that this little girl killed Santa too—especially after everything we've seen today. But I also know that kicking against Masterson is going to get us no-where. So I'm just going to follow up on our leads and see where they take me."

Johnny nodded. "Okay, let's go," he said.

"If you've been suspended, then you need to get out of here before you get fired," Paul said.

"Masterson was on his way out when we had our little chat. If he's gone and we make sure nobody sees me, then as far as he knows, I have left."

Paul was going to argue but realized it would be useless.

❄ ❄ ❄

The guard handed Susie her dinner and said nothing. Ever since her rant earlier in the day, he had not spoken a word to her. Susie took her meal and ate it quietly in the back corner of her cell.

She felt an odd feeling inside, much like she felt when her sister had died. It was not sorrow, though she had certainly felt that as well when her sister had died. She could not put her finger on it. With her sister, she had felt terrible that there was nothing she could do to help her get better. She had tried. She had gone to the doctor with her and held her hand. She had made a snack for her at least twice a week. She had cleaned their room, so her sister didn't trip over anything. And when nothing helped anymore, she had naively and desperately written Santa Claus to ask for his help.

Suddenly, Susie understood what she was feeling now and what she had felt before: guilt. She had felt guilty for being useless to her sister—nothing she tried had really done any good. Now she felt guilty about Santa Claus. Even though she had done nothing to him, she still felt guilty. Guilty for hating him even though he deserved it.

He had not been a nice man, not to her at least. He had never even responded to her outrage after the Village Council meeting. He had just ignored her during their entire sleigh ride back to the house. But Susie couldn't stop thinking about the prison guard and how he had actually started crying when she had gone on her little rant. Santa must have been nice to *some* people, she realized.

Susie picked at her meal. She did not have much of an appetite. When she had eaten what she wanted to, she set her tray by her cell door and lay down on her small bed, staring at the gray ceiling.

Why did you invite me here, Santa Claus?

❋   ❋   ❋

As soon as Johnny punched the bald gunman in the face, Paul stormed out of the holding cell.

The suspect had not been silent this time, and Johnny had recognized the man's voice—he was one of the men who had been sneaking around outside the Claus estate. Johnny asked him why he had been there and what dirt he was supposed to be digging up for Mayor Wassail. The man had then suddenly became silent, a brief look of shock passing over his face.

Again and again, Johnny had demanded to know what the Mayor wanted from Mrs. Claus, but the suspect wouldn't say anything. Finally, in frustration, Johnny had simply punched him.

After Paul stalked off, Johnny followed.

"So that's how you make sure Masterson doesn't know you're still here?" Paul demanded.

"Oh, what's he going to do?" Johnny asked. "Suspend me again?"

"Johnny!" Paul shouted. "This isn't just about rules. I guarantee baldy's going to hire a hotshot lawyer and sue us for what you just did. It won't matter that he shot at us or what else he may have done. He's never going to go to jail now."

"He knows something, Paul!" Johnny yelled back.

"And now we're never going to get it out of him," Paul fired back.

Johnny stalked off, angry with Masterson, with the gunman, with Paul, but mostly with himself. Paul was right—again. Johnny was making everything worse. He idly ran a hand through the gunman's belongings: the gun, lock picking tools, a bottle of ether, a dirty green cloth, and a small, folded piece of paper. Johnny picked the paper up and unfolded it:

Cell 3, Maximum-Security
Last window on the left on the West wall, 2nd floor

After staring at the paper for a moment, Johnny looked up.

"Come on, Paul," Johnny said.

"Where?" Paul demanded.

"Okay, Paul," Johnny said. "You're right. I botched everything up. Now come on. I need a computer."

"You can't go back to your desk," Paul said. "Everyone will see you."

"I'm not going to my desk," Johnny said. "I'm going to Sara's lab."

Paul was about to make a snide comment, but a group of officers walking down the hall caught his attention. Paul recognized them immediately: they were the team that had been assigned to interrogate the gunman.

"We have to get out of here," Paul said, gesturing toward the approaching group. "Now."

Johnny understood, and the two of them quickly headed down a side hall, hopefully before anyone recognized either of them. Quietly, Johnny and Paul walked through the corridors toward Sara's lab. They passed only a couple officers along the way, who simply said "Hi" and walked by. Johnny's suspension did not seem to be well publicized yet.

When they reached the lab, Paul went inside while Johnny waited tensely outside. If Sara's supervisor, or anyone else on the lab team, was inside, Johnny didn't know what he would do next. After a moment Paul poked his head back out the door.

"It's okay," Paul said. "Sara's the only one in here."

"Sara," Johnny said before he had even stepped completely through the doorway, "I need your computer."

"Okay," Sara said. She seemed agitated.

Johnny sat down at her computer and tried to log on, but he was denied access. He swore under his breath.

"Masterson's on the ball, isn't he?" Paul said.

"What's wrong?" Sara asked.

"We've been taken off the case, and Johnny's been suspended," Paul said. He pushed Johnny aside and logged in himself. Paul reached for the mouse but stopped suddenly.

"Why do you need a computer, anyway?" Paul asked Johnny.

Johnny handed Paul the piece of paper.

"This looks like a cell at the Diamond Maker," Johnny said. "We need to find out who's in it and if the description matches the actual location."

"Okay," Paul said.

"And Sara, I need you to do me a favor," Johnny said. "I need you to go to the evidence room and find out if the evidence from Susie Thompson's room matches the cyanide in your toxicology report on Santa's body."

"What cyanide?" Sara said. "The tox screen came back negative. There was nothing in his system."

Johnny was stunned. "You're kidding. Let me see that report."

"I can't, Johnny," Sara said. "The entire autopsy report is gone."

"What are you talking about?" Paul asked, his attention jolted away from the computer.

"It's disappeared," Sara said. "The hard copy isn't where I filed it, it's gone from my computer, it's off the network, and the database shows no record of it. It's gone."

"Who could have erased it?"

"Anyone above me would have access to the file," Sara said. "Limphus, any of the division heads, or the chief."

"Any one of them could have erased it?" Paul asked.

"I swear," Johnny said, "the next time I see Masterson, I'm going to—"

"Johnny," Paul interrupted his partner. "Before you finish that thought and I have to arrest you for threatening an officer, you should look at this."

Paul pointed to the monitor, now showing the layout of the North Pole Penitentiary. Johnny scanned for the four cells that made up the maximum-security sector. Cell three's inmate was Susie Thompson. Johnny swore and slammed a fist on the desk.

"That's not all," Paul said, pointing to the monitor. "The description on the paper—it's accurate. Her window is the last one, second floor, on the north wall."

"So why on earth would baldy have directions to her cell?" Johnny asked.

"I don't know," Paul said. "All I *do* know is that you have to have serious security access to even get that information."

"Masterson," Johnny said under his breath.

"He could have done it," Paul said hesitantly.

"But?" Johnny asked.

"I think you're letting personal animosity interfere with your ability to think," Paul said.

"Paul, it all adds up," Johnny said.

"I know it does," Paul said. "Right now everything is pointing to Masterson, and you're acting as if Christmas has come early. Think about it, Johnny. Masterson's the *chief*. If he's gone bad, that's going to scare a lot of people. It scares me. On the other hand, we have both been cops long enough to know that when all the arrows are pointing at one person, there's a good chance that the evidence has been manipulated."

"Who's Susie Thompson," Sara asked, studying the monitor, "and why would Masterson give out her prison information?"

"Susie has been arrested for killing Santa Claus," Paul said.

"But she didn't do it," Johnny said. "She's an eleven-year-old girl, for crying out loud. I don't even know who made the arrest, but Masterson authorized it."

"So why would he give out directions to her cell?" Sara asked again.

Johnny said nothing. He simply put on his coat and double-checked his gun.

"What are you doing?" Paul asked suspiciously.

"Think about it, Paul," Johnny said. "Masterson gave the information to some thug who tried to shoot us. We don't have time to find out exactly why he did it."

"You think he wants her killed?" Paul asked. "Now you're really jumping to conclusions. Why would he want to kill Susie?"

"To keep her quiet," Johnny said. "To divert everyone's attention from Santa's murder. I don't know. I'm not even sure he wants her killed. All I know is that there's something *very* sinister going on, and Susie's been dropped right in the middle of it. I don't think she's safe."

"So what are you going to do?" Paul demanded.

"Break her out of prison," Johnny said.

"She's in a maximum-security sector," Paul said. "You'll never pull this off, and you're not going to do Susie any good if you're in jail, too."

"I'm not going to get caught," Johnny said.

"Not to be cynical, but we've both arrested hundreds of people who were sure they weren't ever going to be caught," Paul said.

"Then what should I do?" Johnny demanded. "Go home and watch TV for a couple days and just see what happens? Something bad is going on, and I don't care what happens to me. I have to do something."

"'Never let established procedures get in the way of doing what is right,'" Sara said quietly.

"What?" Johnny and Paul asked simultaneously.

Sara pointed to a small plaque hanging above her desk. The phrase was etched in with gold letters.

"I came up with the phrase in college," Sara said. "Back when idealism was much more important than having a decent job."

"It's a good phrase," Johnny said.

Sara blushed slightly. "Well, it's not all mine. It's really from an old science fiction book. I just changed a few of the words so it said what I wanted it to say."

Paul took a deep breath. "You're going to be on your own, Johnny," he said. "I'm not breaking the law based on some theory that this girl is the target of a conspiracy being facilitated by the police chief."

"You do what you have to do, Paul," Johnny said. "It's a lot easier to be idealistic when you have nothing else," he said self-deprecatingly. "I have nothing left, and I honestly don't care what happens to me any more."

"Don't play martyr with me, Johnny," Paul said. "You would be just fine if you'd pull your head out of your—"

"Just do what you need to do," Sara told Johnny, cutting off Paul.

Johnny nodded. He looked at Sara for a moment, his face unreadable, then quickly walked to the door.

"Good luck," Sara said as Johnny opened the door.

"Do you remember the results of the autopsy?" Johnny asked her suddenly.

Sara looked insulted. "Do you remember what you found out at Mrs. Claus's house—even without looking at your notes?"

"Sorry," Johnny said. He felt dumb for asking.

"Johnny doesn't take notes," Paul added.

Sara ignored the penguin's chide. "Cause of death was internal bleeding. My guess is that he was bludgeoned to death. Given the amount of bruising, damaged tissue, and broken bones, probably multiple assailants."

"Will you write it all down again?" Johnny asked.

"What's the point?" Sara asked. "Masterson, or whoever it was, will probably just get rid of it again."

"Don't file it," Johnny said. "Just give a copy to Paul."

"How am I going to follow up on it?" Paul asked. "I'm off the case, remember?"

"You'll just have to figure it out, Paul. I need your help. Susie needs your help."

Paul sighed and nodded.

"If you need anything, you can call me," Sara said. "That number I gave you earlier is my personal cell. Nobody here will be monitoring it."

Johnny nodded. He took a deep breath, walked out, and let the door shut behind him.

CHAPTER TWELVE
—NORTH POLE PENITENTIARY, 8:13 PM

JOHNNY WALKED into the holding area. Usually officers were required to show their badges to enter. Johnny, having quite a bit of notoriety in the department, was able to just walk through. Having left his gun in his car—he figured it would be more accessible there than in a one of the prison's locked stockings—Johnny didn't need to check in any weapons. He simply smiled at the guard and walked through the metal detector blinking with Christmas lights.

The North Pole Penitentiary was not large. The main holding area, which was adjacent to the entrance, had twenty cells: ten on each floor. Cheap red and green confetti paper had been strewn around the flickering fluorescent lights overhead. A faded poster of one of the previous Head Clauses, Johnny thought it may have been Santa's grandfather, hung on a far wall. "He knows if you've been bad or good," the poster caption read.

The entrance to the maximum-security sector was at the end of the hallway. The burly walrus standing guard at the entrance recognized Johnny as well, but demanded to see his identification anyway.

"I was supposed to be off an hour ago," Johnny shouted, faking a small fit as the walrus tried to run his badge through the scanner, "but Masterson demanded that I try to get the girl to cooperate one more time. I don't have time to wait all night for a stinking computer to authorize me."

The guard, aware of Johnny's sharp temper and tendency to do whatever he felt like to get his own way, grudgingly let Johnny through. *Sometimes it helps to have a bad reputation*, Johnny thought. If Masterson had already blocked Johnny's computer access, he had probably changed his status to "*suspended*" in the database as well.

The guard led Johnny up the stairs, where all four cells in the maximum-security sector were held. Johnny spotted Susie in the cell in the back left corner. A polar bear growled in a cell to Johnny's right. As Johnny walked to Susie's cell, the guard followed right behind him. Susie jumped up at the sight of Johnny and started to talk, but Johnny held a finger to his lips and gestured her to be quiet. The guard, watching the quick exchange, hesitated at opening the door. Johnny grabbed the keys from the walrus's flipper and unlocked the door himself. He threw the keys back to the guard and opened the door.

"Well, I'll be! If it isn't the great Johnny Iceberg!"

Johnny looked over and saw an elf in black and white stripes up against the bars of his cell, a wicked grin on his face.

"What's the matter, Johnny? Don't want to pay me a visit? How ungrateful. You'd be nothing without me!"

"Be quiet, Murdock!" the guard said.

"Or what? You'll throw me in prison?" Murdock laughed uproariously.

Johnny had forgotten that Murdock, the elf he arrested nine years earlier for murder, would be in the high security containment area as well. Johnny had no desire to talk to him.

"Come on, Johnny! Let's chat, for old time's sake! It's been so long!"

Johnny ignored his jeers. He could not afford to lose his cool right now, and this slimy little elf was one of the few people that could make him do just that. It had been the Murdock case that had consumed Johnny's entire life nine years ago—so much so that Johnny had literally not spent any time with his family for three months. Murdock had been so coy, so overly confident that the po-

91

lice would never get enough evidence to arrest and convict him.

Johnny had known Murdock was hiding evidence, but he did not know where. Like Paul was now, Johnny had been a by-the-book cop, and he had tried every legal means possible to find the evidence, but nothing had turned up.

One late evening, after spending a week and a half straight at the department, sleeping on a couch in the break room, he had suddenly felt like going home. When he arrived at his house, a modest home on Candy Cane Lane, a taxi was parked at the front curb. Before he could ask the cab driver what he was doing, his wife, Tara, and daughter came out of the house, each pulling two suitcases. *We are leaving*, Tara had said. *I can't stand this anymore*. Johnny had tried to explain that he was trying to solve an important case, but Tara cut him off. *I don't care*, she said. *You don't call, you don't come home. You haven't really been a husband or a father in a long time anyway. This just makes it official.*

Without another word, she pushed herself and Emily into the car, and it drove off.

Furious at Murdock, his wife, and himself, Johnny had immediately taken off to the coal mines where Murdock had worked. When he found the murderous elf, Murdock had smiled and asked Johnny how the investigation was going.

Without a word, Johnny had picked the elf up and threw him against the wall. Before Murdock could even respond, Johnny picked him up again and held him by the shirt over a mineshaft. *Give me the evidence or I'll drop you*, Johnny had yelled. Murdock, still sure of himself, had just laughed. *That's assault, detective Iceberg. You'll get yourself arrested if you do that.* But Johnny didn't care anymore. Without another word, Johnny let go. After he had heard Murdock hit the bottom, Johnny rode the pulley-operated elevator down, where he picked the elf up again, and took him back to the top of the shaft.

You can't force evidence out of me, Murdock had cried, sounding desperate this time. A large gash had been opened on the elf's head, and blood ran down his face. Johnny dropped him again. Once Murdock had hit the bottom, Johnny rode down and dragged the elf back up. He had a broken leg this time.

Before Johnny could do anything else, Murdock shrieked out in pain and fear: *I'll give it to you*, he had screamed. *I'll give it to you.* And he did.

Murdock had been so shaken by Johnny's temper and brutality that, even during the trial, he never even told his lawyer about the assault. Life in prison, Murdock had decided, was better than getting killed by a renegade cop.

And as much as Johnny loathed himself for losing his temper, as much as he hated working with the fear that his tactics would be discovered, he couldn't help but notice how quickly the assault had solved the case. He couldn't help but wonder if he would have been able to spend more time with his family had he been less obsessed with following protocol and procedures.

Johnny turned his back to Murdock as he entered Susie's cell. She had sat back down on her bed. She wore black and white stripes just like the other prisoners.

"Hello, Susie," Johnny said.

Her face was expressionless. "What took you so long?"

Johnny let out a laugh, then cut it short when he realized Susie was serious. "I'm sorry. I had more trouble than anticipated."

"So are we leaving?" Susie asked.

"You're leaving?" Murdock chimed in from the neighboring cell. "Oooh, can I leave, too?"

The guard banged his nightstick against the deranged elf's cell again.

"I'll be taking Miss Thompson here back to the station," Johnny told the guard. "There's some question as to whether she should actually be in here."

The guard stiffened and stood in Johnny's way. "I thought you were seeing if she wanted to cooperate," the walrus said.

He had said that, hadn't he? *Smooth*, Johnny thought.

"She's going to cooperate," Johnny said. "That's why I'm taking her."

The guard pushed Johnny back with a flipper. "No," he said. "You don't go anywhere until I verify this."

Johnny started to protest again, but the guard cut him off. "I don't care who you are, Iceberg, and I don't care about how much you're used to getting your way. I haven't been notified about any of this, and you don't take her anywhere until I verify that this is authorized."

"Fine," Johnny said. "Suit yourself."

The guard started moving back toward a phone on the wall. As he did, Johnny jumped toward him, grabbed the guard's head and slammed it against the wall. The guard slumped to the ground with a heavy grunt. Johnny knelt down and took the guard's keys and gun.

"Hey!" Murdock yelled. "Hey, somebody, in here! Johnny Iceberg just assaulted a guard and now he's going to break out!"

"Shut up, Murdock!" Johnny yelled at the elf, pointing the pistol at him.

"Hey! In here! Quick!"

Johnny bent down and looked Susie in the eye. "Susie, we need to get out of here, quickly. I need you to follow me and do exactly as I say. Can you do that?"

Susie simply nodded her head. She looked scared.

Johnny quickly led her to the stairs leading down to the main holding area. Murdock was still screaming about the breakout. Johnny paused before going down the stairs. He was of half a mind to shoot the elf, but didn't.

Johnny shut the door behind him as he led Susie down the stairs. Luckily, none of the prison staff had responded to Murdock's shouting. Either they hadn't heard him or Murdock's reputation and instability had desensitized the guards.

As he reached the bottom of the stairs, he realized Susie's feet were still chained together, and she was having trouble keeping up. Her hands were still chained together as well.

"Okay, Susie, here's what I'm going to do," Johnny whispered quickly. "If I unchain you, the guards up front are going to be suspicious, so I have to leave them on. What I can do, though, is unlock the chains on your legs so they look like they're still on, but you have to promise me you'll walk slowly unless I tell you to run, okay?"

Susie nodded again. She tried to act calm, but, again, Johnny could tell that she was scared. Johnny tried to give a reassuring smile. He unlocked the shackles on her feet, making sure they stayed in place and looked as though they were still locked shut.

Johnny opened the door at the bottom of the stairs and led Susie through the main holding area. The prisoners all watched them, wondering what was going on. A trashy looking snowman with a mohawk made out of rhubarb and syrupy tattoos all over his torso scowled at them. Both Johnny and Susie did their best to ignore him. Johnny opened the main door and they walked through.

The guards on the opposite side of the door looked at them, obviously perplexed.

"Where are you taking her?" the first guard, an enormous elf nearly as tall as Johnny's shoulder, demanded.

"Back to the station for questioning," Johnny said.

"Nobody said anything about a prisoner transfer tonight," the elf said. The other guards stood up and stood in Johnny's way. The elf walked over to a phone.

"You know," Johnny said to the other guards. "I don't have all night. Why don't you just escort me into the reception area while he makes his phone call. Then, when he finally gets through to Masterson, you can just let me go."

The elf, not wanting do deal with one of Johnny's infamous fits, nodded to the others, who led Johnny out to the reception area. Once there, Johnny moved himself and Susie as close to the exit as the guards would allow.

Suddenly an alarm went off. Red lights flashed around the room and sirens echoed off the walls. The guards moved to grab Johnny, but before they could, Johnny grabbed the nearest officer and held the gun to his head while jerking Susie behind them both.

"How'd he get a gun?" one of the others yelled.

"Back off!" Johnny shouted at the other guards, pressing the pistol into his captive's temple. He slowly moved toward the door, kicking Susie's shackles off as he did. As soon as he reached the door, he shoved the guard straight into the others and fired several shots randomly at the walls.

"Run, Susie!" Johnny shouted.

He and the girl bolted out the door and into the parking lot, pausing only long enough for Johnny to quickly jam the door with the empty shackles.

"Where am I running to?" Susie shouted.

"There," Johnny pointed at his car.

Behind them, the guards had broken through the jammed door. As Johnny aimed his gun at them his shoulder jerked back with a splatter of blood and a sudden sharp pain. He briefly fell to one knee.

"Susie," Johnny said, pulling keys out of his pocket. "I need you to start the car." He threw her the keys. "Just stick the key in the ignition and turn it forward."

"What's the ignition?"

"It's the hole in the side of the steering wheel. Go!"

As Susie ran toward the car, Johnny picked himself up and charged the guards. Taking them by surprise, Johnny knocked two of them down and grabbed their guns. He was grabbed from behind, but quickly elbowed the man in the nose. He pistol-whipped a fourth guard, who fell to the ground in an unconscious heap. Ignoring the pain in his shoulder, Johnny turned and ran toward his car again, which had exhaust coming out its tailpipe.

Good girl, Susie.

More guards rushed through the front door, but Johnny ducked behind a row of cars before they could shoot. Shooting a tire on each of the cars in the parking lot as he went, Johnny made it to his car and jumped in. Just before the prison guards caught him, Johnny peeled out and drove off.

Johnny smiled at Susie, who was panting heavily.

Sirens, coming from somewhere in front of them, rang faintly, though they slowly became louder and louder. Johnny frowned again. He pulled the car onto a dark side road, mostly hidden by a dense thicket of trees. Just after doing so, a dozen patrol cars sped down the main road and toward the Penitentiary, sirens blaring and lights flashing.

Johnny suddenly felt lightheaded. He looked at his shoulder. Blood had soaked through his shirt.

"I need you to drive, Susie," Johnny said.

"I can't drive! I'm only eleven!"

"You're almost twelve."

Susie scowled at him. Johnny got out of the car and walked to the passenger side. He opened the door, shoved Susie to the driver's seat, and sat in the passenger side.

"You can do this," Johnny said. "There are two pedals down by your feet. As soon as I put this stick here on the D, push down on the right pedal as hard as you can and use the steering wheel to steer. Just like a video game. I'll tell you where to go."

"I hate video games."

"Well, this will be a bumpy ride then, won't it?"

Johnny shifted the car into drive. The car idled forward slowly.

"Okay, push down on the pedal."

The car slowly sped up. Susie looked wide-eyed over the steering wheel and out the front windshield. As she drove the car down the small, dark road, she gradually began speeding up.

"Faster," Johnny said. "We have to get out of here as fast as we can."

Susie pushed the gas pedal more, and the car accelerated.

"That's a good girl," Johnny said. "You did it, Susie."

"Mr. Iceberg?"

"Yes?"

"Can you unchain my hands now? I can't steer very well with them on."

Johnny, despite himself, had to laugh. He had completely forgotten about them. He reached into his pocket, pulled out the guard's keys and unlocked her hands.

"Thank you," Susie said.

"Thank you, Susie. We're going to make it." Johnny smiled at her, and she smiled back.

DECEMBER 23

Chapter Thirteen

Paul picked at his breakfast while his two sons, Greg and Harrison, fought over the largest piece of salmon. Finally Greg, the eldest, smushed the larger piece and threw it into Harrison's bowl of cinnamon oatmeal.

"Mom!" Harrison cried.

"I gave you the biggest piece," Greg said defensively.

"You just dip it in your oatmeal anyway," Allison, Paul's wife, told Harrison.

"But I like to break it into little pieces first, then dip it in," Harrison whined.

"Fine," Allison said, exasperated. She switched bowls with Harrison and gave him her piece of salmon. She looked over at Paul, who still had not eaten anything.

"Slow down, Paul," Allison said sarcastically. "You're going to choke."

"Look mom, I'm choking!" Greg put his flippers around his neck and made gagging noises.

"Knock that off right now," Allison said.

"Dad does it," Greg said. "He did it when we went to the hockey game and the Tannenbaums scored three goals in the last period."

Allison scowled at her husband, but Paul didn't seem to notice.

101

"You don't have anything to say to your son?" Allison asked.

"Quit choking yourself," Paul said.

"Why?"

"Because your mother said so."

Allison set her spoon in the bowl and tossed a napkin on the table. "Paul," she said, "we need to talk. Greg, Harrison, finish your fish and oatmeal. No fighting."

Paul followed her out of the kitchen and into the living room. Just like the dining area, the living room had white walls and ice blue carpet. Several dozen pictures of their family hung on one wall, and two custom-designed, penguin-fitted sofas sat against another. The Glacier Lamp in the middle of the room cast an iridescent, faintly bluish light that drifted back and forth across the walls.

The house had originally been built for elves, and it was in a predominantly elvish neighborhood. The previous owner had worked in the Doll and Action Figure Division of Santa's Workshop for thirty-six years. Allison had always maintained that he must have designed the old hippie Barbie clothing—when she and Paul had bought the house the walls had been neon red, the carpet mustard yellow, and the appliances sea green. It had taken Paul and Allison nearly three years to make the interior look and feel comfortable.

"Paul, what is wrong?" Allison asked in a tense whisper as soon as they were in the living room. "It's like you're not even here this morning."

Paul took a deep breath. "Sorry," he said. "It's just … the case," he said.

"You've had tough cases before," Allison said. "But you've never acted like this before. I've never had to wonder whether you know I exist or not."

"This isn't just another hard case, Allison. Santa Claus is dead for goodness sake," Paul said. "I'm doing my best. I'm spending time with you, but I still have a lot on my mind."

"Do you have *any* leads?" Allison asked.

Paul grimaced. He had told her the brief details about the case, but he had said nothing about the specifics—Susie's arrest, the missing evidence, the investigation going on behind his back, Johnny's suspension, or the reassignment to traffic duty. He definitely hadn't said anything about the gunman, the possible threat to Susie's life, or Johnny breaking her out of prison. Knowing that the prison break would be all over the news last night, Paul had spent the evening playing *Don't Break the Ice* with Allison and the kids in order to keep them away from the TV. He had no idea what was going to happen once he went in to work.

"Paul," Allison said. "Are you listening?"

"Yeah," Paul said. "We have some leads."

Allison opened her beak, as if to say something, but the phone interrupted her. Allison picked up the phone and looked at the Caller ID: "*Unavailable.*" She let out an exasperated sigh and clicked *talk*.

"Look, I don't care if your knives can cut through your Aunt Matilda's fruitcake—" Allison began before trailing off. "Oh, sorry Johnny. Yes, we're having a wonderful breakfast. Yes, I'm planning to wear my blue dress at the Department New Year's Eve Party. Yes, you can talk to Paul."

Allison handed the phone to Paul. Paul covered the receiver with one flipper and motioned to Allison to go back to the kitchen. After a long look, she nodded and left the room.

"Good morning sunshine," Johnny said.

"What's going on, Johnny?" Paul asked. "Are you okay?"

"I'm fine," Johnny said. "Susie's fine too."

"Where are you?"

"At the Arctic Hotel. The one out at Star Port."

That would explain the unavailable number on the caller ID, Ever since Paul and Johnny had busted its previous owners, a group of caribou, for running a drug ring, the new owners had maintained the chain's sleazy reputation. Knowing that most of their clientele would prefer nobody to know they had stayed there, the owners cited their *unavailable* phone numbers as one of the services offered to guests.

"I need a favor," Johnny said.

"What kind of favor?" Paul said skeptically.

"Susie needs a place to stay."

"And you want her to stay here," Paul said. It wasn't a question.

"She has nowhere to go," Johnny said. "My apartment isn't exactly a good place for a kid to spend her time. And besides, I guarantee there are at least two cops staking out the place right now."

"No," Paul said. "I am not getting Allison and the kids involved."

"Paul, we both know that Susie is innocent and that she is in danger—"

"We *think* she was in danger," Paul cut him off. "Based on a single clue and a good deal of conjecture."

"And a big load of instinct," Johnny said. "Don't try to pin this all on me. You were just as uneasy about the whole thing as I was."

Paul was pacing up and down his living room. Allison, who had come back in the room, watched her husband uneasily. A rustle of the bushes outside caught their attention. Paul and Allison both rushed to the window. Paul spotted a team of officers setting up surveillance equipment in a tree across the street. Allison bit her bottom bill, her eyes widening in confusion.

"*Frost*," Paul said under his breath as he moved away from the window. "This is no good, Johnny," he said into the phone again. "There's a surveillance team setting up across the street."

"Have they tapped your phone?" Johnny asked.

"I don't know," Paul said.

There was silence.

"Then I guess I'm on my own," Johnny finally said. He hung up.

Paul simply held the phone and stared blankly at nothing. Allison stood tensely at the other end of the room, watching Paul closely.

"Paul, what is going on?" Allison asked quietly. "What are those cops doing across the street?"

"The guys across the street are looking for Johnny," Paul said. "Nobody here's in any danger." Paul desperately hoped it was true.

"What did Johnny do?" Allison asked, having heard dozens of stories of Johnny's rule breaking over the years. "What was he calling about?"

"Johnny's fine, as far as it goes," Paul said. He touched Allison's face gently.

"You're not going to tell me what he did, are you?" Allison asked.

"Allison, don't ask. Please, just don't ask."

❄   ❄   ❄

Johnny sat in a rickety wooden chair in the corner of the hotel room. The walls were covered in gaudy, peeling pastel wallpaper, a rusted out sink dripped nearly frozen water, and the single bed was propped up by busted toys, the throwaways from Santa's Factory. The curtains were stapled to the wall and covered the windows. Two dangling light bulbs swayed back and forth in the icy draft. Susie was still asleep in the bed, and Johnny had moved from the chair only once during the entire night.

Susie had winced at the sleaze as soon as they entered the room, late the previous night. Johnny told her she should just be thankful the North Pole was too cold for cockroaches.

There had been nowhere else for them to go. Johnny had known that his apartment would be watched, so he had never even considered going home. They couldn't stay in the car—they had abandoned it after they had driven far enough away from the prison, and had hidden it in a small ravine. Johnny supposed he could have tried to build a snow cave, but neither he nor Susie was dressed for a night in the forest.

That left the Arctic Hotel. The hotel managers never asked your name and they only accepted cash. There was no way anyone would be able to track him there. There was also no way for any of the guests to be tracked, and both Johnny and Susie were able to see exactly what kind of people the hotel attracted. *Is everyone here a freak?* Susie had asked after seeing yet another heavily tattooed elf with no teeth mumbling to himself and walking drunkenly through the hallway. *Not unless we're freaks too*, Johnny had answered, trying to lighten the mood. Susie had simply looked annoyed in response.

As soon as they got to their room, Johnny had Susie pull the bullet out of his shoulder. All Johnny had was a pocketknife, which Susie used to dislodge the bullet and pry it out. It had felt like his

105

muscle was being pulled off his bones. Susie gagged several times, but each time she did she forced a cough as she tried to hide it. When the bullet was finally out, she just dropped it to the floor and slumped down on the bed. By the time Johnny had thrown the bullet in the garbage and mopped up some of his blood, Susie was already asleep. Johnny watched her for a moment before covering her up with the comforter. It was nearly one o'clock in the morning.

While Susie slept, Johnny had tended to his wound. He took one of the hotel towels to wrap around his shoulder, but the towel was brown and crusted with grime and dirt. He took it to the sink to rinse it clean, but the water that came out was brownish green. Johnny slammed the water shut.

Left with no other options, Johnny pulled out an extra shirt he had brought and ripped it into a long strip. He went outside, locking the door behind him, and walked a hundred yards or so to the coast. He rinsed out the dirty towel in the icy seawater and used it to wipe and clean his shoulder. The salt water stung as it soaked into the wound, but it was not nearly as bad as it had been when Susie had pulled out the bullet. After Johnny felt like he couldn't get it any cleaner, he wrapped his shoulder up with the torn strip of shirt and walked back to the hotel room.

Susie had still been asleep on the small bed when Johnny came back and dozed off in the wooden chair.

Now, having been awake for nearly an hour, Johnny looked at Susie, still sleeping, and wondered what to do. Asking Paul to let Susie stay at his house had been more out of desperation than ideal planning. Johnny had known it was a long shot even before Paul saw the surveillance equipment across the street—Paul was hesitant to do anything that jeopardized his family's welfare, regardless of the cause or need. And Johnny knew that his partner would realize that any threat to Susie would be transferred to his family if she were at his house.

Johnny simply didn't know what else to do. Getting her safe was the first step, but until the real perpetrator was found nothing would really be solved. Johnny had hoped that between he and Paul, working on two different fronts, they would be able to solve the case. To do that, however, Johnny needed to be free to do what was necessary. He did not know how he could do that with an eleven-year-old girl trailing him everywhere he went.

Susie stirred a bit, but not enough to wake up. She was wearing an old outfit Johnny's daughter had once had—just a pair of jeans and a turtleneck. Prior to breaking her out of the prison, Johnny had stopped by his apartment to get the clothes, and Susie had put them on over her prison jumpsuit when they abandoned the car. It was enough to keep her just a little bit warmer and to turn away any attention her jumpsuit would have attracted.

It was odd to see her in Emily's old clothes. Susie looked almost nothing like Johnny's daughter. Where Emily had been tall, light-skinned, and blonde, Susie was short with light brown skin and dark hair.

A pale green rotary phone sat on a small nightstand next to the bed. Johnny had a fleeting impulse to call his daughter, but he didn't have the phone number with him. *Besides*, he thought, *I can't imagine a worse time to try to call than right now*. Like it had for nine years, reestablishing contact with Emily would have to wait. A different girl needed his help right now.

Masterson was partially right—there was an obvious connection between Emily and Susie. Johnny was honest enough with himself to admit that. But Masterson was wrong about the nature of the connection. Susie wasn't Emily, and this wasn't an attempt to somehow make up for what had happened nine years ago. It was simply an attempt to help a young girl whose life had been turned upside down. Johnny had failed to do that once before. Now he had a chance, with a different person and in a very different situation, to do it again, and he was determined to be successful. This wasn't about the past. It was about the present.

But he still had to figure out what to do now. Aside from Paul the only person Johnny trusted was Sara, but Johnny didn't like the idea asking her to watch over Susie. She would probably do it if he asked her to, but it would be … awkward. As brilliant as she was in the lab, she had no experience doing field work. Johnny didn't know if she was could do what was necessary to keep Susie safe, even if she could realistically anticipate it.

Johnny suddenly laughed. He was just like Paul. Suddenly he understood why his partner hated bringing his family into these kinds of situations. It was an awful feeling to ask someone for help who honestly had no idea what the situation was really like—especially when that person would probably say *yes*. That's why he could call and ask Paul to involve his family so easily, Johnny supposed. He knew Paul understood the situation and wouldn't agree to it. And then Paul would go to work and risk his career, his reputation, and his life to do whatever was necessary to help Johnny solve the case and keep Susie safe.

I hate it when Paul makes sense, Johnny had often complained. The truth was he felt lucky to have a partner with his priorities in such working order. Paul did what was necessary, followed the rules, and kept innocent parties innocent at the same time.

The light outside the window, shining through a crack between the curtains, brightened slightly. Johnny winced, but walked over to the window and looked out. The permanent dawn-light had just moved across the horizon enough to brighten the icy harbor and coastline. Despite the trashy reputation and amenities, Johnny had to admit the Arctic Hotel had a nice view. There was nobody in sight.

He still had to figure out what to do with Susie.

CHAPTER FOURTEEN

FROM THE minute Paul had walked in the door, everyone kept asking him about Johnny. *Where's Johnny? What's he doing? Is he staying at your place? Did he help the girl kill Santa?*

"I don't know," Paul kept repeating. "I'm not even on the case anymore. I have traffic duty."

Paul fidgeted with a pen as he sat at his desk. It had seemed clear enough last night that Paul should do everything he could to keep up the investigation behind the department's back, but now that Paul was here, he wasn't sure how to go about doing it.

He had already tried to question the gunman he and Johnny had arrested yesterday. He had been set free and nobody knew where he was. Computer activity was closely monitored, and only those on a case had access to any evidence that had been filed away. Plus, he was interrupted every couple of minutes by another officer asking the same questions. Paul swore he would hurt the next person to bring up Johnny and the prison break.

That opportunity looked like it would present itself soon enough. Masterson was walking towards Paul's desk. *Great,* Paul thought.

Masterson came and hovered over Paul's desk. Paul acted as if he was busy, scribbling several unintelligible notes on a notepad.

"Come with me to my office," Masterson said.

Masterson turned around and began walking without waiting for a response. Paul felt a sudden impulse to just sit there until the chief found the civility to hear whether Paul could come or not, but Paul shook the thought off. *I've been around Johnny too much*, he thought. Paul reluctantly stood up and followed, trying to anticipate Masterson's questions and quickly come up with some good responses. Despite what Johnny thought, Paul knew Masterson was not a fool. His instincts would tell him that Paul knew something about Susie's breakout.

As Paul walked through the department the other officers stopped what they were doing and silently watched him.

As Paul approached Masterson's office, he noticed a picture of the chief wearing an ugly Claus hat and a ridiculous looking fake beard. It was taped on one of Masterson's office windows, just beneath a sprig of mistletoe. A caption read: *"Don't be a Naughty Officer. Chief Masterson is watching you!"* Looking at the picture, just before stepping inside the office, Paul suddenly wondered how much Masterson and the rest of the administration could really monitor Paul's activity. Should he take administrative oversight seriously when somebody obviously considered it a joke?

"Have a seat, detective," Masterson said. "I have a new case for you to work on."

Paul wasn't sure what to say. He had expected a full-blown interrogation to find out what he knew about Johnny, Susie, and the prison break. He sat down slowly, feeling both skeptical and cautious.

"What case is that?" Paul asked.

"Yesterday you reported a fight at The One-Horse Open Sleigh," Masterson said. "I want you to follow up on that and find the guy who started it."

Menial work, Paul thought.

"I want you to do everything possible to arrest the suspect by tomorrow," Masterson said.

Paul frowned. "Why tomorrow? It's just a bar fight."

"I don't like to have open cases over the holiday season," Masterson said. "It makes bookkeeping easier if everything is taken care of by Christmas Eve."

Paul had never heard such nonsense in his thirteen years as a cop. *Since when is bookkeeping the primary concern of a police department?* Paul wondered. Had the NPPD suddenly turned into Yule-Mart? Did they suddenly have stockholders demanding quarterly returns?

Masterson read Paul's face. "I know you think following up on a bar fight is just busy work. You think it's an inappropriate case for a detective of your experience. You think I'm just trying to keep you occupied until we find Johnny and the murder suspect."

Paul stiffened. *Here it comes,* he thought.

"Detective, you need to trust me," Masterson said. "I need this case solved by tomorrow, and there is no other detective I can trust to do it."

"Sure thing, *chief*. At least it's not traffic duty," Paul said half-jokingly.

Masterson gave an ambiguous smile. "I still need you for that. Penguins make good crowd control. Make sure you get to True North Plaza no later than nine-thirty."

"Is that all you had to ask me, sir?" Paul said.

"Yes, that's all, Paul. Don't let me down."

Paul walked out of the office feeling somewhat bewildered. *Let him down?* How was Paul going to let him down? It was a stupid bar fight. Who cared if they threw one more drunk in jail for a couple months?

Again, as Paul walked back to his desk, the other officers watched him. Some looked surprised, as if they had expected the meeting with the chief to go longer. Paul had. He felt uneasy. He didn't like wondering what kind of game Masterson was playing with him. Just as the other officers had all assumed, Masterson had to think Paul would know something about the prison break. Why else would he have set up a surveillance team outside Paul's home?

Regardless of Masterson's agenda, he had given Paul the perfect means to secretly continue investigating Santa Claus's murder. Mitchell, the nervous factory elf, had been involved with both incidents. If anyone reprimanded Paul for getting involved with the Santa case, he could just claim to be investigating the bar fight.

Paul liked the prospect of visiting with Mitchell again, anyway. He and Johnny had probably been a little too easy on the elf when they questioned him yesterday. Now Paul would have the chance to really squeeze some information out of him.

Once he reached his desk, Paul called one of the office secretaries and asked for a composite artist to be sent to the One-Horse Open Sleigh. It was best to look as though he was really working on the case, he had decided.

Once the composite artist was arranged, Paul called his wife. He didn't like that Masterson had set up the surveillance crew outside his house and then pretended not to suspect Paul knew anything about Johnny. Something under-the-table was going on, and Paul did not want his family involved.

"Hello?" Allison answered the phone.

"Honey, it's Paul. Are those officers still across the street?"

After a pause, Allison said, "I don't see anything. I drove the boys to school—maybe they left while I was gone."

"Nobody's approached you or tried to ask you any questions?" Paul asked.

"No," Allison said. "Should I be worried about something?"

"I don't know," Paul said. "It's just been an odd day at work."

"I saw the news this morning, Paul."

"Oh."

"I guess I'm going to have to testify in front of a grand jury."

Paul let out a short laugh, but stopped when he remembered that his phone was probably being tapped.

"I've got to go, honey," Paul said. "My coworkers don't need to listen to me gab to my wife all day."

"I understand," Allison said.

"I love you."

"I love you too, Paul."

Paul set the receiver down. A red light was flashing at the base of the phone: he had a message. He picked up the phone again and listened to his voice mail.

"Paul, this is Sara Albright down at the lab. I just found an addendum I forgot to include with the original autopsy report. I understand you are no longer on the Claus case, but could you just come down to the lab and let me know who should receive the information?"

Paul picked up everything he thought he would need for the day and headed down to the lab.

Sara was waiting for him.

"Oh, come on in to my office," she said, closing the door behind her once Paul had waddled in. She handed him a retyped autopsy report, which Paul hid in his notebook.

"I hope you really have an addendum," Paul said. "If somebody's monitoring my phone, then they'll be looking for it."

"I wrote one up," Sara said. "It's even legitimate. The lab test on the black powder came back."

"Soot?" Paul asked.

"No," Sara said. "Carbon, hydrocarbon, sulfur, and hydrogen sulfide. And traces of both methane and ammonia."

"How about you tell me without speaking Elvish," Paul suggested.

"Coal," Sara said. "Consistent composition with the elves' mine."

"Is this information in the report you just gave me?"

"It's all there."

"Okay," Paul said. "I'll go over it when I'm out in the field today."

"I thought you were on traffic duty today?"

"Sort of," Paul said. "Masterson put me on another case—one that involves part of the Santa case."

"But it's not the Santa case?"

"No. They just … overlap."

"Do you think Masterson did that on purpose?" Sara asked.

"I don't know," Paul said. "Johnny would just say it proves that Masterson's incompetent, but I've never been convinced that our chief is an idiot. I think he knows exactly what he's doing."

"So is that good or bad?" Sara asked.

"I don't know," Paul said. He tucked the notebook away in his coat and walked toward the door.

"Have you heard from him?" Sara asked just before Paul opened the door and walked out.

"Yes," Paul said. "He's okay. At least he was a couple hours ago."

CHAPTER FIFTEEN

"HERE," JOHNNY said, throwing a small pack of cheap powdered sugar donuts next to Susie on the bed.

"What are these for?" Susie asked.

"Breakfast," Johnny said.

"I don't eat junk food," Susie said. "Especially not for breakfast."

"Oh come on, Susie," Johnny said. "They have flour and … potato stuff in them. They're fine. I've been living on donuts and coffee for years, and look at me."

"Isn't there any orange juice or anything like that?"

"What are you talking about?" Johnny asked. "Orange juice would taste terrible with donuts."

Susie let out an exasperated sigh and opened the pack of donuts.

"They taste like cardboard," she said after nibbling on one.

"Of course they do," Johnny said, grabbing on of the donuts for himself. "They're from a vending machine."

Johnny checked his gun and the one he had taken from the prison guard and frowned. There were only a few bullets left among them. He had no idea how seriously he and Susie were really in danger, but he didn't want to take any chances. He also knew that he would be caught the minute he tried to buy more ammunition from a legal firearms dealer, and he didn't know of any illegal ones—he and Paul had broken up the only two black market weapons rings he had known about a year and a half earlier.

"Susie, I hope you're good at hiding," Johnny muttered. They both had to be careful to avoid any kind of open confrontation.

"What are we going to do today?" Susie asked.

"I need to break into the mayor's office," Johnny said.

Susie's eyes widened a bit. "Why?" she asked.

"Yesterday I overheard two men at Mrs. Claus's house. They were looking for something. Just a couple of hours later, one of those men shot at me and Paul. When we arrested him, we found a scrap of paper that had directions to your prison cell in one of his pockets."

"Why did he have directions to my cell?" Susie asked, her face becoming a bit pale.

"That's one of several things I need to find out," Johnny said. "What does the Mayor want with you? Why was Masterson—the police chief, my boss—going behind my back to screw up my investigation? Somehow everything is connected to Santa's death. When I figure out how, then I can get the *real* bad guys arrested and you home."

Susie looked at the drawn curtains covering the window. She rubbed an eye and took another bite of her donut.

Johnny watched, still wondering what to do with her. He knew that dragging her along with him all day would be a bad idea, but he could see no other option. Leaving her alone at the hotel would be worse, and there was nobody who could watch her that Johnny trusted.

Though she might make a better lookout than Paul did at Mrs. Claus's place, Johnny thought.

"Did you like Santa Claus?" Susie asked.

Caught off guard, Johnny just stood with his mouth open for a moment. "Uh–I guess so. I mean, he never did anything to make me *not* like him. Next to Mayor Wassail and Masterson, Santa was a real snow cone."

Susie, still looking away, scowled. Obviously it was not the kind

116

of answer she had wanted. "Did he ever do anything nice for you?" she asked.

Johnny didn't know how to answer. He hadn't really believed in Santa for a long time—so long that he couldn't remember if he ever had. The whole Santa thing had always seemed like something for kids—for other kids. Never for him.

Susie wiped at her eyes again, smudging powdered sugar on her wet cheek.

"My daughter, Emily, she always got something nice from Santa for Christmas," Johnny said.

Susie nodded, but said nothing.

"Those clothes I gave you," Johnny broke the silence, "they don't fit very well, do they?"

Susie shook her head. "They're too big."

"Well, before we do anything else then, we need to get you some new ones. Maybe we should dye your hair too."

"Don't touch my hair," Susie said. "The last thing I want to be is blonde."

"Fine," Johnny said. "Hopefully there aren't thousands of pictures of you nailed to all the telephone poles."

"Aren't you worried about pictures of you being everywhere too?" Susie asked.

"There probably will be," Johnny said. "But this isn't the first time I've been on the brink of losing my job and thrown into jail. I've learned how to get around public places without people recognizing me."

"Then you'll just have to show me how," Susie said.

"You think you're smart enough?" Johnny asked.

"Oh, I'm plenty smart," Susie said. "Smarter than a man and a penguin combined."

Just as Johnny was going to respond he heard several cars outside. Somewhat alarmed, Johnny rushed to the window and peeked out from behind the curtains.

Susie moved to the window, beside Johnny. "What is—"

"Shh," Johnny whispered.

"Don't you tell me what to do—"

Johnny clamped a hand on Susie's mouth and muffled her. She fought for a moment, but Johnny only held on harder.

"I'm trying to see what's going on outside," Johnny whispered. "So be quiet and hold still."

Johnny swore silently. Three police cars, now empty, sat in the hotel parking lot. *How did they find us?* Johnny wondered. He had been afraid when Paul had seen the surveillance equipment being set up by his house—and Johnny had kept close watch for the next hour just in case Paul's phone had already been tapped when Johnny called. But as time passed and still nobody arrived, Johnny had been sure he and Susie were safe.

Johnny turned to Susie. "We have to get out of here, *now*," he whispered. "Put your shoes on."

Johnny gathered up everything he had and threw it into his small backpack. There wasn't much—the guns, Susie's prison clothes, and some money—but Johnny didn't want any trace of them left in the hotel room.

He peeked out of the window again. Six officers, four of whom were snow leopards, were outside arguing with the hotel manager. *Thank goodness for the Arctic Hotel*, Johnny thought. He could always count on them to not cooperate with the police. Unlike most officers, Johnny had long ago decided to use that fact to his advantage rather than fight it.

"Come on," Johnny whispered to Susie. He pulled her to her feet and to the back window.

"There's always a trick latch on the back window," Johnny muttered. After hearing a soft *click*, he opened the window.

"You can always open the back window in hotels?" Susie asked.

"No. Just in Arctic Hotels." Johnny winced as he lifted her up to the window. His shoulder wasn't going to be in good shape for some time, he knew.

Susie jumped from the window to the snowy ground outside. Johnny climbed up after her, breaking the radiator with a loud *clang* as he did, and jumped out of the room with her. Wincing again, now at both his shoulder and at a sudden pain in his knee, Johnny pointed to the thick forest several dozen yards away. Susie ran, and

Johnny did his best to keep up—he must have hit his knee a bit when he broke the radiator.

"I see them!"

Johnny looked back. An officer—Johnny did not know who it was beyond another random elf working for NPPD—was in the hotel room watching them from the window. The elf pointed toward them and two of the snow leopards bounded through the open window and started chasing them.

Ignoring the pain, Johnny broke out into a full run. As he reached Susie he grabbed her hand and pulled her along. His shoulder and knee both throbbed with pain. Behind them, the snow leopards were closing in fast. *They must have been expecting a chase,* Johnny thought. That was the only reason they would assign four of them to investigate the hotel.

Reaching for his belt with his one free hand, Johnny felt for his gun. He didn't want to shoot or accidentally kill anyone, but—

Suddenly, a large brown blur swooped past Johnny's head, and both he and Susie tumbled to the ground. When Johnny looked up and brushed the snow from his eyes, he saw the two snow leopards lying in the snow unconscious and a reindeer approaching them.

"Get on my back, Iceberg," the reindeer said.

"Dasher?" Johnny asked hesitantly.

"Get on."

Johnny helped Susie to her feet but placed himself protectively between her and the reindeer. Dasher had been neither friendly nor helpful at the training grounds, and Johnny did not know whether he should trust him or not.

"There's no time to explain," Dasher said, gesturing behind him. The second set of snow leopard officers had just appeared. "Just get on."

Johnny took a deep breath and hefted Susie to the reindeer's back.

"Are you sure you can hold both of us?" Johnny asked.

"Of course I can," the reindeer snorted. "There's a reason Santa placed me at the head of the team."

Okay, Johnny thought. He climbed on Dasher's back, ignoring the pain in his shoulder and knee, and sat down right behind Susie.

"Hold on tight," Dasher said.

Johnny grabbed a tuft of hair just as Dasher spun around and charged the two snow leopards. Stunned by the reindeer, the two officers stopped their charge and tried to jump out of Dasher's way. The second reacted a bit too late, was knocked in the head, and fell to the ground with a loud *thud*. Just before reaching the hotel, Dasher leaped into the air and circled into the sky, higher and higher, until the entire South Port area was nothing more than a mass of colored Christmas lights among the surrounding forest. To their left, Johnny and Susie watched the rest of the North Pole meld into a single multicolored halo reflecting off the surrounding mountains.

Susie laughed.

"It's like flying at the top of a snow globe!" she shouted above the icy wind.

Johnny, his hands already sore from how tightly he gripped Dasher's fur, did his best to laugh back.

"Yeah," he yelled in a shaky voice. "It's great. Dasher, where are you taking us?"

"Someplace safe and away from town."

"No good," Johnny yelled, trying to steady his voice. "I need to go to City Hall."

"Why?"

"Because I'm still doing the investigation."

Dasher shook his head, but changed direction and flew back toward the city.

Chapter Sixteen

Paul sat on a stool in the same room he and Johnny had used to interrogate Mitchell the day before. The transmission cable to the security camera was still disconnected, and the blinds were still closed. The door opened and Mitchell was shoved in by two burly security elves.

"Hello again, Mitchell," Paul said. "Have a seat."

"What do you want from me?" Mitchell asked. "I've told you everything I know."

"Actually, you told me everything you felt like telling me," Paul said. "You have *not* told me everything you know."

The elf let out a nervous laugh that sounded more like a hiccup.

"Those other elves didn't seem very nice," Paul said. "At least not the way they shoved you in here. Don't they like you very much?"

"They just have this thing against me," Mitchell said defensively. "They're always looking for reasons to shove me around. I don't know why it's always me."

"And your manager, Mundango, he just gave me an earful about what a lousy worker you are: fourteen hours behind on your quota, he said."

"He's out to get me, too," Mitchell whined. "He assigns me triple the work he gives anyone else, then he yells at me when I don't get it done in time!"

Paul leaned in toward Mitchell and stared the little elf in the eye.

"Actually, Mitchell," Paul said slowly and evenly. "I don't care about any of this. I just thought it might be worth reminding you that you're making everybody mad today. Don't do it to me, too."

Mitchell sat down on his stool and whimpered.

"Just tell me what I need to know," Paul said. "And I'll be happy."

"But I don't know anything else about Santa!"

Paul smiled coldly. "I'm not here about Santa. That case has been taken care of. I'm here about your little bar fight two nights ago."

Mitchell did not respond. Paul, who had always enjoyed watching potential suspects squirm, also said nothing. He simply cleared his throat several times, loud enough to jolt Mitchell's eyes back on the penguin, and smiled coldly at the elf.

"Where's the tall guy?" Mitchell finally spoke up.

"He's busy," Paul said. "NPPD thought that it would be better if I didn't have anyone to keep me restrained today. I get answers more quickly when I can do things the way I want."

"Are you going to open the blinds?" Mitchell asked.

Paul ignored the question. "Cut the crap, Mitchell," he said. "I had a long talk with Jim, the owner of the One-Horse Open Sleigh. He told me all about the fight you had two nights ago—the same night Santa was killed. You've already lied to me about what happened that night, and I'm running out of patience. If you don't cooperate right now, then you are going to get hurt."

"What do you want me to do?"

"First, tell me what the fight was about, how it started, and how you were involved. Second, tell me the names of everyone involved. Third, make me completely convinced that you aren't either lying or hiding *anything* from me."

Mitchell took a deep breath and started talking:

"I don't know much. I was at the One-Horse Open Sleigh with a bunch of guys from work, and we were complaining—you know, about the long hours, Santa's ridiculous manufacturing quotas, the fact that only about twenty percent of us pull our own weight at the factory. I said something about Santa being a slave driver—"

Paul raised a feathery eyebrow.

"No, no, no, no, no," Mitchell started talking very quickly. "Don't get me wrong. I don't think Santa was a slave driver—I mean I *didn't* think he was one before he was ... you know ... had his bucket kicked."

"I told you," Paul said. "I'm not investigating the Santa death anymore. If you had paid attention to anything in the news yesterday you would know that there's already a suspect in custody. I just found it very *interesting* that you seem to have had a motive too."

"I was just blowing off some steam," Mitchell protested.

"Go on. You haven't told me anything useful yet," Paul said, thoroughly enjoying Mitchell's flustering. Unlike Johnny, who really did do whatever he felt like when it came to investigations, Paul never really resorted to physical abuse during interrogations. He simply implied that he would like to and let the detainee's imagination fill in all the details. It was a rather effective means to perfectly legal interrogation.

"Okay," Mitchell said. "So, we were drinking a bit and complaining a bit and some guy walks over and sits down at our table. He's loud, like he had a bit too much to drink, and starts telling us how much he hates Santa too. 'Santa thinks he's such a big shot,' the guy said, 'but he's nothing but a tub of lard in an ugly red suit.' Then he asked us if we knew where Santa was. He said he wanted to settle the score.

"Well," Mitchell continued, "we weren't going to take that. I mean, what kind of ungrateful jerk hates Santa? It's one thing for us to complain about the work we have to do, but it's totally different for someone else. Santa only does nice stuff for the rest of the world.

"Besides, he might as well be insulting *us*. After all, we make the toys Santa gives out. I guess they just weren't good enough for this guy.

"Anyway, that's when we started yelling at him, asking him who he thought he was, telling him to get out of the North Pole. One thing led to another, somebody broke a table, Jim had some thugs throw us all out, and the next thing we knew the guy was gone."

"So this guy was looking for Santa?" Paul asked, intrigued.

"Yeah."

"Did he say exactly how he was going to 'settle the score'?" Paul asked.

"No. He looked like a rough dude, though."

"Do you remember what time Jim threw you all out?"

"I don't know," Mitchell said, thinking it over, "around one or one-thirty. Jim let us back in a half hour later. Our ears were turning blue."

That would have given the man plenty of time to get to Santa. "Have you ever seen this guy before?" Paul asked.

"No," Mitchell said.

"Were you too drunk to know whether you have ever seen him before?"

"I only had one drink."

"Yesterday you said you had 'a couple drinks', Jim said you had a dozen and were completely smashed, and now you claim you only had one. Don't give me any crap, Mitchell. Just answer the questions. What did the guy look like?"

"I–I don't remember," Mitchell whimpered. "I think he had blondish hair. You know, kind of dark brown. And red! Maybe. Sometimes things look kind of red in the bar when they're really not red at all."

"Well, at least you are finally being somewhat honest," Paul said. "You have no idea what he looked like. Was he human?"

"Yeah, he was human," Mitchell said firmly.

"Or maybe a walrus?" Paul asked sarcastically. "Sometimes they're hard to tell apart."

"He was human! And he had an accent. It sounded Australian."

Australian? Paul eyed Mitchell carefully, but the elf seemed to be telling the truth. Paul frowned, and Mitchell squirmed in his stool again. Paul ignored it. The bar fight case was lining up too neatly with the Santa case. As Paul had told Johnny the day before, when all the evidence points to a single conclusion, more than likely the evidence has been manipulated.

Paul still wasn't sure of what Masterson's agenda was. Johnny had been very quick to assume the chief was behind everything, probably in tandem with Mayor Wassail, but Paul was a little hesitant to jump to that conclusion. However, regardless of Masterson's intent, Paul knew the chief was deliberately manipulating him, and Paul hated being manipulated. For all of Johnny Iceberg's faults, that was one thing he at least had never tried to do to Paul.

"Mitchell, who else was with you at the One-Horse Open Sleigh?" Paul asked.

"Everyone in the bar?"

"No. You said you were with a group of elves—all workers in the factories. What are their names?"

Mitchell said nothing.

"Santa's Beard!" Paul swore. "I'm not going to arrest them for anything, I'm going to see if they can tell me anything else about this guy you got into a fight with."

"Monterey, Moonwort, Milliken, Mitchell, Mitchell, and Mitchell."

"Four elves named Mitchell, huh?"

"They're all pronounced very differently," Mitchell said, annoyed.

Right, Paul thought.

Before Paul could ask anything else, the door to the room opened. A woman elf made an odd gesture, to which Mitchell responded with wide eyes and a suddenly pale face. Mitchell jumped off his stool and darted out the door.

"Hey!" Paul tried to follow, but the woman stood in his way.

"The manager needed him," she said. "It's an emergency."

Paul pushed past her and into the bustle and chaos of the factory workroom. Paul looked back and forth, but there was no sign of Mitchell. Mitchell's manager, an elf named Mundango Paul remembered, was walking down an aisle near the army tank production team. Paul quickly walked after him.

"Where's Mitchell?" Paul demanded once he had reached Mundango.

125

"I'm sorry, detective," Mundango answered without looking at Paul. "He no longer works here."

"He did five minutes ago!"

"You must be mistaken."

Paul just stood in place, shocked. Slowly, his expression changed into suspicion.

"What about some other elves here: Monterey, Moonwort, Milliken, Mitchell, Mitchell, and Mitchell?" Paul did his best to pronounce the names exactly as Mitchell had.

"They no longer work here, either," Mundango said, still not looking at Paul.

Paul, suddenly feeling like going on an Icebergesque tantrum, turned and looked in the direction that Mundango had been staring for their entire conversation. Three large polar bears, wearing suits and badges that identified them as members of Mayor Wassail's personal security team, stood near the entrance of the factory, arms folded and sunglasses over their eyes.

What are they doing here? Paul wondered.

"Do those three have anything to do with Mitchell's sudden lack of employment here?" Paul whispered.

"Possibly," Mundango said.

"And Mitchell's friends?"

"Possibly."

"Could you tell me where they are?"

"I'm sorry," Mundango said. "All I know is that they aren't here, and the official factory records will show that they haven't been here since last week."

Paul nodded, and walked toward the front entrance. As he passed the three polar bears, not one of them seemed to notice him walking by—but it was impossible to tell what exactly they were looking at from behind their dark sunglasses.

CHAPTER SEVENTEEN

JOHNNY STOOD in the shadows of an alley across the street from City Hall, a five-story refurbished igloo, and watched Mayor Wassail leave the building, escorted by his usual entourage of polar bear security guards. One by one, the lights in the building turned off as the majority of the city staff headed off to True North Plaza to see the mayor's speech. A light-blue flag with a snowflake in the middle flew at half-mast. A large wreath hung from the third floor windows at the middle of the building. Each window was lined with haphazardly blinking Christmas lights. An inflatable team of reindeer was on the roof. Santa had been respectfully removed from the display.

Twenty-two years with the NPPD had made Johnny very familiar with the streets of North Pole Village, and he had little difficulty sneaking to City Hall through back roads and alleys without being noticed. Susie, now wearing a heavy black parka, snow boots, and purple earmuffs, stood by Johnny's side and looked at City Hall, scowling.

"You don't like the igloo?" Johnny whispered.

"No."

"Why not? It's historic," Johnny said. The building was one of the few remaining structures that had been built by the snowmen even before the elves had arrived at the North Pole.

"I know," Susie said sharply. "Santa told me all about it two days ago. I had a tour and everything."

"Oh." Johnny had forgotten that she had been to the building before and that it had been an unpleasant experience.

After Johnny had given Susie a quick shopping spree at Yule-Mart, Dasher had tried to persuade them to come with him to Sphere Valley, the current residence of most of the North Pole's snowmen. *They would be safe there*, Dasher had claimed.

Johnny, however, had no interest in safety. Masterson and the mayor seemed to be heading a conspiracy that involved Santa's murder, and Johnny had to solve it. Hanging out with a bunch of snowmen would do nothing to help him.

Johnny had considered sending Susie with Dasher. He didn't want a kid tagging along while he was doing the investigation, but once Johnny had refused to go with Dasher, Susie refused as well. Dasher had been obviously disappointed but finally took off on his own after telling Johnny and Susie to watch their backs. *The police aren't the only ones after you*, Dasher had said.

As they had watched Dasher disappear into the dark morning sky, Johnny didn't know whether to trust the reindeer or not. He was obviously on the run as well, but Johnny didn't know from whom. Nor did Johnny know Dasher's agenda. It was best that Susie hadn't gone with him.

The old reindeer had claimed that Santa had sat down with all nine reindeer on the team about a week before the murder and told them about his impending plans to change the entire operation of Christmas. According to Dasher, nobody knew exactly what Santa meant, and nearly all the reindeer were agitated by the news. A drastic change in Christmas could mean no more Christmas flight, and that meant the nine reindeer would be out of their jobs. Santa had promised them that they had nothing to worry about, but according to Dasher many of the reindeer, especially Rudolph, had not seemed very reassured.

Then, according to Dasher, Santa had said something strange. While passing around cookies and milk to the reindeer, Santa had suddenly looked forlorn and asked if the reindeer would ever forget him. *Forget you?* Comet had asked, vocalizing the perplexed question all the reindeer were asking to themselves. Santa had simply ignored Comet's question, and finally the reindeer all ate and drank their snack.

It was as if Santa had known he was going to be killed, Dasher had told Johnny.

Johnny shook his head and tried to forget about what Dasher had said. The reindeer had claimed that his icy and unhelpful attitude the previous day was because he had assumed Johnny was connected to Santa's death somehow. He had known someone at NPPD was involved. That, supposedly, was why Dasher had insisted all communication go though him: so that nobody would accidentally tell Johnny anything that would help the conspiracy. Dasher then had claimed that as soon as Johnny broke Susie out of prison, he had known that he could trust Johnny.

Johnny wasn't sure whether he could buy it or not. Dasher had never explained how he had known the details of the breakout or how he had found them at the Arctic Hotel. He had been equally cryptic about why he had risked his life to save them.

"Stay here, in the shadows," Johnny whispered Susie.

"What are you doing?" Susie asked.

"Nobody's come out of the igloo for a while now," Johnny said. "That means that everybody who is going to the speech is gone. I'm going to break in."

"Why?"

"To see if I can find anything," Johnny said.

"Like what?"

"Like … I don't know, something that helps me figure out what is going on."

"What can't you figure out?"

"What, do you think you're the inquisition or something?" Johnny snapped. "I'm breaking in so that I can help clear your name. That's all you need to know."

"You're clearing my name by robbing City Hall?"

"I said cut it out!"

Susie looked annoyed. Johnny looked back at the giant igloo and tried to think of how to get inside. There was a fire exit on the far side, and he figured he could pick the lock to get in without triggering the alarm. Beyond that, though, he didn't know. He would have to improvise.

Johnny pulled out his cell phone and stuck it into Susie's hand.

"You want me to make a phone call, too?" she asked sarcastically, recognizing the coin as the same kind she had been given in prison the previous day.

"If anything happens," Johnny said, "or if I take more than an hour to get back, I want you to call my partner, Paul."

"The penguin?"

"The penguin. Here's his number." Johnny scribbled it down on a piece of paper.

"How do I know if an hour has passed?"

Johnny let out an exasperated breath at both Susie and himself. He unstrapped his watch and gave it to the girl.

"Can you read an analog watch?" Johnny asked.

"I can read it *just fine*," Susie said.

Johnny took a few steps out of the alley and shadows and looked around to see if anyone was watching him.

"How are you getting in?" Susie asked.

"Look, I said to be quiet," Johnny's voice trailed off and he jumped back into the alley. Susie's eyes widened in fear and anger. A car had just pulled up to City Hall, and Masterson got out and walked up to a door on the near side of the igloo. He pulled out a blue access card, swiped it through a scanner, and opened the unlocked door. Before walking in, Masterson scanned the area, including the alley. Johnny pressed himself and Susie against a wall, hoping the shadows hid them well enough.

Johnny peered out again. Masterson was gone. Johnny grabbed Susie and started walking back the way they had come.

"You're not breaking in now?" Susie asked. "Just because your boss is in there? Are you afraid of him or something?"

"Yes, I'm afraid of him," Johnny said. "If he finds me, then we're both going back to prison."

"So what are we going to do now?"

"I need to make a phone call, but I'm not going to do it on City Hall's front sidewalk."

❋   ❋   ❋

Paul stood in the middle of the intersection just outside True North Plaza. The plaza, built over the northern-most square block of the world, surrounded a cylindrical tower, nearly 50 feet high but only ten feet wide. A marvel of 15th century elvish engineering, the tower was painted with angled red and white stripes and sat precisely on the latitudinal North Pole. A large red dome, supported by a single cement post in the middle, capped the tower and covered the open balcony that was visible from all sides of the plaza. A simple black podium stood at one end of the balcony. Dozens of speakers and amplifiers were attached to the lower buttresses, and a large Jumbo-Tron screen hung just below the balcony on one side. Directly above the tower Polaris, the North Star, shone down.

The plaza was filled with humans, elves, and animals. Even a few snowmen had made the trek from Snowman's Land to hear the mayor's speech. The low rumble of several hundred conversations filled the air, most of which seemed to be about Mayor Wassail's decision to make his speech at True North Plaza.

Since the time of Nicholas Claus, the tower had been used only by the reigning Claus for public addresses. The plaza itself, though it had been converted into a public square nearly a century ago, was still used as the launch site for the Christmas Eve flight. The plaza and tower remained private property, though the public had an easement on the property and was guaranteed access.

Nobody knew what Mayor Wassail's reason for making a speech at the plaza was. Some speculated he was going to make a power grab while others assumed it was meant as a gracious tribute to Santa during a time of public mourning. Regardless of the mayor's intention, nearly everyone was surprised that Mrs. Claus, who had sole ownership of the tower, had agreed to let Mayor Wassail use it, and all its amenities, for his first public address following Santa's murder.

131

SANTA CLAUS IS DEAD ❋ JASON TWEDE

With so many people gathering to the plaza, Paul, as the only officer assigned to direct traffic at the adjacent intersection, found his temper getting shorter and shorter. Finally, when an ostentatious looking Volvo pulled out of the line of cars and tried to cut through the intersection, Paul had had it. He jumped in front of the car, which skidded to a sudden stop, and slammed a flipper onto the hood.

"Do you see this?" Paul yelled at the driver, pointing to an upheld flipper. "This means *stop!*"

Standing in front of the car to prevent it from driving off, Paul quickly wrote a ticket and gave it to the driver, who was obviously a little intimidated by the abrasive penguin.

"Have a wonderful Christmas," Paul said as he finally let the Volvo drive through.

I don't know if I could take doing this every day, Paul thought as he returned to directing the line of traffic.

After a few minutes, virtually all traffic on the roads disappeared. The noise at the plaza suddenly quieted, and Paul saw several uniformed polar bears, Mayor Wassail's infamous personal security entourage, emerge in the tower balcony. With no cars on the road anymore, Paul forgot about traffic duty and let his attention wander to the tower.

The speakers and amplifiers at the tower gave off a sudden, loud squeal of microphone feedback. One of the polar bears stepped to the microphone and introduced "*our most dignified, benevolent, magnanimous, and excellent Georg Wassail, Mayor of North Pole Village and representative of its diverse citizenry.*" A loud chorus of the customary fanatic cheers competing against raging boos erupted from the crowd.

Mayor Wassail stepped to the podium in the balcony and basked in the attention. He was a large man—almost as large as Santa had been—with a large nose, curly blonde hair, and enormous fuzzy sideburns. He wore a gaudy purple suit with green pinstripes and a fluffy eighteenth century tie ruffled at his collar. Wearing a deliberately sorrowful smile, Mayor Wassail waited for the crowd to quiet before he spoke:

"Good morning, citizens of the North Pole: my friends, my people, and my constituents," Mayor Wassail started in his smooth voice, "as I am sure we have all heard, our beloved Santa Claus has passed away. A tragic event by itself, but one made even more harrowing by the facts surrounding it.

"Santa Claus was taken from us only three days before Christmas—just three days before the season he had devoted his life to reached its climax. Santa Claus perished alone, late at night, and in the middle of the woods. He was removed from every comfort his life of service had merited. And worst of all, he was killed by a child, one whom he had invited to his home and made his personal guest."

Mayor Wassail paused, and then continued quietly. "Yes, it is disturbing beyond imagination. Santa Claus was murdered by one of those to whom he had dedicated his entire life.

"An appropriate response is grief. An appropriate response is anger. An appropriate response is outrage. An appropriate response is mourning.

"But, my friends and my people, I am not going to respond in such a way, and I plead with you to set your emotions aside, just for a little while.

"Santa's assassin, though just a young girl, was a cold-blooded fiend. She is not representative of the children of the world. She is not evidence that his goal, the happiness of children around the world, was in vain. She *does not* represent a need to revise the idealism upon which the entire North Pole was built.

"Santa Claus is gone, this is true. But it is also true that millions upon millions of other children are placing their trust—their fragile, hopeful trust—in the annual Christmas Eve flight and gift delivery. It is up to us, the people of the North Pole, to fulfill their hope. Together, we can pull through this difficult time and give the world a Christmas never to be forgotten."

The mayor paused again, removed his glasses and dabbed tears that had formed at his eyes.

"With no other heirs," Mayor Wassail continued, "Mrs. Claus is now the Head of Christmas. I know that many of us, myself included, found Santa's remarriage two years ago rather shocking.

Her motives for marrying him were questionable then, and they remain questionable today. Her motives for not providing an heir are likewise questionable."

Murmurs of approval rose from the crowd.

"Nevertheless," Mayor Wassail continued, "while Mrs. Claus may never receive the endearment nor faith we willingly gave her late husband, she is the Head of Christmas. We owe it to the children of the world to support her and ensure that this Christmas is a *great* Christmas.

"The Claus monarchy has served Christmas well in the past, and we must put our faith in Mrs. Claus. She will, of course, most likely never rise to the quality we have all enjoyed during the reign of Santa, without question one of the noblest reigns since Nicholas Claus himself, but with our support Christmas will be successful.

"I plan to invite Mrs. Claus to a meeting in my office later this afternoon to discuss her plans for this Christmas. I will do my best to help her understand that we must have a strong plan of action because unless we do even our best efforts, no matter how diligent, may come up short. I will lend her all my leadership and planning skills, as well as the invaluable experience I have as a two-term mayor of the North Pole.

Mayor Wassail paused dramatically before continuing:

"I know what many of you are thinking. You are wondering what will happen if Mrs. Claus is not up to the task ahead. I wish to emphasize again that we must give her our trust. However, I also wish to do all I can to abate your fears. If the only way to save Christmas is some drastic measure, I will do it. If Mrs. Claus proves incapable of serving the children of the world, I will not stand idly by. The Village Council has oversight authority over the proper execution of Christmas. It also has the authority to impeach the current Head Claus and appoint an interim director.

"I would hate to disrespect the memory of Santa Claus by abolishing his old position, but I would also hate to disrespect his memory by watching an inadequate replacement doing a half-rate job on Christmas. The people of the North Pole deserve better. The children of the world deserve better.

"Let us all resolve now to do whatever is necessary to save Christmas. For Santa."

The crowd erupted in cheers of *"for Santa!"*

Paul felt disgusted. He knew that the only reason Mayor Wassail would impeach Mrs. Claus was so that he could be named interim director of the Christmas Foundation, the nonprofit corporation that made and delivered the toys. Millions of dollars were donated to the foundation each year, and it had billions of dollars in assets. Even a single Christmas season would be enough time for Wassail to change the foundation's bylaws and make himself the permanent Head of Christmas. Paul didn't even want to think about what the mayor would do with the money involved.

Paul scowled and tried to refocus on his job at hand: directing traffic. Paul had known that Mayor Wassail would find a way to use Santa's murder to his advantage. Still, Paul felt a mix of outrage and admiration for the way the mayor had set himself up as the man ultimately responsible for the fate of Christmas—regardless of Mrs. Claus's legal claim.

Paul hoped that Johnny had not been listening to the speech. Between the slip of paper in the bald gunman's hand, the mayor's men who had been sneaking around the Claus Estate, and the secrecy and covert activities that had been going on behind their backs at the NPPD, there was enough to link both Masterson and Mayor Wassail together into some kind of conspiracy. If Johnny got any more circumstantial evidence he would become so obsessed with it he wouldn't be able to find any real evidence to find out what was really going on.

Paul simply wondered why the mayor's goon had shot at them at Frozen Yoga. The only real connection between the mayor and the murder that either he or Johnny had discovered had been the bald gunman himself. If he had never attacked them, all Paul and Johnny would have had was an ever-growing resentment toward Masterson for hijacking their investigation. Why would the mayor risk his entire career by sending the gunman after them?

Then it hit him. The gunman had come shot at them *after* Johnny had retrieved the Naughty List from Santa's office. Johnny had even said that the gunman's voice was the same as one of the voices he had heard outside Santa's office. It could be coincidence, or the mayor could desperately want to keep them from finding something on that list.

As yet another car sped by without paying attention to Paul's directions, he had had it with traffic duty. He pulled several barriers up and blocked off two directions of the intersection. Several cars started honking at him.

"What's going on?" a sea lion asked from his rolled down window.

"Detour," Paul said.

"Where are we supposed to detour to?"

Paul had too much on his mind to answer.

Chapter Eighteen

The grounds surrounding the Claus Estate were quiet. The Christmas lights were still lit, though several strings had burned out. Dozens of tracks were littered across the snow, though Paul couldn't tell how many people had actually made them. The house was dark, and all the windows had their curtains drawn.

As Paul approached the front door, he kept looking around for any sign that he was being watched. Returning to talk to Mrs. Claus would not be as easy to justify as re-interrogating Mitchell had been, and the last thing Paul wanted was to deal with some overzealous officer who may have been assigned to watch him.

Paul knocked on the front door, which swung open to a dark and empty foyer.

"Mrs. Claus?" Paul called into the house. "This is the North Pole Police. I would like to talk with you for a minute."

There was no response.

Paul looked at the door again. The lock looked as if it had been broken off. He stepped through the open door hesitantly. Something was wrong. Mrs. Claus had the entire home locked up yesterday; it didn't make sense for the door to suddenly be unlocked. Paul drew his gun and continued into the house.

Two large red sofas sat on opposite walls. Between them was a large fir tree covered with homemade ornaments. A dark brick fireplace was on the opposite side of the room. Two red stockings hung from the mantle, labeled "*Santa*" and "*Amber.*" Nothing looked out of order.

Paul moved on to the kitchen. Again, nothing looked out of order. A plate of stale cookies and a glass of lukewarm milk sat on the countertop.

Paul scowled. Unless he found some further sign of a problem, Paul knew he was risking trouble by snooping around without a warrant. Cautiously, he walked down a back hall, opening the doors as he went.

The third door, next to a vase that had shattered against the wall, opened into Santa's study. A desk was overturned and its drawers were pulled out and lying on the floor. Hundreds of torn papers and envelopes were scattered all over the room. Paul kicked through several piles of the papers, uncovering a partially unrolled scroll. Paul picked it up and looked at its heading: *Nice*.

A sudden, high-pitched electronic rendition of "Rockin' Around the Christmas Tree" sent Paul fumbling through his coat for his cell phone.

"What?" Paul whispered into the phone.

"Paul, it's me," Johnny's voice said.

"Johnny, this is a *really* lousy time to chat."

"Why?"

Paul reached over and closed the door.

"I'm in Santa's study right now," Paul said. "I'm looking for the Naughty List."

"You broke in?" Johnny asked. "Paul, I never knew you had it in you. Way to go—"

"Oh, shut up Johnny. I came over to see Mrs. Claus. Masterson took the list from you, right?"

"Right. What, did you think he would just give it back?" Johnny scoffed.

"We don't *really* know how much Masterson is involved in everything—"

"I thought you had given up defending him."

"And even if he is the ringleader," Paul ignored Johnny, "there's a chance that he *would* just give it back. It would deflate any suspicion."

No response came over the phone, which made Paul smile. Johnny always hated it when Paul made sense.

"So what are you calling me for, anyway?" Paul asked.

"I need you to do something for me," Johnny said. "I need to get some things out of my apartment."

"Like what?"

"Money, for one. I hadn't really planned on buying Susie an entirely new wardrobe. And some other things."

"I'm not breaking into your apartment for you," Paul said. "There's no way that would work out. I checked the reports out this morning, and it's being watched by four officers."

"I don't want you to break in," Johnny said. "I'll do that myself. I need a diversion—something that will pull everyone off the surveillance just long enough for me to get in and get out. Call Steve at Channel Six."

"Your polar bear reporter friend?"

"Right. Tell him I need a type-six eggnog bomb to go off on the corner of Snow Street and Candy Cane Lane at one o'clock."

"Wait. What is a type-six eggnog bomb?"

"Let's just say that it's big, it's loud, and it won't hurt anyone." Johnny said. "Just tell Steve I'll get him an exclusive interview with the girl accused of killing Santa Claus."

"An exclusive interview?"

"And make sure he knows that we had nothing to do with the press conference or the mayor's speech. I had promised him first word, and he's going to be ticked about that."

"Fine," Paul said tersely. *Why do you always pin stuff like this on me?*

"Great," Johnny said. "Bye."

Click.

Paul looked at the Nice List again. *Not what I need*, he thought as he dropped it back into the pile of papers and envelopes on the floor.

He left the office and carefully walked up the stairs. Like the living room and kitchen had been, everything was clean and tidy. Nothing was out of place in any of the five guest rooms or two bathrooms. Several pictures of Santa hung from the walls—showing his graduation from Kringle University, several vacations to Mexico and Tahiti, and wedding pictures.

The master bedroom, however, was not clean. All the drawers had been pulled out of both dressers, papers were strewn all over the room, the mattress had been pulled off the bed frame, the closet had been rummaged through, and dozens of hangers—each with a little candy cane styled hook at the top—lay all over the room. A six-foot mirror had been shattered, and broken glass was all over the floor. Shirts, pants, skirts, dresses, socks, large Christmas tree boxer shorts, and several pieces of silky red lingerie covered the floor, hung from the bed frame, and lay in piles along the walls. Two lamps had been bumped over, both light bulbs broken.

There was no sign of either the Naughty List or Mrs. Claus.

Shuffling though the mess, Paul could find no blood and nothing broken besides the shattered mirror. He shook his head. It was impossible to tell whether a struggle had taken place in the room or if Mrs. Claus had merely created the mess in a mad rush to get out. From what Johnny had seen and heard yesterday either scenario was just as plausible as the other.

As Paul walked out of the room, several large blotches on the carpet caught his eye. Looking closer, he could see that they were more than simple blobs—they were hoof prints.

They were all over the house. Paul's attention was so focused on finding Mrs. Claus and the Naughty List that he hadn't noticed them before. Though there was no clear pattern upstairs, once Paul got downstairs they led down the hall and to the laundry room. The window was broken.

Paul rushed outside. Just as he had expected, there were more hoof prints in the snow. They all pointed in the same direction—toward one of the small clearings in the large yard—and became farther and farther apart. Then they ended.

As if a reindeer had taken off, Paul thought, but he refused to let himself get too caught up in the theory. Reindeer were not the only hoofed animals in the North Pole, and it was best not to jump to conclusions. He needed a forensics team to gather the evidence and get real conclusions.

From behind a tree Paul saw a small, flashing red light. A security camera. It was pointed directly at the clearing the footprints were in.

❄   ❄   ❄

"I need you to run a Ph test on this broccoli juice sample," Limphus, the NPPD lab manager, told Sara.

"Broccoli juice?" Sara asked.

"For a domestic violence case," Limphus said. "A caribou accused her husband of deliberately altering the acidity of the juice so that it would react with the dish soap and cause an explosion in their kitchen sink."

"Did the sink actually explode?" Sara asked.

"No. She claimed that she intercepted the juice before anything could react."

Sara took the vial of murky green juice and set it on the table. "Isn't there anything more important I could be working on?"

"Like what?"

"A rather significant case came up yesterday," Sara said. "I thought that with the missing autopsy report—"

"It's taken care of," Limphus cut Sara off and, with a tight smile, walked out of Sara's office.

Broccoli juice, Sara mouthed sarcastically to herself. Typing up the report, which would take probably two minutes, would take longer than actually doing the test.

At least it was something to do, though. Limphus had spent the entire morning keeping Sara in her office while making sure she had absolutely no work to do. Sara had become so sick of it that she had even asked if she could take some PTO. Limphus had simply ignored the request.

Sara sat down and put her feet up on her desk. Idly, she picked up the free copy of *The Northern Lights* that had been delivered earlier in the morning and browsed the front page. Elf has twenty-pound baby. Vixen and Prancer come out of the closet. Mrs. Claus and the Abominable Snowman caught having an affair. Santa spotted in Vegas with Elvis. Elf and Snowman marry despite racial barriers.

Why on earth am I reading this? Sara wondered as she turned to page two. Beneath the headline, "Santa's Body Bound in Forest", was a half-page picture of Santa's hat sitting in the snow. The forest and several police officers were in the background and out of focus. The caption read: "Fallen hat and single footprints are only clue". The rest of the article was nonsense—speculation about a love triangle between Santa, a snow-woman, and an elf that went bad—but Sara couldn't stop looking at the hat.

Her phone rang.

"Sara Albright, NPPD," she said.

"Sara, this is Paul."

"Paul, have you looked at today's edition of *The Northern Lights?*"

"Sara, I already knew about Prancer and Vixen. With names like that they never had a chance."

"Not that," Sara said irritatedly. "It's on page two. A huge picture of Santa's hat in the snow. Did you recover the hat from the crime scene?"

"No," Paul said, suddenly interested. "It could be an archival picture."

"It's clearly in the forest, and there are several NPPD officers in the background. One of them looks like a walrus, and another looks like it might be you."

"Are you sure?"

"No. The focus is on the hat. Everything else is fuzzy."

"Okay," Paul said. "While I go check it out, I need a favor."

"What?"

"I need a forensics team to go through the Claus Estate," Paul said. "The study and master bedroom have been torn apart, and I need them to get fingerprint analyses. There are also several hoof prints. I need an ID on them, too."

"Why don't you call this in to dispatch?" Sara asked.

"I'm not supposed to be over here. I've been taken off the Santa case, remember?"

"So, you're doing things like Johnny now?"

Paul ignored the chide. "Just tell them that you got an anonymous tip. And make sure that you do the analysis. I don't want this report to evaporate into the fog before I can look at it."

"Limphus isn't going to make that easy to do, but I'll do what I can."

"Great. Let me know what you find out."

Sara started to dial dispatch, but before she did her phone rang again.

"Sara Albright, NPPD," she said, slightly exasperated.

"Sara, it's Johnny."

"Johnny!" Sara's whispered, trying to keep from being overheard. "Where are you? Are you okay?"

"I'm fine," Johnny said. After a long uncomfortable pause he continued, "I need a favor."

CHAPTER NINETEEN

JOHNNY AND Susie knelt behind several bushes and a mound of snowplowed snow. Behind them was a "Fur-Only" barber shop with iron bars in the windows. Across and down the street a hundred yards sat a dark brick apartment building with two sunning balconies jutting out the front of all three stories. One window had a single string of Christmas lights nailed outside, five of which actually worked.

"You live there?" Susie asked for the fourth time.

"Yes," Johnny said. "On the second floor."

"Which one?"

"The one to the south" Johnny joked, suddenly pleased with how clever he was.

"Why was that funny?"

"We're at the North Pole. All the directions are south when you're at the North Pole."

"I know that," Susie said. "But we're not really on *the* North Pole. That's just a single point, and I learned in math that a single point actually takes up no space, so there's no way possible that a person could actually be on the North Pole and have all directions be south."

"I ... really?" Johnny asked. "They teach you stuff like that in

American schools?"

"Don't they at the North Pole?"

"I don't know. I didn't really pay attention to school very much when I was a kid."

"Really?" Susie asked sarcastically.

"Look, kid, it was just a joke. I was being funny. You were supposed to laugh and think I had a great sense of humor."

Susie laughed—a startlingly crisp and joyous sound—and quickly covered her mouth to try to stop the sound from coming out.

"Now you're really being funny," she said.

A sudden gust of wind blew specks of ice and snow through the bushes and into their faces. Susie shivered and tried to press herself more firmly into her parka. She breathed heavily into her mittened hands, and pressed them against her cheeks. Johnny, aside from brushing a bit of snow from his face, ignored the breeze.

"I thought winters were cold in Colorado," Susie said.

"They aren't?"

"Not compared to here," she said. "I never really believed my teachers when they said that up here you go days and days without the sun ever coming up."

"It's about three months," Johnny said. "And three months in the summer when it never goes down."

"That's what my teachers said when we were studying astronomy. I really did believe them, because they were teachers and teachers teach stuff the way it really is, but I kind of didn't really believe it at the same time."

"You mean that you knew it was true, but you couldn't really imagine what it would be like?"

"Yeah. Does that ever happen to you?"

"Yep. Like this one time when I broke a little girl accused of murder out of prison," Johnny said, smiling slightly. "That wasn't anything like the TV shows made it seem like."

Susie said nothing.

"What time is it?" Johnny asked after a moment.

Susie looked at the watch Johnny had handed her earlier. "A

couple minutes past one," she said. "Is your friend really going to set … it off?"

"Steve?" Johnny asked. "Yes. He's never let me down."

"What's the thing called again?"

"A type-six eggnog bomb, and don't even think about asking for any details."

An enormous boom thundered in their ears. The ground shook for a moment, and Johnny had to grab Susie's arms to keep her from falling. An odd smell, like a mixture of chocolate, ash, and pine with a little dash of tinsel, slowly emerged.

Johnny's cell phone rang.

"Yeah," Johnny said.

"You're clear," Sara said. "All four officers left their post to investigate the explosion."

"Thanks, Sara," Johnny said. He stood up and pulled Susie to her feet.

"Has Masterson come back yet?" Johnny asked Sara.

"Not yet."

"Well … good luck when he does."

"Don't worry about it. I'll see you later this evening."

"Uh … right," Johnny said uncomfortably.

"Be careful."

"I will."

Johnny closed his cell phone, nodded to Susie, and both of them ran across the street to his apartment building. Susie stumbled once along the way, and Johnny wished she had stayed hiding behind the bushes. But Susie had refused. *I'm going wherever you're going*, she had told him more than once since he had broken her out the previous night.

The main door to the building had neither a lock nor a doorknob. Johnny pushed it open and led Susie up the stairs to his apartment on the second floor. The front door's paint was peeling off. Johnny inserted his key and then stopped. He knelt down and looked Susie in the eye.

"The door probably has some kind of alarm fixed to it," Johnny whispered. "It will trigger as soon as we walk inside. Everybody is focusing on the nog bomb, so it should take a few minutes before anyone realizes we're here. Then it will take another few minutes before the officers can get back to the building. We have to be gone before anyone can get here."

Susie nodded.

"I'll tell you what we're doing," Johnny continued. "I am going to get some money out of a little pocket under the sink. Then I'm going to break a hole in a wall. While I'm doing this, you need to get a frying pan out of the cupboard. It's in a drawer right by the sink in the kitchen.

"As soon as you see me break through the wall, you need to throw the pan through the window above the kitchen sink. I'll get my stuff and lift you up to the window. Jump through it. There's a little balcony on the other side with a fire ladder. I'll follow you out the window, we'll climb down the ladder, and then we'll run down the back alley."

"Okay," Susie whispered.

"Any questions?"

"Why do I have to break the window?" Susie asked. "And why do you have to break a hole in your wall?"

"The window rusted shut, and I have to get some stuff out of the wall," Johnny said.

"What stuff?"

"Susie," Johnny said, getting annoyed. "This isn't the time."

"So you don't really care whether I have any questions?"

"I guess not," Johnny said as he held up his fingers and counted down. *Three … two … one …* "Go!"

Johnny unlocked the door and pushed it open. Just as he had expected, a wire and some kind of motion detection device had been attached to the inside of the door frame. The device was blinking a small red light. NPPD would know he was there.

Johnny pointed to the kitchen sink, and Susie ran to get the pan. Johnny rushed to the bathroom, searched beneath the sink until he felt the small pocket hidden behind the pipe. He pulled out the money and ran back to the living room.

Susie held the pan and was looking at something on the countertop. Johnny knelt beside the brown and gold striped sofa—the only piece of furniture in the living room besides a TV, a lamp without a lampshade, and a portable heater with several large dents in the side. A blanket and set of sheets lay crumpled on one cushion of the sofa.

Knocking softly against the wall, Johnny searched for the right spot. When he found it, he stood up and kicked a hole in the wall.

"Now, Susie!" Johnny said.

She threw the pan into the window, which shattered with a large crash.

Johnny peeled back the drywall and pulled out the computer and various types of detective equipment. He had always had a feeling that he would need equipment NPPD wasn't aware of. He just had never expected that he would use it with so much at stake, nor had he ever expected to be in such serious trouble. He was just glad he had it.

Be prepared, he thought to himself. Though he doubted that the Klondike Scout committee had ever envisioned a situation like this when they came up with the motto.

He stood up and ran to the kitchen, where Susie was waiting anxiously. He hoisted her up and shoved her through the broken window head first. He heard a thud and a grunt from outside. *Well, at least there's snow to catch her fall*, he thought. He climbed up the sink and felt a sudden jolt of pain in the knee he had hurt at the Arctic Hotel earlier that day. He shook his head as he climbed out, surprised to think that it was really the same day.

Once outside, he leaned back through the window and closed the blinds. Hopefully the hole in the wall would distract the officers from noticing the broken window until it was too late.

Susie picked herself up from the floor of the balcony and looked annoyed at Johnny. He ignored her and pushed her toward the ladder. They quickly climbed down and ran down the alley—one of three back alleys that he had expected to be free from snow. They would leave no tracks.

Once they got to the alley, Susie stopped and looked back. Johnny shook his head.

"No time," he said between heavy breaths. "Just keep running and follow me."

Susie nodded and ran.

They changed direction with nearly every alley and back street they came to, and Susie became completely disoriented. Finally, ducking behind a set of dumpsters, they stopped. Both of them were breathing heavily.

"My chest hurts," Susie said.

"It's the cold air," Johnny said. "Unless you're used to running in it, it'll hurt a bit. You did good, though."

"We're safe?"

"You can never be completely sure," Johnny said. "But I think so. We'll have to wait here for a while, though."

Sirens rang from several directions, but they were all faint and distant. Johnny smiled.

The alley was strewn with torn wrapping paper and bows, as well as a few nativity flyers from the local Methodist church. The walls had a few bits of graffiti, the bright red angular snowman caricatures often drawn by a local elf-supremacist gang. *Melt the Snowmen* was written just above the dumpster.

"Mr. Iceberg?" Susie asked. "Who is this?"

She was holding a small framed picture of Johnny's daughter—one he had kept on the kitchen counter near the sink. Emily was sitting on Santa's knee, wearing a green elf hat and a lavender shirt. When the picture had been taken neither he nor Tara, his ex-wife, could believe how badly the shirt and hat clashed. But that was Emily. She always did things her own way. Johnny supposed that was why the picture was one he had kept out and framed. It reminded him of who she really was.

"That's Emily," Johnny said. "My daughter."

"The clothes you gave me last night, they were hers?"

"Yeah."

"They were kind of out of style."

"Well, they were in style when she wore them," Johnny said defensively.

"That was a while ago?"

Johnny nodded. "She's twenty now. Or nineteen."

"You don't know?" Susie couldn't believe it.

"It's been a while since I've seen her." Johnny's brow became lined. "I'm pretty sure she's twenty."

"You really don't know, do you?"

"I know it's been nine years since she left with her mother," Johnny said. "I just don't remember exactly how old she was when she left. I didn't pay attention to things like that very well. That's kind of why they left."

"You haven't seen her in that long?"

"No," Johnny's voice became quiet. "Tara—that was her mother's name—said that Emily didn't really want to see me for a while. She said that Emily would be happier if I didn't try to pop back into her life for a day or two every month. And Tara's always been very honest. No matter how many problems we had, I have to say she was always completely honest. And she always tried to figure out what was best for Emily. I hadn't worried about what was best for her for years, so who was I to say any different?"

Johnny swallowed hard. "Then, when Tara said Emily was ready, that she wanted to see me, I didn't know how to do it. I didn't know what to say—what to talk about. And the next thing I knew, nine years had gone by."

Susie said nothing for a long time. Finally she spoke up again. "Emily—your daughter—she liked Santa?"

"She did," Johnny said. "Most people did."

CHAPTER TWENTY
—THE NORTHERN LIGHTS, 1:19 PM

LOCATED IN the basement of the historic Randall P. Claus building on the corner of Main Street and Holly Jolly Avenue, *The Northern Lights* had made its main office difficult to find. No signs announced its location, and no phone book included its address. Paul had even heard rumors that interviews were always conducted off-site. Unless a person had somehow learned where it was, he would never find it.

Paul and Johnny had, during the Arctic Hotel investigation, made it their business to find it. Finally, after Johnny had employed his usual interrogation efforts on a punk elf, they had learned the location. While Johnny had just cared about solving the case, Paul had different plans for the knowledge.

He knew that there were probably hundreds of outraged North Pole residents who had, at one time or another, been libeled by one of the paper's rumors and photo doctoring. As soon as he and Johnny met Ferguson Lombarton, a walrus and publisher of the tabloid, Paul started giving him what had become regular reminders that Paul knew their location. He had received all kinds of eager help from *The Northern Lights* because of those frequent reminders.

Paul walked through the side door and down the stairs that led to the office. Having reached the locked double door, Paul buzzed the intercom system.

"Handy-Elves Incorporated," a voice spoke the cover business name over the speaker.

"Good morning Liberacette," Paul told the elf he knew manned the office security. "It's Paul Penguin, NPPD. Let me in."

"We're always so happy to have you visit," Liberacette said in an unhappy monotone.

The doors clicked open, and Paul stepped into the tabloid office.

The place was decorated with worse taste than NPPD had been. Red and green orbs hung from every cubicle corner. The ceiling lights had red and green fluorescent bulbs, and the entire place reeked of pine. Nearly every employee wore fake antlers, which looked particularly ridiculous on the elves, who were shorter than the antlers, and the reindeer, who already had real ones.

Liberacette, whose hair was styled into six inch-long red, purple, and pastel blue spikes, met Paul when he came in.

"What do you want, Paul?" Liberacette asked in the same unhappy monotone. "Lombarton's in a staff meeting, so if you want to talk to him you'll have to wait."

"I need to know where this is," Paul said, picking up a paper and pointing to the picture of Santa's hat on page two.

"That's the North Pole forest," Liberacette said, annoyed. "How do you investigate a crime scene and not know where it is?"

"No, not the location of the crime scene," Paul snapped. "The hat. Where's the hat?"

"I don't know. Ask the photographer."

"Where is he?"

"In the staff meeting. If you want to talk to him you'll have to wait."

"Miss Liberacette," Paul said, "of all the people in town, I am the one penguin who doesn't *have* to do anything you say when I pay a visit."

He left the sullen elf and walked to the back of the office to a large pair of heavy doors. Along the way he tripped on a couple of presents that had been left on the floor, and he deliberately kicked a couple others. A sign posted at the doors was labeled "*Bored Room*" with cutesy, curly letters.

Very clever, Paul thought sarcastically.

He flung the doors open, and they banged against the walls inside the board room with a loud crash. An ornament fell from the Christmas tree in the corner of the room and shattered. Everyone sitting at the conference table turned around and stared at him. Lombarton, who was an even more enormous walrus than Paul had remembered, was dressed in his typical green tux and top hat and stood at the head of the table. He was obviously in the middle of a presentation to his staff.

"Jack Frost, Paul!" Lombarton swore. "What on earth are you doing?"

"I'm not in a good mood," Paul said. He held up the paper and pointed to the picture again. "I need to know who took this picture."

"Tweedles did," Lombarton said, pointing to a man who was slouching in his chair. Paul recognized him immediately—he was the obnoxious photographer from the crime scene who Paul had whacked in the knee with a branch.

"*Tweedles?*" Paul asked the photographer.

"Actually, the name's Bill," the photographer said.

"What do you need him for?" Lombarton asked. He never bothered to remember the names of most of his staff, instead calling them by whatever ridiculous nickname popped into his mind at any given moment.

"Santa's hat is in the picture," Paul said. "We never recovered the hat from the crime scene, which means *Tweedles* here must have it."

"What?" Lombarton roared at the photographer. "How many times have I told you—all of you—that when Iceberg and Penguin are on a case, you can't snitch anything from a crime scene?" The large walrus took a deep breath and straightened his bow tie. "I'm sorry, Paul," he said. "Go ahead and take him back to his cubicle, and I'm sure he'll do everything he can to cooperate. And if you have to arrest him, could you fudge over who he's affiliated with?"

Paul nodded. It was a fine line between getting Lombarton to do what he wanted and making the publisher believe it wasn't worth the hassle any more.

"There's one more thing," Paul said as the photographer got up and walked over to the doors. "I need to see video from the security cameras at the Clause Estate. Mrs. Claus is missing, and I'm trying to figure out what the deal is."

"Reindeer training grounds," Lombarton said. "They volunteered to oversee security three or four years ago. It got them a heck of a pay raise. But don't get your hopes up. We've been trying to get some good footage of Mrs. Claus for two years, but they've taken out most of the cameras that were inside."

"Thanks," Paul said. "I knew you would be the one to ask."

"Knowing things like that sells the papers."

"Right," Paul said. He escorted the photographer out of the room. "Have a nice meeting," Paul said as he closed the doors.

The photographer slowly led Paul back through the cubicles and to his desk, a mess of papers and pencils. A picture of Santa with his arm around an alien was thumb-tacked to one of the cubicle walls. The photographer opened a drawer, removed the false bottom, and pulled Santa's hat out.

"So why does Lombarton do whatever you tell him to do?" the photographer asked sullenly.

"He doesn't want me to tell anyone where this office is, and he doesn't want me to do anything to interfere with his deadlines. He also doesn't want me to shut down the paper and arrest the entire staff—which I could easily do with all the evidence stashed away at NPPD."

Paul held out a plastic bag, and the photographer dropped the hat inside.

"So was that photograph completely legit?" Paul asked. "You didn't doctor it at all?"

"Well, I did a few color enhancements."

"That's it?"

"Yeah. Why?"

"You didn't wipe out any foot prints or anything else from the snow? The hat was really just lying like that with nothing else around? No sign that anyone had walked over and put it there?"

"No. It was just like how it is in the paper."

Paul pulled out a flash drive.

"Can you find all the formats of the picture on your computer and put it on this?"

"Why?"

"From what it looks like in the picture, that hat was about a hundred feet from Santa's body. If there's no evidence that somebody walked over and put it there, then that's important."

"Important enough to let me off the hook if I give it to you?" the photographer said hopefully.

"Do you remember that polar bear we arrested for mauling two elves out by the coal mines last year?" Paul asked. The photographer nodded. "He really needs a cell mate right now. The prison guards think it will calm him down a bit. He spends all his time biting and clawing at the cement walls and metal bars right now. If you cooperate and give me the files right now, I'll make sure that cell mate isn't you."

The photographer glowered at Paul, but finally grabbed the flash drive and put the files on.

"There," he snapped as he handed the flash drive back to Paul.

"Thanks," Paul said. He put the drive back in his pocket, pulled out a set of handcuffs, and slapped them on the wrists of the photographer.

"You're arresting me right now?"

"What, did you think I was going to come back and do it later?"

Paul led the photographer out of the building, past stares from all *The Northern Lights* staff. Paul reached up and pulled the antlers off the photographer's head. *Might as well keep him from looking like an idiot in his mug shot*, Paul thought.

"Have a good day," Paul told Liberacette as he and the photographer walked out.

The elf said nothing.

"Why'd you take the hat, anyway?" Paul asked the photographer once they were outside.

"It guaranteed an exclusive take on the story. You have no idea how cutthroat the journalism business is. That photo got me a major promotion."

"Does *The Northern Lights* really count as journalism?" Paul asked.

"Ha ha," the photographer said. He stopped and looked around at the empty road. "Isn't there a patrol car you're taking me in?"

"They haven't got a decent model for penguins to drive—not one that can hold a suspect, anyway. We get to use the North Pole's renowned public transportation."

Paul pulled out his gun, stuck it at the photographer's back, and led him to the corner. Hopefully, the dog sled wouldn't be too long. He had to get to the training grounds.

Paul smiled. He had no intention of throwing the photographer in prison. After a few days in jail, Paul would work with the prosecutors for a deal—probably a small fine. After all, if the photographer hadn't taken the hat, it would be locked away with the other evidence Masterson had cut Paul's access to. Besides, Paul had found it very useful to know a network of petty crooks who were both afraid of him and owed him for getting them off easy.

And Paul, for whatever reason, was suddenly in a better mood. He got to rough up the photographer and get what he wanted. He hoped Lombarton would still give the photographer his promotion.

Chapter Twenty-One

The Igloo, a small diner downtown, was known throughout the North Pole for its outstanding baked salmon, extra greasy fries, low prices, and terrible service. Johnny, though not terribly fond of fish, had long ago decided that unless he wanted to cook something himself the famous Igloo baked salmon was just about the best he could do on a cop's salary.

A counter ran along the back wall that separated the dining room from the kitchen, and a single row of booths sat along the others. As always, the large TV mounted above the counter was turned on—now playing reruns of the *Adventures of Yukon Joe*. Johnny had always thought it a stupid show, though during the past nine years he had probably seen every episode at least twice. Johnny could never figure out why, besides the obvious need to attract a male audience, the producers seemed to think that all women native to the far north were tribal, desperate for men, and wore nothing but skimpy togas made from yak hides.

The waitress, a teenage harvest seal chomping on at least three sticks of gum, set their food down with a thud. As Johnny did at least twice a week, he had the baked salmon. Susie got a hamburger and fries.

"Can I have some ketchup?" Susie asked the waitress.

"It's over there," she said without pointing anywhere.

"Can you get it?" Susie asked.

"What, you think this is the Gingerbread House or something?" the waitress said, referring to the North Pole's only five-star restaurant. She walked away without another word. For once, Johnny was grateful for the terrible service. This was the only place he could think of that they could eat at without worrying about being remembered by anyone.

"I'll get you some ketchup," Johnny said. He walked over to the dispenser, a bizarre container that looked like a bloated candy-cane with a pump on top. As soon as he brought a bit of ketchup back, Susie seemed to inhale her food. Other than the pack of donuts Johnny had bought from the hotel vending machine, this was the first food Susie had eaten since he had rescued her the night before.

As she ate, Johnny picked at his salmon and watched everyone else in the restaurant, still somewhat worried that they would be spotted, but less so than he had been earlier in the day.

A little less than an hour earlier, he and Susie had still been sitting in the alley by the dumpster. As they sat, a snowmobile had roared to a stop at the intersection with the main road. Johnny pushed Susie behind him and reached for his gun but relaxed when he saw a familiar polar bear jump out of the snowmobile.

"I always know where to find you," Steve laughed. "I don't know how, but I always do—usually hanging around a pile of garbage somewhere."

Johnny smiled at his friend, now sporting a beige hoody and sunglasses.

"Why were you looking for us?" Johnny asked.

"Don't worry, nobody's followed me," Steve said. "I just wanted to see a little evidence that everything your penguin friend told me is true." Steve pointed behind Johnny with a giant shaggy paw. "That's the girl, huh?"

"This is her," Johnny said, letting Susie come out from behind him. "Susie, this is Steve. He's a reporter, and a friend."

"You set off the egg ... bomb?" Susie asked.

"A genuine type-six eggnog bomb," Steve said. "Johnny and I

invented the things back when we were in high school. They don't hurt anyone, but when they go off the sound, the mess, and the smell make you think Armageddon has come."

"Why are you wearing sunglasses?" Susie asked. "The sun never comes up here."

"Because I'm cool, kid," Steve said. "Cool as a snowman's backside." He motioned for Johnny to come closer.

"I also wanted to give you a little heads up," Steve said, more quietly now. "Something kooky's going on."

"Oh really?" Johnny asked. "You mean besides the fact that they arrested an eleven year old for a murder she obviously didn't commit?"

"Yeah," Steve said. "Besides that. Your boss and Mayor What's-his-tail have both forbidden any of the media from reporting your little adventure last night. They got a judge to uphold it, under some law about open criminal investigations, and we've all been threatened with multi-year imprisonments if there's a leak about the girl's escape."

"So nobody knows about it?"

"The people who woke up early enough to catch the morning news do," Steve said. "After that, they shut the story down."

"That doesn't make sense," Johnny said. "The best way to catch somebody on the run is to let everybody know about it."

"I know," Steve said. "I assume that's why you're spending your time playing with garbage in back alleys. But you don't need to worry about it. There are no flyers circulating with your pictures, there are no updates on TV, there's nothing. As far as the public knows, nothing has happened, and the kid's still sitting in prison waiting for the trial to start."

"That's why you were looking for me?"

Steve nodded. "You still need to be careful, but don't be too worried about being seen in public. Few people are looking for you."

Steve took a few steps back toward the snowmobile.

"So I'll get an exclusive with the kid?" the bear asked.

"By the time this is over, you'll be getting the scoop of the decade," Johnny said.

"I better."

"You will."

Steve looked at the girl and smiled. "I'd offer you a ride, but I can't. Cops are watching reporters like me a little too closely for me to buzz you around town."

"That's okay," Susie said. "I don't have a helmet anyway."

Steve smiled and got back on the snowmobile.

"Steve!" Johnny called out as the snowmobile started. "Thanks!"

"Anytime," Steve said as he drove off.

Johnny stood there for a moment, looking in the direction Steve had driven off in. *Why on earth would Masterson and Wassail keep the public from knowing about our escape?* Johnny had wondered.

"Mr. Iceberg," Susie pulled on Johnny's coat.

"Susie, just call me Johnny."

"Johnny, I'm really hungry."

"Then let's get something to eat," Johnny had said.

Now, after a long walk, he and Susie were there, at the Igloo. Johnny still wondered why their names and pictures hadn't been circulated among the public. It made no sense at all. Johnny shook his head and put a large piece of salmon in his mouth.

"Why did you rescue me?" Susie asked.

Taken completely off guard, Johnny gagged on the fish and had to wash it down with a drink of water before he could answer. Before answering, he put a finger up to his mouth and reminded Susie they had to talk quietly.

"Because you didn't do anything wrong," Johnny said.

"Everybody else thinks I did something wrong. A big something."

"What everybody else thinks isn't what really matters," Johnny said. "It's the truth that matters. And what's true is that you didn't do anything wrong."

"Then why do I feel bad?"

"I don't know. Why do you feel bad?"

"Those people on the street, they were crying. And everybody is so quiet—like they're afraid to talk to anybody."

Johnny frowned, wondering what Susie was talking about, until he remembered the two elves they had passed on their way to the Igloo. They had been sitting on a bench wiping at their eyes. And Susie was right. Nearly everyone they had passed seemed very somber and subdued.

"Santa meant a lot to a lot of people," Johnny said.

"I know," Susie said crossly. Her stern face softened a bit. "He didn't mean that much to me. I mean, he used to, when I was a kid, but not anymore. But then he died and … I don't know. I didn't really wish he was dead."

Johnny was not sure what she was talking about. He was not sure how to respond, either. He was no good at this heart-to-heart stuff. He decided to tell her the only thing he thought he could say sincerely, the one thing that he knew for certain.

"Sometimes you don't realize the good stuff people do for you until they're gone."

Susie looked at Johnny intensely. He could tell she was thinking hard about something. After a moment the silence became awkward, and Johnny took another bite of the salmon and looked over at the TV. Yukon Joe was climbing a glacier, being pursued by the evil CIA, and a bikini-clad tribes-woman sang love songs while she sat stranded on a cliff. *This is such a stupid show*, Johnny thought, for what must have been the hundredth time in his life. Suddenly, the scene cut to a news flash and a reporter standing in front of a large crowd at True North Plaza. Johnny almost turned away, assuming it was a rehash of the mayor's speech, until he saw the word "*Live*" on the screen. He stopped the waitress as she walked by.

"Can you turn the TV up?" he asked.

The waitress let out an exaggerated sigh, but did actually walk to the TV and turn the volume up.

"… here in True North Plaza where Mayor Wassail is about to make another announcement," the reporter said.

Johnny watched intently. The screen panned around the crowd several times until it finally focused on the balcony in the tower that marked the precise north pole of the world. Mayor Wassail walked to the podium, and Johnny suddenly felt tense. All he could think about was what Steve had said—that they hadn't announced Susie's escape from prison. Johnny quickly ate the rest of his fish, anticipating that he and Susie might have to get out very quickly.

The mayor cleared his throat and began: "My friends, my fellow citizens of the North Pole, the outpouring of public support since this morning has been phenomenal. I can say with complete confidence that you are prepared to do all that is necessary to make this Christmas great. The children of the world owe their happiness to you.

"However, all is not well here at the North Pole. I told you earlier today that I would meet with Mrs. Claus to discuss and plan what needs to be accomplished to make this Christmas successful. I am very displeased to report to you that this meeting never took place. Mrs. Claus did not show up.

"Police officers have searched everywhere for her, but she is nowhere to be found. There is no evidence of foul play, so the only possible explanation is that Mrs. Claus is on the run and hiding from law enforcement officials.

"It is becoming more and more evident that Miss Thompson, the girl currently in custody for Santa's murder, did not act alone. She was a guest of Mrs. Claus's on the night of the murder. It appears their ties are more entangled and more sinister than that.

"I give you my word, and the word of Chief Masterson of the NPPD, that Mrs. Claus will be caught and brought to justice. However, we have other matters that we must address right now. Even with your support, unless we take drastic measures this Christmas will fail. Mrs. Claus cannot be allowed to take her late husband's position, but unless it is filled all your efforts will be for naught.

"There is a solution, however," Mayor Wassail paused for effect. "I have called for an emergency meeting of the Village Council. It will take place tonight at seven o'clock. With approval of the Council, the Claus monarchy will be dissolved and I will be appointed interim Head of Christmas.

"It is a tragedy that Santa's memory must be maligned in this way. I do not have words to express my sorrow over these recent events. I assure you, however, that ever since I received word of the murder, I have been preparing myself to take over Christmas, should it prove necessary. My friends, it has now been proven necessary.

"I appreciate your support. I appreciate your work. I appreciate your belief. Together, we will make this a Christmas to never forget. *For Santa!*"

Mayor Wassail waved to the cheering crowd, many of whom were in stunned tears. The scene cut back to the live reporter, who continued with her commentary.

I'll bet you've been preparing to take over ever since you received word that Santa was dead, Johnny thought. The pieces were starting to fall into place. The mayor had killed Santa in order to take over Christmas. As much as the idea angered Johnny, he couldn't help but feel sad when he wondered how Masterson had fit into the scheme. No doubt Wassail had promised something to the chief, probably a boat-load of money. Johnny shook his head. Masterson had been a decent detective nine years ago. As much as Johnny disliked him now, it still hurt to see a good cop go bad.

"Did that man kill Santa?" Susie asked.

Johnny was surprised that she had been paying attention. "There's a good chance he did," Johnny said. "Or, more likely, he paid someone else to pay someone else to do it."

"And now he's going to deliver presents to kids around the world."

"Unless something happens soon," Johnny trailed off. He hadn't thought of that. Unless he, Paul, and Sara could figure out something fast, a murderer would be entering the homes of millions upon millions of sleeping kids. That would be a far worse and more notorious disaster than even the fabled decade of Groucho Claus back in the 1880's.

Johnny looked at his watch. The Christmas sleigh lifted off at 6:00 PM on Christmas Eve. They had a little less than twenty-seven hours until then. If they didn't have hard evidence against Wassail by that time … .

Johnny didn't know what they would do. In fact, there wasn't much of anything he *could* do until after he met Sara later this evening.

Johnny's cell phone vibrated. He picked it up and looked at the text message:

> "*Masterson back. Blue keycard in pocket. Wish me luck. Sara.*"

CHAPTER TWENTY-TWO

"COME IN."

Sara opened the door to Chief Masterson's office and walked in. He looked surprised. Sara usually stayed down in the lab.

"Hello, Ms. Albright," Masterson said. "To what do I owe this visit?"

"Uh–" Sara was not sure what to say. "I was just checking up on the status of the Santa case. I was on the original lab team, and I *did* do the autopsy."

"The case has been closed, Sara. Don't you worry about it," Masterson said with a smile.

"Well, I, um–I wanted to know if you got the toxicology report I ran on Santa."

Masterson's face lost its smile. "I was under the impression that Mr. Sarvis had done the toxicology report. Limphus had clearly specified how the lab work on the case was divided, and I followed up with Sarvis personally. Cyanide matched the sample recovered by Detective Porter. Why are you bringing this up?"

"Um …" *Think, Sara, think!* She had to distract him, and her communication skills obviously were not going to work.

"Are you okay, Ms. Albright?" Masterson asked.

She froze. *Come on, Sara! He's going to know something's going on.*

Suddenly all she could remember was the conversation she had had with Johnny more than two hours ago.

"How am I going to get it?" she had asked.

"Distract him," Johnny had said.

"How?"

"Lock him in the bathroom, try to seduce him. I don't care."

"Try to seduce him? Is that what you would do?"

"Uh, no. I don't think it would be all that effective coming from me."

Try to seduce him. Sara, looking straight back at Masterson, tried not to laugh. *I've never seduced anyone in my life.*

She reached behind her and closed the door to the office. She pursed her lips and walked to each window, swaying her hips and closing the blinds. Masterson stood perfectly still, his eyes fixed on Sara. She walked back to the chair in front of Masterson's desk.

"It's a little hot in here, don't you think?" Sara asked. "Do you mind if I take off my lab coat?"

"Okay," Masterson said very slowly.

She slowly took off the coat. Arching her back, she let her tight V-neck blouse loosen at the neckline, showing a bit of the camisole underneath. She sat down, leaned forward, and crossed her legs, letting her skirt ride up just past her knee. Biting her bottom lip, she looked Masterson straight in the eye.

"I'm sorry, Tom," Sara said, suddenly hoping that she had remembered his first name correctly. "I shouldn't have called it *my* tox report. I just had a little time and helped Sarvis out with it. I thought you might appreciate somebody double-checking everything. I know that with important cases you need everything to be … unblemished."

Sara laughed softly. "I shouldn't have brought it up. I don't want you to think I'm just a silly girl."

"Honestly, I don't know what to think," Masterson said, again very slowly.

Sara stood up again, took a few steps toward Masterson, and sat on the corner of his desk. Her skirt rode up her leg a bit higher. Masterson coughed and looked away uncomfortably. *Perfect.* Tilting her head to one side and leaning in a bit more, her eyes quickly scanned the room. *There!* Masterson had put the keycard on top of a filing cabinet on the opposite side of the desk. This was going to take a little more work.

"Look, Sara," Masterson said. "It's okay. I trust that you did a fine job on the autopsy and a fine job helping Sarvis with the toxicology report. And I don't think you're just a silly girl. I don't think anyone in the department is a—*whoa!*"

Sara swung herself up onto Masterson's desk. *This is so ridiculous*, she thought. *I don't even want to know what he's thinking right now.* At least she was keeping him distracted. She pulled her knees forward, knocking pens, pencils, a stapler, and several papers on the floor as she did. Masterson pushed himself away from the desk.

"Look, Ms. Albright, I don't know what has gotten into you, but I'm going to have to ask you to leave my office *right now.* This is completely inappropriate."

Sara let her lip quiver slightly. "You thought … ?" she asked softly. This was it. She had to make her move now.

Trying to look shocked, Sara scooted off the desk and pulled her skirt back over her knees, suddenly losing her balance and crashing to the floor. On her way down, she grabbed both a desk drawer and a file drawer and pulled them down with her. The file cabinet and desk both toppled over in a massive crash.

Tears welled in Sara's eyes, and she bit her lip to keep from crying out. Her hip had hit something hard.

Masterson, who had jumped to his feet as the furniture crashed to the floor, took Sara by the arm and helped her stand up. Her hip *really* hurt.

"I'm so sorry," Sara said without any need to fake embarrassment.

"It's okay, Sara. Just—just don't worry about it. I'll get it cleaned up. You just get back to the lab."

"No, I'll help," Sara said, stooping down and gathering papers into a stack. *Where was the keycard?*

"Ms. Albright, please let me take care of this," Masterson said. "You're mixing up all the papers. Just let me do it. I know where they go."

"Then let me pick up the pencils," Sara said. "This is my fault. I don't know what I was thinking. I just—" her voice trailed off as she spotted a blue card with a magnetic strip sitting beneath the mug. *That's it!*

"Sir?" a detective had entered the office. Masterson stood up immediately and started smoothing out his suit. Sara quickly grabbed the keycard, struggled to her feet, and held it carefully behind her back while trying to straighten her hair with her other hand.

"Is there a problem, chief?" the officer asked.

"No," Masterson said. "No problem. Why?"

The detective looked around the room, a very confused expression on his face.

"I think I should go now," Sara said abruptly. She grabbed her lab coat, stuffed the card in a pocket, and briskly walked out of the office.

"What happened?" she heard the detective ask.

"I have no idea," Masterson said.

Sara quickly walked through the department and to her lab. Closing the door behind her, she pulled the card out. There was no label. Just a black magnetic strip on one side. Hopefully it was the keycard Johnny needed.

I'll see you at Mistletoe Lane, Johnny, she thought.

CHAPTER TWENTY-THREE

WALKING PAST the giant ice sculpture of Rudolph and Santa, Paul looked at his watch and shook his head. He had hoped to have moved on in the investigation, but, as had been typical since he and Johnny had started the investigation the day before, NPPD was not cooperating.

Paul had little trouble getting the photographer taken care of. Paul didn't know whether he was still afraid of penguins or if employees of *The Northern Lights* had simply learned that he and Johnny tended to let them off easy when they cooperated. Whatever the reason, the photographer had done exactly what Paul had told him to do—even during the chaos that had ensued when a couple of huskies leading the dog sled started chasing after a snow leopard.

The problems had started at NPPD. Dispatch raised a small fit when it heard where Paul had been and what he had been doing. A report was filed to one of the sergeants, and Paul was accused of neglecting his assigned case to pursue a personal issue. *This is biting me in the butt, just like I told you it would*, Paul wished he could tell Johnny.

Paul had explained that he wasn't investigating the Santa case. Concealing evidence and tampering with a crime scene were crimes in and of themselves. When he had seen the picture in *The Northern*

Lights, he had decided to investigate himself because of his personal connections with the editor-in-chief.

Apparently, his story was good enough. He got out without even a verbal reprimand.

Still, Paul had put the hat in his coat. He had not wanted to file it as evidence yet, fearing it would disappear along with everything else in the Santa case. Not knowing what else to do, he had taken a lesson from the photographer he had just booked and hid it in the bottom of a file drawer.

It was then that he had learned whose hoof prints had been all over the Claus Estate. Looking for Sara, Paul had walked down to the lab. She wasn't there—someone had said that she had gone to talk to Masterson about something. But there was a small forensics report lying on a table. Another lab assistant walked in and asked what Paul was doing, but not before Paul had seen one item on the report: the hoof prints belonged to Dasher.

So here he was, at the Reindeer Training Grounds again, with two things to follow up on instead of just one. The fleet manager had again balked at issuing Paul a penguin-fitted patrol car, so Paul had rode another dog sled.

"Where's Dasher?" Paul asked as soon as he opened the door to the stables and walked in.

The four reindeer playing poker ignored him, as did another one resting on a sofa. *Do these guys do any work?* Paul wondered. He didn't even want to think about what their salary was.

"I said where's Dash—"

"Detective," a voice cut him off from down the hall. "May I speak with you for a minute?"

It was Rudolph. Paul groaned slightly but walked over to the red-nosed reindeer anyway. Rudolph was annoying, but at least he was willing to talk. Rudolph nodded back toward the hall, and Paul followed him into his office.

"About Dasher," Rudolph said after closing his door. "I know why you're here."

"You do?" Paul asked.

"Of course. I've suspected that Dasher was up to something

ever since he disappeared yesterday evening."

"He's been gone that long?"

"He was acting odd all yesterday, and then he told us he was going out for a jog. He's been on the run ever since." Rudolph sighed. "Honestly, I never liked Dasher all that much. He always seemed to *think* he runs the place, he never treated me with due respect, and he has always been unpleasant. But until now I had never, *never* thought he could have been involved with this … situation we're in."

"Dasher's involved?" Paul was incredulous. "With Santa's murder?"

"It sure looks that way," Rudolph said. "He and Mrs. Claus. They wanted to take over."

Paul just sat there dumbfounded. Yesterday Rudolph had been the only one that had given Mrs. Claus any support, and now he was reciting the same clichéd theory about the young bombshell killing her husband.

"I assume you know this already," Rudolph said, puzzled by Paul's bewilderment.

"I don't know what you're talking about," Paul said.

"The mayor, during his press conference two hours ago, said that Mrs. Claus was on the run and NPPD was conducting a manhunt to bring her to justice. I assumed you were here because you had figured out that Dasher was a party too."

"No," Paul said. "All I knew is that I needed to talk to Dasher about his whereabouts today and that I wanted to see the security videos you have of the Claus Estate."

"I already sent them in to NPPD," Rudolph said. "You didn't see them?"

"No," Paul grumbled. "But that shouldn't be shocking at this point."

"I have a copy here," Rudolph said. He put a video into a small TV sitting on a shelf.

A scene from the grounds at the Claus Estate appeared on the TV—apparently from the same security camera Paul had seen in the bushes. A running log of year, hour, minute, second, and micro-

SANTA CLAUS IS DEAD   ❄   JASON TWEDE

second was in the bottom right hand corner.

"That's from today isn't it?" Paul asked.

Rudolph nodded. "From this morning. You have to be quiet, though, the sound is not very good."

For nearly a minute the scene was both silent and empty. The hoof prints Paul had seen at the house were not in the snow yet.

Very faintly, the sound of voices arose—though nothing had appeared on the screen yet.

" … what about the girl?" Paul recognized Dasher's gruff voice.

"There's nothing I can do for her right now," a woman's voice replied. *Mrs. Claus*, Paul realized.

"And you seriously don't have the Naughty List?"

"It's gone," Mrs. Claus said. "I'm not sure who took it."

"You know that list looks bad for both of us. All NPPD has to do is put two and two together and they'll link you with the girl and the boy."

"I know, Dasher," Mrs. Claus said. "Can you think of anything to do about it, though?"

"No. Let's just get out of here. I'll do whatever I can to take care of this mess, but you need to keep out of sight. I don't know if you'll be able to make the flight tomorrow."

"That's okay," Mrs. Claus said. "We both know this has never been about delivering toys."

"It's about the money," Dasher agreed. "And doing whatever it takes to get control of it."

Suddenly Dasher, with Mrs. Claus on his back, ran on screen, leaped into the air, and flew away.

Rudolph stopped the tape.

Paul didn't know what to think.

"There's just something that doesn't quite add up," Paul finally said. Between Susie's arrest, the mayor's shenanigans, the gunman with directions to Susie's cell, Masterson inhibiting the legitimate investigation, and the bogus cause of death, it just didn't make sense to suddenly be able to pin everything on Mrs. Claus and Dasher.

"Detective," Rudolph said. "I know your job is to catch the real killer and compile all the evidence in a way that actually makes sense, but that isn't the only issue we have to worry about. Christmas Eve is tomorrow, and it *has* to be pulled off. We have never missed a Christmas flight since I joined the team, and we are not going to miss it now."

"So what are you going to do?" Paul asked.

"Just wait. Mayor Wassail announced that a special session of the Village Council will be held tonight. The only item on the agenda will be the dissolution of the Claus Monarchy and appointment of an interim Head of Christmas."

"And who will that be?" Paul asked.

"Who do you think?" Rudolph said with disgust. "Mayor Wassail."

"Of course," Paul said. "Do you really think Mrs. Claus was involved with Santa's murder?"

"I don't know," Rudolph said, obviously uncomfortable with taking an official position. "I told you before that I have always liked her. She always treated me well. Yesterday, I thought she was the best option to take over. But the more I hear and see … I just don't know."

"So are you happy with Mayor Wassail's plan?"

"Let me tell you something, Detective Penguin," Rudolph said. "About a week ago Santa sat down with all of us reindeer for an evening of milk and cookies. Do you know what he talked about? He wanted us to remember him after he was gone. I'm sure he didn't know the end was coming as soon as it did, but that really isn't the point. The point is he wanted us to remember him, to remember what he stood for, to remember what Christmas was about, and to make sure it continued in the same way after he was gone.

"I don't like what's going on any more than you do. The mayor's just about as sleazy an opportunist as they come. His motivation is all wrong, but the fact is he is the only one who is focusing on what ought to be focused on: taking care of this Christmas right now. Everybody else is either obsessed with solving a case or taking care of themselves.

"It is a sad, sad way to honor Santa's legacy, but I think the

Claus monarchy must be dissolved, and I think Mayor Wassail needs our support. I know he's just taking advantage of Santa's death. I know he's in it for purely selfish purposes. But that doesn't really matter. What matters is whether Christmas happens this year. We can hack out the politics and ethics after the children get their gifts. That's what would have made Santa happy."

A thought occurred to Paul. "Did you know that Santa was considering a complete overhaul of Christmas? That he was advocating a complete change from how he had been running things for the last fifty years?"

Rudolph huffed. "Santa mentioned something about it."

"Are you sure that you really want the same thing Santa would want?"

"I'm sure that I want what he spent his entire life trying to accomplish."

CHAPTER TWENTY-FOUR

—MISTLETOE LANE, 5:57 PM

SARA SAT beneath a softly glowing lamppost on one of nearly a hundred elegantly crafted benches that lined both sides of Mistletoe Lane. Across the back of the bench, in gold plated letters, was written "*A Love in December is a Love to Remember.*" It was just one of nearly three thousand sentimental phrases that had become a part of the now infamous street.

Fabio Claus, whose reign had lasted all of three years before he ran off to Norway after becoming involved in a notorious love triangle, was responsible for Mistletoe Lane. The road had originally been Kitsch Avenue, but it was changed when Fabio decided that the youth of the North Pole needed a spot to romance, woo, and make out. The road was turned into a pedestrian walkway, the name was changed to Mistletoe Lane, and Kitsch Avenue was designated to a new road on the other end of town.

The work of creating the walkway took nearly the entire three years of Fabio Claus's reign. He hired skilled metal smiths, carpenters, and weavers from Switzerland and Germany to fill the entire place with comfortable benches, secluded little gazebos, and elaborately draped tapestries that hung from the lampposts—which had then held oil-burning lanterns. The tapestries, of course, didn't even last a single winter, but the benches and gazebos had proven astoundingly resilient. Mistletoe Lane was, even today, the hot spot for teens on Friday nights and after the annual North Pole High Junior Prom.

Sara still couldn't believe she was waiting for Johnny here. He had picked the place because nobody would ever think to look for him here, the lighting was much dimmer than most of the rest of town, and the entire place was designed to give ample privacy—but Sara couldn't help feeling like a girl waiting for a date. *I thought I grew out of this kind of thing when I turned fifteen.* She felt both ridiculous and defensive at the same time.

She checked her pocket again. The keycard was still there. *Just get here before I start breaking out into zits or something*, she silently demanded from Johnny. She looked around the area, which was filled with teenage couples completely oblivious to the outside world.

She felt somebody slide next to her on the bench. It was Johnny. Susie stood next to him.

"You know, Johnny," Sara said. "I'm really not the kind of girl that usually meets guys on a bench at Mistletoe Lane."

"I know it's stupid," Johnny was flustered. "I felt so dumb asking it. I–I don't want you to get the wrong idea."

Sara smiled somewhat bitterly. "Well, don't worry about that. I won't." She pulled out the keycard. "Here it is."

"No markings on it?"

"Nope. If that's not the right one, I don't know where else it could be."

"Then let's hope this *is* the right one."

Sara nodded and looked at Susie, who was breathing into her mittened hands to keep them warm.

"You must be Susie," Sara said. "I'm Sara. I've heard about you from Johnny."

"You work with Mr. Iceberg?" Susie asked.

"Sometimes," Sara said.

"You're friends with him?"

"A little bit." Sara turned back to Johnny. "Where are you staying tonight?"

"I don't know," Johnny said. "We were at the Arctic Hotel last night, but I don't know if I want to go there again."

"Pretty gross?"

"That and the fact that Masterson found us there. If we're not going to be able to go incognito, we might as well stay at the Ritzy Sugar Plum."

Silence. Susie's eyes darted back and forth between the two of them.

"Have you heard about the mayor?" Sara asked.

Johnny nodded. "He's trying to take over. We've got to stop him. Do you realize what could happen if we put a killer in kids' homes this Christmas Eve?"

"I know."

"You heard from Paul lately?" Johnny asked.

"No. I don't know what he's been able to dig up," Sara said. "I've decided to go to the Village Council meeting tonight. Maybe I'll see him there."

Johnny nodded.

"Are we going now?" Susie asked.

"Yeah," Johnny said. His face tensed. Up the walkway, nearly a hundred yards away, two police officers were approaching. He looked around, but there was no place he could get to without drawing attention to himself.

"Oh no," Sara whispered. She had seen the officers too.

Johnny started to stand up, but before he could Sara grabbed his coat and pulled him down to the bench on top of her. Wrapping her arms around Johnny's neck, she kissed him. After a quick moment Johnny relaxed a little, but he was still as stiff as an ice cube.

"Oh, geez," one of the cops said as they walked by.

"What kind of person drags their kid to Mistletoe Lane with them?"

"What kind of person even comes here when they're older than sixteen?"

Neither Sara nor Johnny moved.

"They're gone," Susie whispered.

"Right," Johnny said, taking a deep breath and getting back to his feet. "Uh … thanks," he told Sara. "That was close."

Sara just looked the other way. "Anytime," she said. Johnny wasn't sure whether the sarcasm in her voice was directed at herself or at him.

"I didn't even have to pretend to be embarrassed," Susie said.

Johnny put an arm on the girl's shoulder and started leading her away.

"Good luck," Sara said.

"You too," Johnny said.

Sara watched them walk away. *I wonder where they'll go tonight,* she thought. She wrapped her coat tightly around herself and walked alone in the other direction. There were enough couples kissing on the benches that nobody would have given her and Johnny a second thought.

"Run, Susie!" Johnny's voice rang out.

Sara spun around and saw Johnny on the ground struggling with two men and an elf. *Where had they come from?* she wondered. Using both hands and legs, Johnny held them back as they tried to go after Susie, who was running toward the thick woods that ran on both sides of the walkway.

"Susie!" Sara called out. The girl stopped suddenly and looked at Sara, who started waving for Susie to come. She understood and started running again, this time toward the lab assistant.

Who decided women are supposed to wear skirts and heels to work? Sara thought as she tried to run toward Susie. Suddenly, from behind a gazebo, two polar bears dressed in black and wearing the mayor's insignia, started lumbering toward Sara. She stopped, tried to take a step backward, and tripped. The two bears, having positioned themselves right between Susie and Sara, separated. One went after the little girl, and the second kept coming toward Sara.

Something swooped down out of the sky and crashed into the bear, who fell to the ground unconscious. Stunned, Sara realized that one of the reindeer had saved her. It put its head down and ran after the bear chasing Susie. Before the bear knew what was happening, the reindeer slammed his antlers into his back.

Johnny, having knocked out and tied up three people he had

been struggling with, ran toward Susie and the reindeer.

"Dasher?" Johnny called out.

"You okay?" the reindeer asked.

"Yeah."

"What do you want to do about the girl?" Dasher asked.

"Susie? You gave both of us a ride earlier."

"No," Dasher said, pointing his antlers at Sara. "Her."

"I wouldn't really call her a *girl*, Dasher," Johnny said.

Sara climbed to her feet and walked toward Johnny and the reindeer. "I'll be fine," she said. "They're all after you and Susie. I doubt anyone that just attacked us even knows who I am."

"You sure?" Johnny asked.

Sara nodded. "I have the Village Council meeting to go to anyway. It's not far." She looked at Dasher. "Aren't you going too?"

Dasher shook his head. "No. Long story. Whatever Wassail does will be done whether I'm there or not. I'm taking these two with me."

"Where?"

"If nobody knows, then nobody can find out," Dasher said. "We don't want to do this morning all over again."

Sara looked back at Johnny. "You'll be okay?" she asked.

"I'll be fine." He tried lifting Susie to Dasher's back, but winced with pain. The bullet wound was still sore.

"Let me help," Sara said. Together they lifted the girl up.

"Be careful," Johnny told Sara as he climbed up.

"You too."

"Miss," Dasher said. "I'd try to get out of here before any of them come to." The reindeer reared up and sprinted down the walkway. Just before hitting a gazebo, the reindeer rose into the air and flew away.

CHAPTER TWENTY-FIVE

"DETECTIVE PENGUIN," the lab aide said when Paul picked up the receiver.

"Yes."

"We've conducted the DNA analysis of the hair sample you sent us."

"Do you have any results?" Paul asked.

"The hair belonged to Santa Claus. Because you are not assigned to that case, the sample has been filed under the Santa investigation."

"I thought the Santa investigation was closed," Paul said.

"We're still compiling evidence for the trial," the aide said.

Click.

Paul sat at his desk. He had gone through every change the photographer had made with the photographs, and he had received as much lab analysis as Paul could risk on the hat. Everything looked genuine. It was Santa's hat, and as far as Paul could tell it had really been found by itself, without any tracks or other disturbances in the snow, more than a hundred feet from the body.

But what good did it do to know that? Paul wondered. He looked at the clock and winced. He was usually home by this time in the evening. He picked up the phone again and dialed his home number. After five rings he heard his own voice: *You have reached the Penguin residence. We are not at home, so you'll have to talk to a tape recorder, but please wait until after the beep.*

"Allison, this is Paul. It's a little past six right now, and I'll probably be working another couple of hours. See you when I do." Paul set the receiver down.

That was odd. Allison hadn't said anything was going on this evening. Both Allison and Paul usually did a good job letting each other know where they would be.

Then again, Paul thought, *I should have called her about an hour ago to let her know I would be home late.*

Paul closed his eyes and leaned back in his chair, trying to put everything he knew about the Santa case out of his mind. He had another case he was supposed to be working on, and he might as well make a show of working on it. Besides, Paul was very curious to find out what kind of person visited the North Pole from Australia in the winter. *You've got to really be into Christmas to do that,* Paul guessed. *Or really mad at Santa,* Paul added, remembering what Mitchell had said about the fight.

The artist's composite taken from the witnesses to the fight at the One-Horse Open Sleigh had been dropped in Paul's box, and the North Pole International Airport had just faxed over a list of all travelers from Australia in the past month. Just as Paul had expected, the list was short—only four names: Thomas Kane, Cynthia Day, Chad Tyler, and Greg Norrisson.

Chad Tyler. The name sounded familiar to Paul. On a hunch, Paul accessed the police records and databases of the major Australian metropolitan areas. One of them, from Melbourne, brought up a match. Three arrests—two for drug charges and one for assault and battery. The mug shot matched the composite sketch. It looked like this Chad Tyler was the right guy. Paul quickly read through the rest of the records: no time served in prison, three probation sentences, one of which included assignment to a partially closed youth correctional facility. Age: sixteen.

The guy's just a kid! Paul realized. Suddenly Paul remembered where he had seen the name: his name had been circled on the

Naughty List. The kid was still young enough to be on the list, and Santa had circled it. Unfortunately there were thousands of reasons the name could be on the Naughty List, and another thousand reasons why Santa may have circled it. Paul couldn't jump to conclusions and assume it had anything to do with the murder.

But something kept echoing in Paul's mind. *It's gone*, Mrs. Claus had said about the Naughty List. *I don't know who took it.* Then Dasher had spoken: *You know that list looks bad for both of us. All NPPD has to do is put two and two together and they'll link you with the girl and the boy.*

The "girl" had obviously been Susie. Was this Chad Tyler the boy Dasher had been talking about?

How did this kid get here, anyway? Paul wondered. He did a quick airline ticket price search from Melbourne to North Pole International Airport. $2099. That was the cheapest round trip airfare. Paul couldn't think of an honest way a sixteen year old could pay more than two thousand dollars for a little trip, no matter how much he disliked Santa.

Following his instincts, Paul called the airline Chad had flown in on. After going through several different operators and divisions within the airline, Paul finally had an answer. Mrs. Claus's Give a Naughty Kid Christmas Foundation had paid for Chad Tyler's airfare.

That was the connection Dasher had been talking about. Mrs. Claus had brought Chad Tyler to the North Pole … to kill Santa? Paul shook his head. It still didn't add up. *What about all the evidence against Wassail?*

Maybe Mrs. Claus and Mayor Wassail had all been in it together, and something went wrong. Then it was everyone for himself—a task Mayor Wassail was obviously most proficient with. But that still didn't explain why Dasher had referred to Susie and the need to distance themselves from her.

Paul pressed his flippers into his forehead. The questions were giving him a headache. He looked at the clock again. The special session of the Village Council was starting soon. Paul felt a masochistic urge to go and watch Mayor Wassail be named interim director of Christmas. *Kind of like watching an avalanche rushing down a glacier right toward you, your skis stuck in the ice*, Paul thought.

❄ ❄ ❄

Sara arrived at City Hall just before the Mayor's bodyguards closed the room off from further public access. It was just as well they did. The public seating was so crowded that the chairs had long since been folded up and shoved to a corner to accommodate standing room only. She saw a black flipper waving slightly from across the room, and she saw Paul. There was no way she could push through all the people and get to him before the meeting began.

Mayor Wassail sat at the head of the large, circular conference table at the head of the room. He kept turning his head, flashing his well-known smile for each of the dozens of cameras in the room. Beside Mayor Wassail were three empty chairs, followed by Morgan, President of the Elvish Labor Union and the elves' representative on the Village Council. The elf, who slouched in his chair, had wild red hair and a hook-shaped nose. He looked even more sullen than usual.

Sara looked over to Paul. *Where are the other council members?* she mouthed silently. She could see Paul shake his head and shrug.

Mayor Wassail stood up.

"I, Mayor Georg Wassail, in accordance with city ordinance 105 section B, do hereby call this special session of Village Council to order. Will those present please stand and state both their names and positions?"

Morgan slowly rose and, following elvish tradition, stood on his chair. "Morgan, Village Council Member representing Seat 2 and the elvish population." He sat down.

"Council Recorder," Mayor Wassail said. "Rise."

A scrawny man near the main table rose.

"Were notices of meeting sent to the absent council members, Frosty of the snowmen and Dasher of the animals?"

"Notices were sent. All notices are verifiable and documented." The man sat back down.

"Then, in accordance with city ordinance 105, section D I hereby declare the present member of the Village Council a complete quorum with rights to dictate and execute laws according to city ordinance 4, section A. Should any ties occur in the voting," Wassail chuckled good naturedly, "the City Recorder shall ask for the mayor's vote, which shall decide the issue."

"On today's agenda," Mayor Wassail paused and smiled at the crowd. "Item one: Proposal to dissolve the Claus monarchy and remove it from sole directorship of the Christmas Foundation, Inc. According to the entire text, this proposal includes a provision, should the monarchy be dissolved, to appoint the current Mayor of North Pole Village as interim director of said Foundation until the council appoints, by unanimous approval, a permanent director. This proposal is set forth according to city ordinance 47, which defines the Village Council's authority over operations of the Christmas Foundation.

"All in favor."

Morgan scowled at the mayor, but finally raised his hand and said, "Aye."

"Those opposed." Mayor Wassail winked at several cameras. "By unanimous vote, the Claus monarchy's directorship of the Christmas Foundation is hereby dissolved, and Mayor Georg Wassail assumes the role of interim director of said Foundation."

Mayor Wassail stood up and let out a big sigh. He looked into the crowd. "And that, my friends," he said, "is the only item on the agenda. Special session of Village Council is adjourned, and I am the new Head of Christmas."

The roar of deafening applause erupted from the people in the room. Mayor Wassail meandered through, shaking hands with everyone he could find. Behind him, Morgan slunk away through the back doors.

Sara glanced back over to Paul, who motioned for her to meet him outside.

"So that's that," Sara said once she and Paul were away from the crowd.

"Right," Paul said.

"Do you still think the mayor was involved with the murder?" Sara asked.

"Yeah," Paul said. "But the truth is I don't have any hard evidence against anybody."

"So what's going to happen?"

"Tomorrow I'm going to do everything I can to get that quack arrested and Christmas in the hands of someone else. Though, at this rate I don't know who it will go to. Frosty can't take over. He'd melt going down the first fireplace. Maybe they'll give it to Morgan."

Both Paul and Sara burst into hard—almost painful—laughs at the idea.

"Well, at least he'll have no trouble fitting down the chimneys," Sara said, wiping away tears.

"And we will go down in history as the people who lived during the reign of Shrimpy Claus," Paul said.

After they both calmed down, Sara became somber again.

"So you don't think Mrs. Claus is an option anymore?" she asked. "Do you believe what the mayor said about her this afternoon?"

"No, I don't believe the mayor," Paul said, "but there's something shady going on with Mrs. Claus. I don't know what's going to happen to her."

They walked away from City Hall.

"Where have you been, anyway?" Paul asked.

"I knew this was going to come up," Sara said wearily.

"What would come up?"

"I met Johnny down at Mistletoe Lane."

"You're kidding? *Mistletoe Lane?* You and Johnny?" Paul laughed again. "I wish I could have seen that."

"It wasn't anything," Sara said. "I stole a keycard from Masterson this afternoon—one Johnny saw him use to get into City Hall. Johnny wants to get in there to find some dirt on Mayor Wassail. Mostly just to figure out what is going on and how much Masterson is involved, I think. Anyway, we met at Mistletoe Lane, and I gave it to him."

"And whose idea was the location?" Paul asked.

"His," Sara said. "He said nobody would ever think to look for him there."

Paul nodded. "Well, that's true. You got him the keycard?"

"Yes. But then we were attacked by some of the mayor's people."

"Are you okay? Is Johnny okay?"

"We're all fine. Dasher came and took care it."

"Dasher?" Paul asked, suddenly alarmed. "Are you sure it was him?"

"Yes. He took Johnny and Susie with him."

"To where?"

"He wouldn't say. He said it would be someplace safe. What's wrong, Paul?"

"Dasher's no good. I think he's one of the main players in Santa's murder."

"What?"

"I'll explain in a minute," Paul said, digging through his pockets. "First I *really* need to make a phone call."

CHAPTER TWENTY-SIX

–SPHERE VALLEY, 9:16 PM

DASHER LED Johnny and Susie through a desolate, snow-covered path that wound through the icy ruts of the treeless glaciers. The reindeer kept promising that they were almost there. Out of courtesy to the snowmen, Dasher claimed, he had set down nearly two miles away from Sphere Valley, where he was taking them.

Despite keeping herself wrapped in an extra blanket, as well as the winter clothes Johnny had bought her earlier that day, Susie's teeth kept chattering. To try to help her stay warm, Johnny had long ago pulled her off Dasher's back and forced her to walk. Luckily the moon was nearly full and the Aurora Borealis seemed to shimmer unusually bright blues and greens. With the never-ending expanse of snow and ice, they had no difficulty seeing the path.

Finally, after they climbed over yet another ridge, a large valley nearly forty miles across in each direction stretched out in front of them. Johnny could see a few wooden huts dotting the snowy expanse. There were no lights shining from inside.

As Dasher led them down into the valley, they were stopped from behind by two snowmen holding long black poles with sharpened icicles attached to one end and intertwined with a flickering jagged line of electricity. Dasher walked with them until they were out of earshot.

Johnny had never before realized how big snowmen were. Both of the ones talking to Dasher were over seven feet tall. Their bodies were made out of three completely round snowballs. Their arms were large tree branches, their eyes were coal, and their noses were carrots. Somehow, though he couldn't figure out how, Johnny could tell the difference between the two of them. One looked fierce—as if he was ready to pounce at the slightest provocation. The second, a female, looked friendly.

They both came back with Dasher.

"We're okay," Dasher told Johnny. "But don't make yourselves annoying guests. Asking them to hide you two *and* Mrs. Claus is a bit much. They don't usually take well to outsiders."

Mrs. Claus was here? Johnny and Susie both looked at each other. Seeing a sudden flash of anger in Susie's eyes, Johnny put his hand on her shoulder. He wanted her to believe that everything would be okay.

The two snowmen, sentinels Johnny assumed, led them further into the valley. More and more snowmen were around them now. Just over a small hill, Johnny could see two of them rolling snowballs and stacking them on top of each other. On the top snowball, which only came up to the others' waists, they stuck in two small chunks of coal.

"Mating season," Dasher said, noticing the detective's perplexed look.

Johnny laughed softly. "Should I cover her eyes?" he asked, pointing to Susie.

Dasher smiled and shook his head.

"I can hear you talking," Susie said. "I'm not dumb, you know."

"Kid," Johnny told her. "I think a lot of different things about you, but dumb isn't even on the list."

"What's on the top of the list?" Susie asked.

"That for the most part, you can take care of yourself because you know what you want."

"I can even hang out with a detective all day—even when he doesn't know how to get me a decent breakfast."

DECEMBER 23 ❄ 9:16 PM

"That's all the evidence anyone would need."

As they neared the huts at the bottom of the valley, Johnny could make out the layout of the village better. The huts were fairly simple—walls made out of tightly-packed logs and roofs that were thatched with pine branches. They had holes for windows but no glass. Probably to keep the buildings cold and prevent melting, Johnny suspected. The lack of lighting around the village was likely for the same reason.

Just before they reached the village, Dasher turned to Johnny. "This is as far as I go. I have other things I need to attend to. These two will provide you with a warm place to stay for the evening. In the morning, they will take you to see Frosty."

"And we're safe here?" Johnny asked.

"You are," Dasher said. Without another word he walked back the way they had come.

Johnny still couldn't figure out the reindeer. The day before he had seemed like a petty leader who had an overstuffed ego. Now he seemed like a humble idealist, trying to do what was best for himself, them, and apparently Mrs. Claus too. Then, he would mutter something that hinted of a conspiracy behind Santa's murder, yet he never offered any explanation as to how he knew about this conspiracy. And Johnny really didn't like his tendency to take off and run errands he never explained.

When two snowmen finally led Johnny and Susie to a hut at the edge of town, he was suddenly very grateful. The windows were covered, the air was heated, and there were blankets and two small cots. He was cold and tired, and the accommodations were enough to make him drowsy.

"Thank you," Johnny told the two snowmen.

They nodded, their coal eyes faintly reflecting the dim rim of sunlight that was always on the horizon. Without a word, they left.

"Come on," Johnny led Susie inside and closed the door. He helped her out of her coat into a cot, and before he had even set the blanket on her she was asleep. He pulled his computer and phone out of a small pack and placed them on the floor. A light on the phone was blinking.

He picked it up. *One new message.* It was from Paul. He had called sometime when Dasher was still leading them across the glaciers, when they were far from cell phone service. Johnny was actually surprised to see that he had service in the village.

"Johnny, it's Paul. Call me as soon as you get this message, and I'm serious. *Don't brush it off.*"

Johnny frowned. Paul sounded very serious. He dialed his partner.

"Johnny, where are you?" Paul asked before the first ring had even finished.

"Calm down, shorty," Johnny said. "I'm fine. Dasher brought me and Susie to—" Johnny cut himself off. The only way the mayor's bodyguards could have known he had been at Mistletoe Lane was if they had tapped into Sara's personal phone. If Sara's had been tapped, the Paul's probably was too. "Just don't worry about it, Paul," Johnny said. "Dasher took us someplace safe to spend the night."

"That's the problem," Paul said. "Dasher's no good."

"What are you talking about? He seemed fine. He said he's brought Mrs. Claus here too, to keep her safe."

"I told you, Johnny," Paul said. "He's no good. And if Mrs. Claus is there too, then you might be in even worse danger than I thought."

"You are not making any sense, Paul," Johnny said.

As quickly as he could, Paul told Johnny about the security video he had seen with Rudolph. Before he could explain the connection between Mrs. Claus and Chad Tyler, Johnny cut him off.

"Paul, this is a ... really bad time," Johnny said. The last thing Paul needed was someone from NPPD to hear everything he had put together.

"What?" Paul shouted. "Have you even been listening to me?"

"Yeah," Johnny said. "Bye."

He ended the call and turned off the phone. Knowing Paul, he would be irritated and try to call back, but Johnny didn't know how to explain the problem without tipping off whoever would be eavesdropping on their conversation.

Johnny stood up and started pacing around in the room. Paul

had said enough about the video to make Johnny feel nervous. He hadn't really trusted Dasher—the reindeer had been too enigmatic from the beginning—but after the attack at Mistletoe Lane there hadn't been many other options.

Johnny looked out the window from the hut. The scene was icy, still, and beautiful. Spruce groves grew around the white hills and the dim hint of sunlight on the horizon danced just above the rim of the valley like fire. Overhead the northern lights shimmered among the stars and the snow-covered ground, blemished only by a single pair of footprints, mirrored the aurora's glimmer.

Johnny suddenly stared at the tracks. He and Susie had made all of them when they had entered the valley. There were no other footprints.

Just below a nearby grove, a single snowman glided silently along the snow. He left no tracks behind.

Only a single set of tracks had been at Santa's murder scene, but Sara's autopsy suggested that multiple assailants had attacked him. Johnny looked in horror at the two isolated set of tracks leading up to the hut.

Paul had been right. He had just been led into a trap.

❄   ❄   ❄

As mad as Paul had been when Johnny had hung up on him, he completely forgot about it as soon as he had stepped into his house and realized something was wrong.

Now he knelt in the middle of his living room, shaking with rage and fear, his head in his flippers. A crumpled note sat on the floor near his feet.

Detective Penguin—

Your wife and children have lovely blue eyes. If you ever want to see them again, back off the case.

DECEMBER 24

CHRISTMAS EVE

CHAPTER TWENTY-SEVEN
—1414 SILVER BELL BLVD., 8:36 AM

PAUL WOKE up sitting awkwardly in a recliner in his living room. His back and neck were both sore, and his eyes were bloodshot. He didn't know how Johnny could sleep on living room furniture every night—Paul didn't feel nearly as rested as the four hours of sleep should have made him feel.

He stood up and winced at the headache piercing him right behind his eyes. The house was dark and silent. Paul's family was still nowhere to be seen.

Paul had searched through every drawer, beneath every table and chair, and rummaged through every paper in the house for some kind of note or anything that could tell him where they were.

Once he called in a missing person report, he had spent several hours helping the officers conduct a search for some sign of them.

They had found nothing.

Finally the other officers had sat down with Paul and gone through the standard missing person questions: *Was there any kind of marital dissatisfaction? Was there anyone who would want to hurt your family? Were there any signs of erratic behavior during the past few days? Are there any relatives nearby that may know of their whereabouts?*

And on and on. The more questions the officers asked, the

more Paul thought about the explanation he couldn't tell the officers: It had to do with the Santa murder. Paul felt sick inside. His job had finally come back to hurt his family.

That could only mean that Paul was getting close. He had certainly felt close last night—though everything didn't add up yet, the pieces were falling into place and Paul could start to see how everyone was connected: Mrs. Claus, Dasher, Mayor Wassail, Chad Tyler. Even Masterson, if he assumed that the chief was the mayor's goon. And, as Mrs. Claus had said on the security video, it was all about the money.

Paul looked out the window. *Now what do I do?* he wondered. The other officers had recommended Paul take the day off—*Didn't he usually take Christmas Eve off anyway?* Paul had simply scowled at them.

Across the street, Paul noticed an enormous suburban parked conspicuously along the curb in the predominantly elvish neighborhood. A polar bear in the passenger-side window was wearing sunglasses.

I knew it! Paul thought as he ran out the door. *Mayor Wassail and his goons are watching to see if I give up on the case or not.* Before Paul even made it to the sidewalk, the suburban drove off.

As Paul stood there, a beat-up silver Nova pulled up to the curb. The window rolled down, and the face inside was probably the last one Paul had expected to see.

"Get in the car, Paul," Masterson said.

Paul was stunned—initially just to see Masterson in such a clunky car. The police chief was rather infamous for the all-wheel drive, black Mercedes he had bought just a year earlier.

But Paul's shock quickly turned to icy cold anger. "Where are they?" he demanded.

"Just get in the car," Masterson repeated. "Do you have your gun and badge?"

Paul instinctively reached down and felt for them. They were there. He must have slept with them on.

"Not until you tell me where they are," Paul said.

"Detective, I know exactly what you're talking about, but I

know much less about it than you probably expect. Now *get in the car.*" Masterson pointed a gun at Paul. Very slowly, Paul complied.

As soon as Paul got in, Masterson put the gun away and sped down the road. The tinsel hanging from the street lights seemed to whiz by in a multicolor stream.

"In general, I like headstrong detectives," Masterson said. "But sometimes it can make you a real pain to deal with." He handed Paul a piece of paper.

"What is this?" Paul asked.

"An address. I've been closely monitoring all your work during the past few days. You're making all the right connections. Now, if you want to solve this case, go to this address. You'll find what you need there."

"And what case are you talking about, *chief?*" Paul asked sarcastically. He was sounding more like Johnny all the time.

Masterson looked annoyed. "We both know what case I'm talking about."

"I'm not really interested in a bar fight case right now," Paul said, ignoring Masterson's obvious double entendre.

"I know exactly what you're interested in right now," Masterson said. "You need to get it into your head that these aren't all separate issues. Everything is connected. You take care of one of them, and you'll take care of all of them."

Paul did not reply.

"Just make sure you have your gun ready," Masterson said.

Masterson stopped the car at an empty back street in the industrial sector of town.

"Get out here," Masterson said, pulling his gun out again. Obviously he wasn't going to waste time listening to Paul argue about it.

"Fine," Paul said.

Once he was out, Masterson sped off, splattering grey slush everywhere.

Wiping the cold drizzle from his head, Paul looked at the address: "*77905 Vermillion Sparkles Way, #14.*" It was a room at the Arctic Hotel in South Port. That was on the other side of town.

That made Paul mad. Masterson had been acting like he was in a big hurry, and then he specifically dropped Paul off nearly an hour's walk away from where he was going. When the welfare of his family was at stake, Paul did not like people playing games with him.

CHAPTER TWENTY-EIGHT
—SPHERE VALLEY, 8:57 AM

JOHNNY HAD stayed awake the entire night, and he was tired. During the long night in the isolated hut in Sphere Valley, Johnny's anger with the snowmen had changed—from despising them for the likely threat they posed, to loathing them because there probably wouldn't be a decent cup of coffee within ten miles of the place. By the time Susie finally woke up, Johnny was even more irritable than usual.

Outside, several snowmen were working in one of the temperature-controlled huts in which they harvested carrots. Adamantly devoted to the traditional carrot noses, the snowmen used the huts to grow the vegetables during the winter—thus saving dozens of lives every year from freak melting accidents.

Many people in the North Pole speculated about whether the snowmen would develop a similar innovation to mine coal for their eyes. Ever since Eliza Claus had first developed the concept of the Naughty List, the elves had taken over the coal mines. Because of the melting issue again, the elves were simply better suited to extracting the vast amounts of coal that the number of naughty children around the world required.

As every child in the North Pole public education system had learned, the elvish takeover of the coal mines sparked the beginning of interracial animosity between the two groups. The snowmen hated being dependent on the elves for basic sensory needs, and the elves hated the mandatory reduced fees imposed for coal sales to snowmen.

In fact, most snowmen refused to take coal from the elves anymore, preferring to use the eyes of deceased ancestors for the eyes of their children. To call a snowman "*Elf-eyes*" was considered a nearly unforgivable insult.

"Are you okay?" Susie asked Johnny, seeing his red eyes and shaking hands.

"I'm fine," Johnny lied. "Look Susie, we're going to have to be careful here, and I'm going to figure out a way to get out as soon as possible.

"Why?" Susie asked. "What's wrong—"

The door to the hut clanged open, and the two snowmen who had escorted them the night before stood in the entry. They still had the odd electric powered ice spears. They wanted Johnny and Susie to follow them.

"Do they ever talk?" Susie whispered to Johnny.

"Well, snowmen usually can," Johnny said. "Maybe they had their tongues removed or something."

Susie laughed. "Do snowmen even have tongues to remove?"

"Yeah," Johnny joked. "I think they grow tomatoes that they slice up and stick in their mouths."

"Not only can we talk," one of the snowmen said in a harsh and oddly metallic voice, "but we can hear, too."

Both Johnny and Susie instantly silenced and followed the snowmen outside. They were led down another icy, snow-covered path. It was impossible to tell whether it was the same one they had used yesterday. Once they reached the edge of the village, the path turned toward the high, rocky mountains that bordered one side of the valley. They were going to the caves.

The walk took about twenty minutes. Both Susie and Johnny shivered again, but the extra blankets given them by the snowmen and the fact that they were moving kept them warm enough.

Though the caves were, from the outside, little more than holes in the side of the mountain, from their first step inside it was obvious that they were something more. Elaborate stone sculpting covered the inside—giant granite-carved murals, ornately designed stalagmites, and complex tiled floors filled the vast chamber. Dozens of sconces lined the walls, with flames large enough to give light but small enough to keep the temperature below freezing.

"What are these caves for?" Susie asked, looking at a scene depicting one of the early snowmen clan wars. A snowman chieftain wielding a torch was shown using it to cut through the middle of his opponent.

"The snowmen use them to hibernate in during the summer," Johnny said.

"Don't most things hibernate during the winter?" Susie asked.

"Not snowmen," Johnny told her. "In the summer the sun is up all day, and they have to stay in the caves to keep from melting. I think they used to head into the caves around mid-May, but for the past few years, global warming has forced them into the caves sometime in April. I never knew the caves were like this inside, though," he added, pointing to another stone mural. A soldier was eating his opponent's carrot nose, a sign of victory and bravery among some of the ancient snowmen tribes.

At the end of the chamber, they entered a smaller passage that steadily ascended higher and deeper into the mountain. Though absent the ornate stonework of the original passage, the passage was perfectly shaped, without any bits of stone jutting out from either wall or ceiling. The floor had been covered with some kind of black substance that gave Johnny's shoes the friction needed to climb through the passage, but it also allowed the snowmen to glide along effortlessly.

Once through the passage, the cave opened up into another large chamber, though still smaller than the first. Here the giant stone murals reappeared, though this time they were simply a collection of portraits—apparently of various snowman statesmen and women from the past fifteen hundred years. The masonry here was embellished by hundreds of finely crafted jewels laid throughout the murals. Amethysts, rubies, emeralds, sapphires, and turquoise were all embedded in the murals and reflected the light from the sconces.

A throne sat at the far end of the chamber. Standing in front of the throne, protected by two guards similar to the ones that had led Susie and Johnny, stood a strikingly large snowman with a black top hat, a scarf, a button nose, and a corn cob pipe. He was talking to a small group of snowmen that had apparently already approached the throne.

"Frosty the Great," one of the escorts spoke to the snowman standing in front of the stone. All the snowmen turned and looked toward him. "We have brought the guests to you."

"Thank you," Frosty said.

The two escorts bowed, and as they did Johnny lunged and grabbed both spears from them. Setting himself between Susie and the snowmen, Johnny held the spears up defensively. He backed toward one of the sconces, where he could easily catch the handle of the spear on fire.

"Put down the spear, Mr. Iceberg," Frosty said. "Or is this how humans have been taught to treat their hosts?"

"Before I do anything," Johnny said, "I want you to tell me exactly what you intend to do with us."

"Mr. Iceberg, we intend to discuss with you and Miss Thompson exactly how to best ensure your safety and help your investigation reach a satisfactory conclusion."

"And what if I tell you that 'my investigation' strongly suggests that snowmen were responsible for the murder of Santa Claus?" Johnny asked.

The snowmen throughout the room suddenly looked angry. The two guards at the throne lowered their spears and glided a few feet toward Johnny and Susie. Frosty, however, seemed unfazed.

"And how did you reach this conclusion?" Frosty asked.

"I'm not going to recite all the details," Johnny said. "Just that Dasher and Mrs. Claus have been strongly linked to the killing. Whoever murdered Santa Claus has attacked me several times, and Dasher persuaded Susie and me to come with him, even though he did not tell us he was taking us here until after we had no way to let anyone else know. Then we learned that he brought Mrs. Claus here earlier in the day.

"Finally," Johnny said, "there are the details of the murder scene. Santa's death was caused by significant internal injuries, most likely from beatings from multiple assailants. But there was only a single set of tracks at the scene. The only people who could get to Santa without leaving footprints are snowmen."

The snowmen were silent. Frosty motioned for the two guards to set their spears aside.

"So, how'd I do?" Johnny asked. "Pretty accurate assessment?"

"You are very good at linking evidence together to form a logical conclusion," Frosty complimented him. "But there are a few questions that appear unresolved. Why did you go with Dasher when he was linked to the murder? What is our motive for the murder? Do you have any hard evidence that we were involved with Santa's death, or do you base your accusations on circumstantial evidence alone?"

Johnny took a deep breath. *He's good*, he thought, impressed with Frosty. *Brings all my questions and uncertainties out into the open.* "First, I did not realize that Dasher was implicated until after we arrived in Sphere Valley."

"And who did you suspect at that time?" Frosty asked.

Johnny gritted his teeth. "Mayor Wassail and Chief Masterson."

"Am I to take it that you no longer suspect them?"

"I have plenty of evidence against them too," Johnny said.

"Such as?"

"No. If I tell you, you'll tell Masterson, and the evidence will *mysteriously* disappear."

"And how exactly do you figure that we are in on this scheme of the police chief and the mayor?"

"That is what I intend to find out right now," Johnny said.

"Let me explain our perspective," Frosty said. "You can then decide whether it correlates with your theory."

"Go for it," Johnny said.

"My friends would appreciate it if you lowered your spear and pulled it away from the sconce," Frosty said.

Johnny set the spear to his side, but did not move away from the sconce. "It stays right here," he said, "but I'm listening."

"As you probably know," Frosty began, "in the days leading up to the death, there was some talk of changing how Christmas is operated. That is why your friend was invited up to the North Pole."

Susie glared at the snowman.

"What you may not know is how each member of the Village Council felt about the proposed change."

"I can tell you that," Susie said angrily. "Nobody liked it except Santa Claus, and he only liked it because it would make him even richer."

"Miss Thompson," Frosty said gently, "what you describe is how the meeting must have appeared to anyone who was not a member of the council, not how any of us really felt about the proposal."

"So, I'm just a dumb kid?" Susie demanded, not backing down. "I don't *really* know what is going on? I was there. Nobody said anything to support the idea except Santa, and he only did for all the wrong reasons."

"I do not doubt your intelligence," Frosty said. "I simply doubt that you have all the information. The Village Council meeting was not the first time Santa brought up his proposal. We first became aware of it a few weeks after he had received your letter."

"You know about my letter?" Susie asked.

"I have a copy of it, and I have read it several times," Frosty said. "You see, Miss Thompson, you were not brought up here to help Santa propose the change. You were brought to help him convince those who were against it."

"Like who?" Susie yelled. "You? You didn't say a thing!"

"You must not mistake silence for dissent. The way the Claus family runs Christmas has enormous effect on nearly everyone in the North Pole. It affects the economic welfare of the elves, because they are responsible for most of the work. It affects the economic welfare of the humans and animals, who rely heavily on the tourism brought in by Christmas. It affects the welfare of the snowmen, because of both the elvish control of the coal mines and the pollution caused by the prosperity of the North Pole.

"Santa's proposed change would *greatly* benefit the snowmen. With the reduced pollution that would come from reducing and closing various factories, it would decrease the time we need to spend in the caves each year—possibly by as much as a month. This would enable us to interact with the other species of the North Pole with greater frequency, which in the long-term will foster greater mutual respect. There is no downside to this proposal for us.

"The animals had concerns. They expected reduced tourism activity with a Christmas less devoted to the commercial side. However, because of his long relationship with Santa, Dasher had agreed to support the proposal.

"Morgan, as head of the Elvish Labor Union, was adamantly opposed to the proposal. Few elves working in the factories currently have the education necessary to work in medical research or social services fields. Changing Christmas could potentially have a devastating effect on thousands of elves. Santa had worked out a very thorough transition plan that would enable ninety percent of the elves to become qualified to work in the new areas of focus and either retain or increase their current salary. However, Morgan was not yet convinced.

"Mayor Wassail, as you probably can guess, was also opposed to the change. However, his motives had little to do with the well-being of his constituency and everything to do with his own power and wealth."

"If you and Dasher supported the change, why didn't you speak up?" Susie asked.

"Because Santa had asked us not to," Frosty said.

"Why on earth would he do that?" Johnny asked.

"Because Mayor Wassail and Morgan already knew our opinions. Santa had hoped that a new focus on the proposal—one brought about by Miss Thompson's presence—would persuade Morgan to vote for the change.

"You see, the elf was the key to the whole thing. According to our laws, any significant change to Christmas requires majority approval from the Village Council. Obviously, Mayor Wassail would vote against Santa's proposal. If Morgan did so as well, then it would fail. However, if Morgan voted for it, then the proposal would pass."

"Was Morgan coming around to Santa's side?" Johnny asked.

"I don't know," Frosty said. "Nobody could tell if Mayor Wassail was manipulating Morgan to get him on his side or if the elf was with the mayor of his own accord. Santa was trying to find out.

"Unfortunately," Frosty looked at Susie, "everything backfired when Miss Thompson threatened Santa at the council meeting."

"Did what?" Johnny turned to Susie.

"I didn't threaten him," Susie shouted. "I said that I wished he was dead instead of my sister."

"For our purposes here," Frosty said, "the specific words do not matter. The point is that from that point on, the meeting became a chaos of baseless accusations bouncing back and forth. Santa's plans for the meeting could no longer be accomplished."

"So, now what?" Johnny asked. "I understand that you don't have a motive, but based on what you have said nothing fits the evidence any better than what I told you earlier. Nothing can explain the reasons why Mrs. Claus, Dasher, and the snowmen are so strongly linked to the murder."

"I know you linked the snowmen to this crime through our ties with Dasher and Mrs. Claus," Frosty said, "but I do not know why you are convinced they are involved."

Johnny stood there, not knowing what to say. He had not heard enough from Paul to be able to explain the security video.

"Why should I tell you why I suspect them?" Johnny bluffed.

Frosty stiffened. "Perhaps I can explain why Mrs. Claus and Dasher are not involved with the crime. Then you can tell me if it's a 'pretty accurate assessment.'"

"Go for it," Johnny said.

"Let me start with the most important fact first," Frosty said. "Miss Thompson was not the only child invited to the North Pole this Christmas."

CHAPTER TWENTY-NINE

AS PAUL approached the Arctic Hotel in South Port, he suddenly felt sorry for tourists. South, as well as east and west, could literally refer to any part of town. South Port had originally been a separate city, and its name had been chosen to distinguish it as the only port in the area. As the North Pole grew, several other ports had been built within the city. When South Port was officially annexed into the North Pole, the name had become ambiguous.

However, South Portans still considered themselves a separate community from the rest of the North Pole, and they had staunchly refused to change the name of the area.

Now, tourists and immigrants often became perplexed when they heard residents refer to South Port, particularly when the two other major docks, Star and Holly Ports, were farther south. Paul, like all residents, felt no confusion. To him South Port simply meant sleaze.

Paul stopped walking once he reached the parking lot of the hotel. It would be useless to talk to the manager on duty, he knew. Even if the guest in room 313 had given a name when checking in, the manager would balk at disclosing it. Even with a search warrant, which Paul had not had time or evidence to obtain, the administration at the Arctic Hotel was a pain to deal with. Paul had yet to get the kind of personal leverage on the new owners that he would have liked.

The only option, Paul decided, was to break into the room and hope the guest was both inside and too surprised to react quickly enough to fight back. Paul did not like that idea. Masterson had told him nothing about who or what he would find.

The thought lingered in the back of his mind that his family might be captive in the hotel room. Masterson had said he did not know where Paul's family was, but the chief had given Paul little reason to trust him.

He walked up the stairs to the third floor, found room 313, and drew his gun. The door was unlocked. He slowly pushed the door in, trying to keep it from squeaking, and held his gun ready.

The shower was running in the bathroom. Looking around the room, it was again obvious that The Arctic Hotel had worked hard to earn its sleazy reputation—the bed, the carpet, the chairs, and the lamps were all in disrepair and painted in gaudy, peeling, faded paint. A large trench coat hung on a shoddy wooden chair by the door. There was no sight of Paul's family.

Next to the bed was a burlap sack. As he got closer, Paul could see the heel of a gun sticking out. He kicked the sack away. It was a rifle.

Before he could check to see what else was in the sack, the shower turned off. Seeing nowhere to hide, Paul stood in the corner near the bathroom door and held his gun up. The door opened, and a young man walked out, wearing only a dingy towel. His back was facing Paul.

"Hold it right there!" Paul yelled. "I've got a gun pointed right at your back! One step and you're—"

The young man quickly jerked to the left and ran to the window. *Frost!* Paul swore. *He knows about the windows.* He jumped at the man's feet but was kicked into the dresser, his gun knocked to the floor. The man lunged for the gun, but before he could get it Paul grabbed his neck. Climbing on the man's back, Paul held his flippers in a choke hold and partially restricted the man's airway.

"Who are you?" Paul demanded. "Do you know anything about

my family?"

The young man put his hands behind his head and tried to grab at Paul. Paul doubled his grip and began twisting the man's head. *I'm not going easy on anyone today.*

"Start talking!"

The young man whispered something, but Paul could not hear him.

"Speak up!" Paul said, releasing his grip a little.

The man jerked his head backwards, and Paul was knocked off. The man ran out the front door, grabbing his coat off the chair as he went. Paul jumped up and chased after him.

The man was already down the stairs and running towards the docks. Paul followed as quickly as he could. *Stupid penguin legs*, Paul thought as he fell farther and farther behind. When he finally got to the bottom of the stairs, the man was already to the docks. He jumped into a small fishing boat, started the motor, and headed off into the sea.

As he reached the edge of the dock, Paul threw off his hat and coat and dove into the water. He went deep, knowing the water was murky and hard to see into from the surface, and torpedoed toward the boat.

As he approached it, Paul suddenly swam up toward the surface, letting his natural buoyancy help propel him, and rocketed out of the water, into the air, and straight into the man's chest.

The young man hunched over in pain. *Good!* Paul thought. He got on top of the young man, held one flipper into his neck, and punched him in the face with the other. In desperation, the man finally pushed Paul away, teetered to his feet, and fell over the side of the boat into the freezing water.

Paul jumped after him, grabbed the wildly splashing man by the coat, and dragged him back to shore. Once there he pulled the man, now shivering and convulsing with cold, back to the hotel. *I can't let this guy die of hypothermia*, Paul thought.

"Where is my family?" Paul demanded as they approached the hotel.

"I—I don't know, mate," he said through shivering teeth and a thick Australian accent.

"Who are you?"

"Chad—Chad Tyler."

❄　　❄　　❄

Sara knew from the moment she walked into the lab that something was wrong. Something was missing. One noticed when a large corpse was no longer in the freezing vaults.

She confronted Limphus when she entered the lab.

"Sergeant," Sara said. "Do you know anything about Santa's body being moved?"

The curt elf woman looked stunned. "No—isn't it in one of the freezing vaults?"

"That's where I sealed it yesterday," Sara said. "But it's not there."

"Are you sure?"

"It's pretty hard to miss."

Limphus was flabbergasted. "Go talk to Masterson," she told Sara. "See if he ordered something done with it."

Sara nodded and walked out of the lab. She actually felt very relieved after talking with Limphus. The elf's surprise seemed genuine, which meant that it might not be somebody crippling the case behind her back again.

Chief Masterson's office was open. He was agitated, tapping a pencil on the desk and staring at nothing. His eyes were narrowed and his forehead was creased.

"Chief," Sara said, stepping inside.

"Ms. Albright," Masterson said, startled at her voice. "Ah … no need to close the door," he added.

Sara let herself smile ever so slightly. Her performance yesterday had obviously had an effect.

"Chief, did you have Santa's body removed from the lab?"

"No. Why? Isn't it there?" Like Limphus, Masterson looked stunned by the news.

Sara shook her head. "My first thought was maybe somebody had had it removed to the mortuary."

"I'll look into it," Masterson said.

"Sir, I could help—"

"That's all," Masterson cut her off. "Thank you, Ms. Albright."

As she headed back toward the lab, she wondered if Masterson would really look into it. He *had* seemed genuinely surprised, but Sara did not trust him—not after so much else had happened with the investigation.

Once back in her office, she sat down at her computer. The screensaver had a series of elves doing cartwheels off a cliff. She quickly logged onto the telephone company database and found the number to Tundra & Son's Mortuary, the only mortuary in the North Pole.

She dialed the number.

"Tundra and Sons," a deep male voice said on the other end of the line.

"My name is Sara Albright with NPPD. I need to know if Santa's body has been transferred to your location."

"Is there some kind of problem?"

"No. I just need the information."

"I'm sorry ma'am. Unless you have a warrant, we can only disclose that information to the deceased's immediate family. Have a wonderful day, and remember that at Tundra and Sons, we treat every funeral as if it was Christmas."

She slammed the phone down. *Morticians!*

The whole situation was weird. *Granted,* Sara thought, *it was only the second murder NPPD had ever had to deal with, but come on. You don't just lose a body.*

She couldn't think of any way to get into the mortuary without a warrant, but she hadn't seen Paul yet and Johnny was who-knows-where with Dasher. She didn't trust any of the officers to do it.

Suddenly she smiled. She had just had the most ridiculous idea of her life.

CHAPTER THIRTY
—ELVES' COAL MINES, 10:53 AM

MORGAN WALKED out of the mine entrance and toward his car. Ever since Santa's murder had become known to the public, several episodes of unrest had broken out among the elves working in the mines. Concern over succession, their jobs, and the well-being of Christmas had taken its toll on members of his union. Now, someone had started a rumor that the snowmen were going to take over the mines, and the workers didn't even bother verifying the rumor's plausibility before attempting to start a riot. It had taken all the schmoozing skills he had to help the supervisors retain order.

He climbed into his car and started the engine. He always hated visiting the coal mines. Between the dusty air and the sweaty, crude, and vulgar elves working there, he always felt grimy until he could take a shower. On top of that, the mines were so far out of town, and the roads tended to be so bad, that it took nearly an hour to get back home. Irritated about having to visit for the fourth time in the past two days, he drove down the narrow road that led back to the city.

It started snowing again. The road was already difficult to follow, but now Morgan had to squint and concentrate. The great spruces of the Evergreen Forest lined both sides, so Morgan could tell that he was at least still on the road.

As he turned a bend, he saw an enormous pile of snow just in front of the car. He slammed on the breaks, and the car skidded straight into the giant snow bank.

In a panic, Morgan opened the door and climbed out as more and more snow slid down on top of him. Finally he clawed free. *Did I go off the road?* he wondered. No. As he stood up and looked at the car he could see that the mound of snow was in the middle of the road. *A drift?* That didn't seem right. There was little wind, and there had been nothing in the road an hour ago when he was driving to the mine.

Whatever it was, the entire front of the car, from the bumper to the windshield, was buried in it. He swore at the car and walked to the trunk to get a shovel.

"Don't move," a voice spoke from behind the elf's back.

Morgan spun around and instantly recognized the tall grey-haired man pointing a gun at him.

"The police are looking for you, Iceberg," Morgan sneered.

"Tell me something I don't know," Johnny said.

"I'd be more than happy to call them right now," Morgan said.

"I told you to tell me something I don't know," Johnny cocked the gun. "Like a detailed list of everyone involved with Santa's death."

"I don't know who killed Santa Claus," Morgan said. He stared straight into the gun without flinching.

"Maybe," Johnny said. "Maybe not."

"But which is it?" Morgan smirked.

"Don't give me any attitude. I know about Santa's proposal to change Christmas. I know that Frosty and Dasher supported the measure, and that you were the only hold out. I know Mayor Wassail was doing everything possible to keep you on his side. I know that the elves would have the most to lose from the proposal, and that it wouldn't be that hard for you to find a group of them to do something about it."

"I'm impressed, Iceberg. That's five whole things that you know. I had never thought your brain could handle more than three at one time."

"I don't have time for this," Johnny yelled at the elf.

"I have all day."

They glared at each other. Finally Johnny shook his head and took a step forward.

"I'm already a felon," he muttered. "What's one more dead elf?"

For a moment—just a brief moment—Morgan believed that Johnny was really willing to shoot him. The image of Murdock nine years ago, body broken and bloodied, flashed through his mind, and Morgan suddenly realized what Johnny Iceberg was willing to do when he had lost all else.

Morgan crumpled to the ground, hands suddenly shaking and voice trembling.

"What do you want to know, detective?" he asked.

"Whose side are you on?"

Morgan looked up, eyes scared but fierce.

"My own," he said.

Johnny's face softened, and he lowered the gun slightly.

"What do you mean?" Johnny asked.

"I was holding out my vote for Santa's proposal for my own reasons, not because I do what the mayor tells me to do. That's really what your question was, wasn't it?"

Johnny nodded.

"Look, Iceberg," Morgan said. "There are a few things you should know about the little political world I live in. If you had spent a little more time learning them, maybe you would be chief instead of Masterson.

"First, I make all my decisions based on what is best for the elves. I may not be the nicest fellow around, I may not be the most honest or well-liked, but I do represent my people and their interests exclusively.

"Second, Mayor Wassail gets what he wants. It may not be in the best interests of anyone else, it may seldom be ethical, it may often involve bullying, blackmailing, or backstabbing, but the fact remains: he gets what he wants. And the fact is as soon as Santa Claus came up with this proposal to change Christmas, Mayor Wassail wanted one thing: control of the Christmas Foundation."

"And does he have control?" Johnny asked.

"I voted him into power last night. He runs Christmas."

"And you're okay with that?"

"No, I'm not," Morgan said, "but that's just how it is. Because I have acted the way I did, my family is safe from his … tactics. My people are safe from possible retaliation, and they will keep their jobs. And in the end, Mayor Wassail will pass on too. Nobody who lives the way he does lasts long. He makes too many enemies, and sooner or later someone will get rid of him."

Morgan stood up again and approached Johnny. The arrogant, snide, scheming act was gone and all that was left was the elf's suddenly commanding confidence.

"I do not sacrifice what I hold dear in order to pursue a cause," Morgan said.

"Will you answer the rest of my questions?" Johnny asked.

"Yes, but I will tell the mayor whenever I see him next. I won't go out of my way to find him, but I will tell him eventually. My life, the lives of my family, and the welfare of my entire people depend on me being forthright with him."

"Fine," Johnny said. "How much do you know about the mayor's plans?"

"I know the general idea. He doesn't let me in on all the details, but during the past month, while he was busy trying to manipulate me into voting against Santa, I was able to learn enough about his little conspiracy."

"Is Masterson involved?"

"Yes."

"Is Mrs. Claus involved?"

"No."

"Is Dasher involved?"

Morgan hesitated. "Dasher is difficult. He's always very secretive, has his own plan and agenda, and is impossible to read. I believe it's unlikely he is involved, but it's impossible to really say. Santa trusted him, though."

"Did Mayor Wassail kill Santa Claus?"

"No. He would never do it himself."

"Did Mayor Wassail arrange to have him killed, then?"

Morgan took a deep breath and looked away, as if thinking carefully. "Iceberg, because I kept myself somewhat aligned with the mayor I know a few things about your investigation. I know what the autopsy report said. I know the details of the crime scene. Wassail would have to have hired a gang to kill Santa, judging by the way he was beaten. If he did hire that many people, I know nothing about it."

"What about Chad Tyler?" Johnny asked.

Morgan smiled. "I guess that's six things you know, Iceberg."

Johnny lifted his gun again. "You didn't answer my question," he said.

"Please," Morgan said. "We both know you're not going to shoot me because you need me to testify against Wassail."

"You're willing to testify against him?"

"If you can find a way to remove him from power first," Morgan said, "yes, I will testify against him."

"Then why not come forward now?" Johnny asked.

"You may be willing to recklessly stick your neck out," Morgan said, "but I'm not. I have my family and my people to worry about."

Seven snowmen carrying their electronic ice spears materialized from inside the forest.

"So I take it you're not letting me go," Morgan said.

"No. Did you think I was going to?"

"Had I thought for a moment that you would, I would not have told you anything. The mayor would have killed me for it." Morgan smiled at Johnny. "It pays to know the people you are dealing with."

Johnny didn't know what to say. The elf was so open about being a self-preserver that Johnny found it both maddening and refreshing. At least he was upfront and honest.

"Remember, Mr. Iceberg," Morgan said. "Remove his power, and I will be the best friend you have—especially if you can help my people."

"I'll remember," Johnny said. He pulled out the blue keycard Sara had given him. *Time to get to work.*

CHAPTER THIRTY-ONE

"SO, MATE," Paul said, "what exactly are you doing at the North Pole? Wanted to see some arctic penguins?"

Chad Tyler sat on a chair in the otherwise empty holding room at NPPD. Paul paced back and forth, glaring at the boy.

"None of your business," Chad said.

"Let me explain something to you," Paul said. "We already have you for underage drinking, assault, destruction of property, possession of a firearm without license, and resisting arrest. I've read your file from Melbourne, Chad. This isn't going to go over well with your parole officer or with the judge. There was something about trying you as an adult for any further infractions."

Chad did not respond.

"You know, most kids—even the naughty ones—try to be at least a *little* good on Christmas Eve. So I'm giving you a chance."

"And what's my chance?" Chad asked.

"Dropping any charges not associated with Santa's murder. But you have to answer my questions. And I have to like your answers."

"What are they?"

"Why did you have a gun? Why are you here in the North Pole? And why did we find your blood and hair on Santa's body?"

Paul stood in front of Chad and leaned in menacingly.

"How about you start with the gun, *mate*," Paul said.

"Warranty issue," Chad said.

"Warranty issue?"

"The gun's broken," Chad said. "I got it for Christmas last year, and it's never worked. I wanted Santa to fix it, so I came here to track him down."

"Santa gave you the gun?"

"Yeah."

"Son, unless that gun shoots Nerf balls, you're lying," Paul said.

Chad sat there again in silence, a defiant look on his face.

"You want to try another story?" Paul said.

"Look, I know what you think."

"That's great. Tell me what I think."

"That I killed Santa Claus."

"Did you?"

"No."

"Explain."

"Before I do," Chad looked nervous, "I want to know if you have a witness protection program or something."

Paul looked puzzled. "Maybe," he said.

"If I talk, I want in."

"Fine. If it's warranted, you can get it."

Chad took a deep breath. "It's like this. Santa and Mrs. Claus invited me up here—a new "Give a Naughty Kid Christmas" program or something. So I came. I wanted to see how they planned to make up for fourteen years of coal for Christmas. Nothing, it turned out. Just a bunch of counselors telling me to straighten out my life, blah, blah, blah. I've heard it all a hundred times."

"Santa offered you nothing else?" Paul asked, skeptical.

"Oh, he said he'd put a couple thousand bucks in some scholarship fund for me if I could get on the Nice List for the next two years," Chad scoffed. "Like I'm going to college."

"Go on," Paul said.

"So, I'm not happy, right? Well, I get picked up by some polar bear goon, who drives me to City Hall. They take me to see the mayor. He tells me that he has a proposition. A hundred fifty thousand bucks to kill Santa.

"At this point, I'm madder at Santa than I've ever been, so I say 'sure.' One hundred fifty grand is a lot more than Santa's crappy scholarship. The mayor gives me the gun. Tells me it has to be done by the twenty-first. Fine. I go to a couple pubs, find out where Santa probably is from a bunch of elves, and then I follow the guy into the forest. Then, all of the sudden, he disappears.

"And I'm like, 'what happened?' I mean he's a big guy, how does he just up and disappear? So I just wander around the forest looking for him for a couple hours, and then I hear this big *thud*. I go to check it out, and there's Santa face down in the snow. Somebody beat me to him.

"Well, I was mad. Mad because I knew this mayor dude would figure out that I didn't do the job, and then he wouldn't give me my money. And I was kind of sad, too, seeing him in the snow—I don't know why. I guess part of me believed in Santa the whole time, and I couldn't handle it.

"So, I had my sack of coal, see? I brought it with me—all fourteen years worth. So I just kind of flip out and start hitting Santa's body with it and yelling and crying until I can't do it anymore. I was in a fight earlier that night, and I guess some of my blood got on the body.

"So there was nothing else I could do. I stood there for a while, and then walked away. I stepped back in my footprints so it kind of looked like Santa had just wandered out there and fell over dead from a heart attack or something. I tried to catch my boat—the mayor said he'd have one for me ready once I did the job, but it was gone. I don't think it was ever there in the first place."

"And that's what happened?" Paul asked.

"That's it," Chad said miserably. "I've been hiding in that hotel ever since."

"That's why you want to be in a witness protection program?"

"Mate, I know all about Al Capone and Lucky Eddie. Your mayor's the same type. Anyone who talks is going to get payback."

"Will you sign an affidavit swearing to all this information if I work out a deal with Australia and their witness protection program?"

"Yeah."

Paul left the room and ordered a notary with the statement. As ridiculous as the story sounded, for the most part it fit the evidence. A gang hadn't beaten Santa; he had been beaten by one person repeatedly.

It explained what Mrs. Claus had said on the security video too. Chad was connected to her. She had invited him up to try to reform him, and the mayor had taken advantage of the situation. He had hired the kid, so that the murder could be tied back to her by his speeches and the investigation by NPPD.

And Chad's story explained the Naughty List. Santa had circled his name because he had been chosen for this "Give a Naughty Kid Christmas" program.

But Paul wasn't completely certain. Could Chad have beaten Santa to death without leaving a trace of a struggle at the crime scene? Then again, maybe there had been signs of a struggle and the other officers had simply trampled all over them by the time Paul and Johnny had arrived. Chad's claim that somebody else got Santa first seemed completely ridiculous. How could someone else have done it without leaving a set of tracks? And that was the one fact that was consistent with every account of the crime scene: a single set of tracks led to the body.

An officer returned with the notary, as well as a written report on the ownership of the rifle Paul had confiscated. It belonged to Mayor Wassail.

Got you! Paul thought. He had enough for an arrest—and he had gotten it before anyone at NPPD could interfere.

NPPD policy required Paul report the findings and obtain an arrest warrant, but Paul decided against it. If Paul followed the procedures, the mayor would get news of his impending arrest and probably do something drastic. Feeling certain his family was being held by the mayor's people, Paul wasn't going to take that chance. He would have to go after the mayor himself.

Paul shook his head. He was becoming more like Johnny every day.

Chapter Thirty-Two
—Sphere Valley, 11:50AM

When Johnny had left to finish solving the case on his own, Susie had been upset. Johnny had done his best to calm her, but nothing he said had really helped. She just did not want to be left alone again.

But she was.

Seven or eight snowmen had escorted Johnny out, leaving Susie alone with Frosty.

"Miss Thompson," Frosty had said gently. "Since you are here, would you like me to show you around Sphere Valley?"

Susie just glared at the snowman.

"I see," Frosty had said with a chuckle. "You wish to test the patience of a snowman. Very well."

Without another word, Frosty had stuck the corn cob pipe in his mouth, stuck his arms out perfectly to the side, and stood completely still. A minute passed. Susie suddenly started laughing. He looked exactly like the ideal snowman she and her sister had tried to make two winters ago.

"That did not take long," Frosty said. "Come with me."

He had taken her through the caves and told stories about each of the giant murals—the great clan wars of the sixth and seventh centuries, the myths about the North Wind creating the world, and the great epic legend of Whisteran the Great, who had supposedly journeyed far across the arctic to defeat the great Ice Dragon and save the snowmen race from early extinction.

"Why are there so many pictures about wars?" Susie had asked.

"You could ask the same question about your own country's museums," Frosty had replied. "I suppose we all believe that true heroes only appear in times of great conflict."

"Could you teach me how to carve the stone like this?"

"Perhaps during another visit, when you have more time."

Frosty had introduced Susie to several prominent snowmen, including Abominable, captain of the snowmen's private militia.

"Why do you have your own army?" Susie had asked.

"Because the other races of the North Pole have never been overly anxious to address our needs," Frosty had said. "Until the animosity that exists between snowmen and the others is resolved there is always a chance that we will have to protect ourselves. We have already had to do so many times during the past ten years. Elvish supremacy gangs seem to be attractive to a portion of elvish youth."

Then Frosty had taken Susie to see the last person she wanted to see: Mrs. Claus.

"I suppose you're not happy to see me," Mrs. Claus said when she saw Susie.

Susie did not answer.

"I'm sorry," Mrs. Claus said. Susie could see that here eyes were red and rubbed raw. "It has been an awful few days for all of us."

"You didn't do anything to help me," Susie said.

"The mayor is very good at forcing people to choose between several bad options. I believed that I could try to help you and get myself killed, or I could let you stay in prison for a time and escape with my life. Dasher persuaded me to choose the latter. I am not proud of the choice, but I still believe it was the best one I had. As miserable as prison must be, you were at least fairly safe."

"Detective Iceberg has informed me that the mayor has taken over," Frosty said.

Mrs. Claus nodded. "It was expected," she said.

"But very temporary, we hope," Frosty said.

Susie suddenly remembered how alone she was. Johnny had abandoned her again, she was surrounded by strangers she did not like, and she was thousands of miles away from home. She wanted to scream at them all.

Instead she started crying.

Mrs. Claus knelt beside Susie and gave her a hug. Despite how much Susie wanted to push away, she did not. She buried her head into Mrs. Claus's shoulder, let the long blonde hair brush against her face, and sobbed.

"Do you want to stay with me?" Mrs. Claus asked.

Susie pulled away and wiped her eyes. She looked at Mrs. Claus and shook her head. "No," she said.

"Stay with Frosty, then," Mrs. Claus said, standing up. "He'll make sure you're okay."

"Come, Miss Thompson," Frosty said. "Let me take you back to your hut in the village."

For most of the long walk back to the village neither of them spoke. The snow was falling again, but Frosty helped Susie through the difficult parts. Once they could see the village again, Susie spoke up:

"I don't understand something," Susie said. "I guess Santa only started talking about money at the council meeting to try to convince the mayor and the elf, right?"

"That is right," Frosty said.

"But, that doesn't make it a good thing to do, does it? I mean, is it okay to toy with people's emotions, to use somebody's death for your own purposes, and even to let people profit from it because it helps you get what you want—even if what you want is good?"

"You did not like Santa Claus, did you?" Frosty said.

"No," Susie looked away. "But everyone else seemed to. When I was in prison, one of the guards started crying about it. I saw lots of people who looked real sad all over the North Pole. But then he didn't seem to mean a whole lot to Mr. Iceberg, either."

"Santa Claus was a very kind man," Frosty said. "Every year, just as he started preparations for the next Christmas, he would come to

Sphere Valley and ask for feedback from us. He was the first Claus to do so since Nicholas. Santa was concerned about what we felt even though we had very different interests. In fact, when you get right down to it that is Santa's greatest legacy. He cared a great deal about how others felt—even strangers and opponents."

"He never cared about how I felt," Susie said.

"Are you sure?"

"He didn't at the council meeting. All he cared about was getting what he wanted. Maybe he really didn't just want the money, like you said, but he still just did whatever it took to try to get what he wanted. He did not care about how it felt for me to hear it."

"That is true. Perhaps he did not consider how you felt about what was going on. Or maybe he thought you would catch on to what he was doing. Whatever the case, I would like to suggest that maybe you shouldn't be so hard on him for this. Sometimes people choose to do things that seem wrong in order to accomplish what is right."

"That doesn't make any sense," Susie said.

"It did to Johnny Iceberg," Frosty said. Susie looked puzzled. "He went against his chief's orders, he violated every policy of the NPPD, he broke you out of prison, and he has conducted an illegal investigation to find the true killer. Why?"

"Because he thought someone was going to kill me," Susie said.

"Exactly," Frosty said. "I do not want to advocate a simplistic ends-justifying-the-means mentality. I believe that a less volatile detective could have figured out what to do without turning himself into a felon.

"But at the same time, it is often impossible to judge anyone's actions without first understanding why he is doing what he is doing and what it is that person is trying, in his heart of hearts, to accomplish."

"And what was Santa trying to accomplish?" Susie snapped. She did not like Frosty's attempts to compare Johnny with Santa Claus.

"Santa was deeply troubled by your letter, Miss Thompson. It made him realize that the world has changed since the time of Nicholas Claus and that today's children needed more than toys.

He also knew that the Christmas Foundation was not capable of meeting those needs. He wanted to change Christmas in order to give today's children what they *really* need.

"And," Frosty added, "he had hoped that by doing so he could help you believe in Christmas again."

"Why does it matter if I believe in Christmas?" Susie asked. "What is the big deal?"

"Because to believe in Christmas is to believe that no matter how hard your life is, no matter how nasty some people can be, no matter how much you are being hurt, there are still people who care about you, both friends and strangers. If you lose that belief, then you lose hope that life is worth living in the first place."

There was a knock on the door, and a guard entered.

"Frosty, we have brought the elf," the guard said.

"You can stay here if you like," Frosty told Susie.

"No. I'm not being shut away," she said.

Outside a crowd of snowmen had gathered around the guards escorting Morgan. Some of the smaller ones, children, Susie guessed, were throwing snowballs at him. Several of the larger snowmen were shouting insults and heckling the small elf.

Frosty glided over to a small drift near the crowd, Susie following closely behind.

"This must stop!" Frosty said.

Everyone froze and looked at their leader. Susie could see Morgan between the guards, bits of snow on his hair and face, but otherwise looking both calm and almost noble.

"I have never called Morgan, nor any other elf, a friend," Frosty said. "But he is my colleague, and I have always and will always show him respect. He has always done so to me.

"I will not represent a people who have forgotten how to show respect to those who are not friends," Frosty said. "Our interests are often *very* different than those of the elves, but their welfare matters as much to them as ours does to us. It is not differing interests that creates enemies, it is the inability to treat strangers with respect."

The snowmen bowed slightly toward Frosty. Satisfied that they had listened, Frosty turned around and headed toward the village.

"Bring Morgan to the heated hut," Frosty said.

The guards complied, and the elf was brought along without further incident. Once inside, the snowmen left Morgan alone with Frosty and Susie, who had followed along. Morgan sat on the cot.

"Thank you, Frosty," Morgan said. "If everyone else on the council could be like you we wouldn't be in the mess we are in now."

"And if all our people could act as you, I expect there would be much less animosity between us," Frosty said.

Morgan looked at Susie. "And so we meet again, Miss Thompson. I regret you were imprisoned falsely, and I hope you are doing as well as possible."

"You did not do anything to help me or support the change," Susie accused him.

"No, I did not," Morgan said.

"I must get straight to the point," Frosty said, "before I lose a little more weight than I would like. Are you working with Wassail?"

"I voted to give him control of Christmas," Morgan said, "and I knew the vague details of his plan to kill Santa Claus. I did not participate in his plan, nor did I know enough to stop it. I told detective Iceberg everything I know and hope he is successful in stripping Wassail from power."

Frosty was silent. Susie did not know what to think.

"I wish you had been more willing to oppose the mayor," Frosty finally said.

"And I wish you had been less willing to risk the welfare of my people when Santa first proposed the change," Morgan said. "But there it is. Because I acted as I did, my people and my family are not the ones currently in danger."

"There is the welfare of others to worry about," Frosty said.

"Yes there is," Morgan said. "But because nobody can help everybody all the time, we must all choose who to help at a specific time. I made my choice, and I do not apologize."

"Nor have you ever," Frosty said. "And in the end, while I disagree, I cannot blame you."

"Nor have you ever." Morgan smiled. "It would be nice if everyone was as simple as the two of us. When you get right down to it we are very easy to work with."

"Our interests are clear, our goals are obvious, and neither of us acts only for ourselves," Frosty agreed.

"So how long will I be here?" Morgan asked.

"Until the situation is resolved," Frosty said.

"Let us hope that it resolves quickly then," Morgan said.

"And in a way that is favorable to both of us," Frosty added.

Morgan looked at Susie. "It would probably be best if you kept me in a different hut," he said. "I don't think she would enjoy spending time with me, and I am much more capable of handling your cold huts."

Frosty nodded. "Come with me," he said, and Morgan followed him out the door.

Susie watched them leave, still unsure of what to think about the elf.

As Frosty escorted Morgan to a nearby hut, a guard glided up to them, obviously concerned.

"Frosty," the guard said. "I bring urgent news from the village."

CHAPTER THIRTY-THREE

JOHNNY, CARRYING a bag with the computer and private detective equipment he and Susie had taken from his apartment, walked up to a side door at City Hall and slid the blue keycard through the scanner. The light stayed red.

Great, Johnny thought. *It's the wrong card.*

He looked at the blue keycard and realized he had swiped it the wrong way. *Way to go, genius,* he laughed quietly to himself. He flipped the card around, swiped it again, and the red light changed to green. Johnny walked inside.

Though he couldn't see any surveillance cameras, he assumed they were there and kept his face down. *No need going out of my way to announce that I'm here*, Johnny thought.

He found a stairwell and headed up to the top floor. The mayor and his staff were supposed to be at the Toy Factories supervising the last-minute preparations for Christmas. When Johnny reached the top floor, he saw that the office was dark and empty.

He walked past the receptionist's empty desk, searching for the mayor's private office. It was easy to spot—like the door outside it had a card scanner.

Johnny swiped the keycard again. The light stayed red. He flipped the card over and tried again, but nothing happened. He tried the door, but it was locked. Johnny winced.

So it comes down to this, he thought. His only option was to break into the office, which would send out a high priority alarm to NPPD. He would probably have about ten minutes to find what he needed to find.

He pulled out the computer and booted it up. He put on a pair of latex gloves and pulled out his fingerprinting equipment and a flashlight. When he was completely ready, he pulled out his gun, shot the lock off the door, and stepped inside.

The office was spacious and immaculately clean. A large oak desk sat in the middle of the room. The Great Seal of the North Pole, a large snowflake against a light blue background, was emblazoned on the front. Shelves and file cabinets lined the walls. *Good. Everything should be easy to find.*

The file cabinets were locked, so he simply kicked them open. Just some redevelopment plans for the new curling stadium project downtown. More of the same in the other drawers—though a plan to rezone the city according to species caught Johnny's eye. But nothing to implicate the mayor in Santa's death.

There was also nothing in the desk or on the shelves. Frustrated, Johnny kicked over a plant in the corner. A black briefcase was hidden behind the pot. As Johnny had expected, it was locked. Knowing there was little time left, Johnny simply shot the latches off.

The Naughty List was inside. Johnny quickly dusted the scroll for fingerprints and uploaded the results to his laptop. He felt relieved. He had exactly what he needed. The only other object was a small audio device attached to a computer cord. Johnny pushed the play button.

" … you have the penguin's family?" the mayor's voice sounded from the device. Johnny frowned. *Are they talking about Paul's family?* He felt sick.

"We got them," said another voice. "Where should we take them?"

"The warehouse," Wassail said.

"Which one?"

"Tinsel Drive."

Johnny stopped the device and let out a low whistle. The Village Council had recently passed a law requiring all conversations at City Hall to be recorded. It was part of an open government policy. Wassail must have removed the recordings from City Hall records and to this device. Very quickly, he attached the device to the laptop and copied the files to his computer. Hopefully there were more specific directions to the warehouse somewhere on the recording. As the audio file copied, a window popped up giving the results of the fingerprint scan. Among several others, the name Georg Wassail came up.

The office lights turned on and footsteps sounded from just outside the door. Johnny quickly stood up between the door and the laptop, which was still copying the audio files to its hard drive. He squinted at the light and held one hand up to block it. Two officers, one human and one elf, kicked open the door and walked through, guns pointed at Johnny

"Hands in the air, Iceberg!" the human shouted.

"They are in the air, Lewis," Johnny said, his hand still blocking the light.

"Both of them!"

"Okay." Very slowly, Johnny raised the other hand in the air, too.

The elf approached Johnny and started frisking him. "By the way," the elf said, "I'm Lewis. He's Layton."

"That's wonderful to know," Johnny said.

Lewis found the extra gun strapped to Johnny's leg. Layton circled around and cuffed Johnny's wrists. A small chime sounded from the computer. The audio files had finished copying.

"What's all this?" Lewis asked about the laptop and fingerprinting equipment.

"I thought they covered what those things are at the police academy," Johnny said. "It's called a computer. That's a flashlight, and that thing is a fingerprinting kit. Though they have very different functions, each one can be very useful in detective work—"

Layton hit Johnny in the back of the head. "Can it, Iceberg," he said. "Nobody at NPPD is going to deal with your attitude ever again."

"Do these things belong to Mayor Wassail?" Lewis asked, pointing to the audio device and the Naughty List.

"Maybe," said Johnny. Layton hit him in the back of the head again.

"Here," Layton said, handing his partner several large evidence baggies. "Put everything in here—the computer and other stuff too."

"You might as well know," the Layton said. "There's no way to weasel your way out of this. We're taking you and the evidence straight to Masterson."

"That is exactly what I had hoped to hear," Johnny said, smiling smugly.

❄　　❄　　❄

Sara sat in her car, parked at the curb just outside Tundra and Son's Mortuary, and looked at herself in her small make-up mirror. *I look ridiculous*, she thought, running her fingers through her dyed blonde hair. She adjusted the neckline of the tight red blouse she had just bought, lowering it just a bit. She squirmed in the tight black mini-skirt, also a new purchase, and tried to decide how high it had to be to be believable.

Nobody is going to fall for this, she thought.

But there was nothing she could do but try. She shut the mirror, put it in the glove box, and got out of the car. Her heels clicked against the sidewalk as she walked into the mortuary.

The receptionist looked surprised to see Sara.

"Oh, Mrs. Claus," the receptionist said. "Where have you been?"

Sara let out a quick breath of relief. Thankfully, all most people knew about Santa's wife was her body and revealing clothes. "With some family," Sara said, trying to make her voice sound breathy.

"But the mayor said—"

"The mayor does not know everything," Sara said. "I would like to see my husband, please."

"Of course," the receptionist said. "Let me call the mortician and make sure he's not working on the body right now. But I'll tell you, Mrs. Claus, everyone is going to want to hear from you."

231

Sara waited patiently, trying not to let the receptionist think that the tight, skimpy outfit was making her self-conscious and uncomfortable. *I haven't dressed like this since high school,* she thought, feeling rather annoyed that she had just spent nearly a hundred dollars on an outfit she was just going to donate to the Sub-for-Santa secondhand store as soon as she was done at the mortuary.

"Mrs. Claus," the receptionist said. "There's a small problem. According to our records, the body was transferred here last night, but the mortician told me that he can't recall receiving it."

"Well, where would it be if it had come in?"

"Either in the vault or the coffin."

"Will you take me to them?"

"Of course," the receptionist said. She led Sara down the hall to a refrigerated vault. Checking the records, she turned back to Sara. "It looks like he isn't in here," the receptionist said. "The body must have been placed in the coffin."

Leading Sara back down the hall and to a different room, the receptionist pointed out the coffin that belonged to Santa.

"Thank you," Sara said. "Would you let me have a bit of time alone with him?"

"Yes, Mrs. Claus."

Once the receptionist was gone, Sara slowly approached the coffin. For a moment, she just stood there quietly, looking at the huge, elegantly carved box. Somehow it felt different to think about Santa's body here than it had been in the lab.

She slowly lifted the lid.

CHAPTER THIRTY-FOUR
—SANTA'S WORKSHOP, 1:23 PM

MAYOR WASSAIL wore a red Claus hat and smiled as he oversaw the mass of scurrying elves working in the Intricate Toys Division. In truth, he had done very little to keep Christmas on track. The factories had, over the years, been developed and modified until they ran without significant problems. However, Mayor Wassail also knew that, despite how little he had actually done, to the people of the North Pole he was single-handedly responsible for saving Christmas. His reputation and future were completely secure.

Even when he made changes to the daily operations of the Christmas Foundation, maximizing personal profit and eliminating costs, all he would ever be remembered for was how he had saved Christmas after the death of Santa Claus.

He watched as elves assembled model kits in one production line and robots in another. It was amazing how quickly the elves could move their little hands. He would never have thought, having personally known no elves except Morgan, that they could do so much so quickly.

One of Mayor Wassail's bodyguards approached him.

"We have bad news, sir," the bodyguard said. "Morgan is missing. There's a rumor that he's been taken captive by the snowmen."

"We'll deal with it," Wassail said. He had never trusted Morgan anyway. He could never figure out what the elf really wanted. He had been a staunch holdout when Santa had made the change proposal, but Wassail could never get a straight answer as to why.

But this rumor about the snowmen could play into his hands. It alone would justify an attack on Sphere Valley, and the elves would willingly go along. It would then be a simple matter to ensure that someone took out both Morgan and Frosty in the course of the battle. In one move he could remove two of the major threats to his power.

After that, it would be a small matter to take care of Dasher. And when he did, he would have complete control over the entire North Pole.

"Wassail!" a voice shouted from somewhere in the factory, interrupting the mayor's thoughts. The entire factory stopped, and all eyes jolted toward the source of the shout: a penguin in a trench coat and hat standing on a crate near the entrance to the factory.

"It's over, Georg," Paul said, his eyes fierce and clearly enraged. He held a gun and pointed it at Wassail's chest.

"I would have thought," the mayor said, "that you would have moved on to a different case by now—considering recent events in your family life."

"Don't even think about it," Paul said through a tense, gritted bill.

"I have no idea what you are talking about," Wassail said. "But I have clearly been threatened, so please understand that my bodyguards have no choice but to take care of you."

Paul laughed. "I don't think so," he said. "You see, when I said that it's over, I meant that it's over. I have a sixteen-year-old Australian in custody right now. He has given us a very interesting statement that I went ahead and had notarized before anyone could get to it."

"I would very much like to see that statement," Wassail said, his voice slightly betraying his anger.

"You will," Paul said. "In tomorrow morning's paper, I expect. I have a friend in the media who was very happy to take care of it while I came by to arrest you."

The elves in the factory had stopped working. Aside from the hum of the machinery, the entire building was suddenly completely quiet.

Georg Wassail, though very concerned, smiled calmly at the penguin. The affidavit would be a problem, but nothing big enough that Masterson couldn't clean up the mess.

"Security," Wassail spoke to his bodyguards, eight polar bears and seven humans, "please take care of this penguin. He is threatening the mayor of the North Pole and Head of Christmas. The people of the North Pole do not deserve to go through the anguish of another high profile assassination."

The guards, all fifteen of them, pulled out their own guns and slowly approached Paul. All at once, they fired at the penguin.

Instantly the entire factory became chaos. Paul jumped to the ground and rolled behind a stash of sheet metal. Elves started screaming and running madly to the exits. Even as it was all taking place, Wassail's mind raced, thinking up several positive spins he could give the media once the penguin was caught.

The bodyguards closed in on Paul, who was now hiding behind a production belt for dinosaur skeleton models. He shot at a crane, severing the cable and sending a box of Legos crashing down on two of the polar bears.

Enraged, the remaining bodyguards charged Paul. Seeing no other option, Paul scrambled over a mess of broken model kits and out the front door of the factory.

Santa's Beard! Paul swore. He had not expected fifteen bodyguards to be protecting Wassail in the toy factory, nor had he expected the mayor to fight back after he knew that the media was going to circulate the incriminating evidence. Paul was definitely becoming more like Johnny, deluding himself into thinking he could do this by himself.

One of the bodyguards threw a model train at Paul, which smacked him in the head and knocked him down in the snow. Two others picked the penguin up and pinned him against a wall.

Mayor Wassail sneered at Paul.

"I have a proposal for you," Wassail said. "If you rescind the affidavit, I'll call off my bodyguards and merely charge you with attempted murder instead of treason. You'll rot in jail for the rest of your life, but at least your family can visit you." The mayor smiled. "That is, if they are still around."

Paul spat into the mayor's face.

"That is not the choice I would have made," Wassail said. "But I have heard that penguins are dumb animals."

Just then a booming shriek sounded from around the factory building. Nearly a hundred snowmen had materialized, each holding an ice spear with convulsing electric jolts dancing on each point.

"Fire!" Wassail shouted as a few snowmen launched their spears at the bodyguards. A few shot at the snowmen, but the bullets passed through harmlessly. They advanced on the mayor and his bodyguards, backing them against the factory building wall.

"Don't fire your weapons," the mayor shouted. "Start a fire. Melt the savages."

Three men and two large polar bears shoved a car toward the oncoming snowmen. Just as the car reached them, the bodyguards shot directly into the gas tank. A deafening explosion sent flames high into the air. A few snowmen were scorched and started melting. They rest slowly retreated away from the burning car.

The bodyguards rushed toward the snowmen, waving burning bits of wood at them. Paul, no longer pinned down, spotted a fire extinguisher right by the factory door. Mayor Wassail lunged at the penguin and tackled him before he could reach the extinguisher. Paul squirmed in the mayor's grip until he could peck at his eye.

The mayor shrieked and shoved Paul away. Breaking the glass box with a robot from the factory, Paul pulled out the extinguisher and ran toward the burning car. One of the human bodyguards saw him approaching with the extinguisher and fired several shots at him.

Paul ducked behind a large crate and pulled out his gun. When he jumped out to fire at the attacker, a sudden wave of flying building blocks was already beating the mayor's bodyguard back. Dozens of elves, throwing whatever they could find at the mayor's men, had rushed to the rooftop.

As the bodyguards fell back, Paul pulled the pin from the extinguisher and sprayed out the fires. Once they had died down, a rush of snowmen came from the other direction and grabbed the bodyguards, pinning them to the ground.

Mayor Wassail, stunned by the elves and snowmen, started backing away, his eye and head throbbing with pain. Two of his guards, both human, stood by him. He tried to duck back inside the factory, but before he could take more than a few steps, an enormous snowman, nearly nine feet tall, lunged at him. His bodyguards fired their guns into the snowman, but the bullets simply passed through the large snowballs as if nothing had happened. The snowman knocked the bodyguards unconscious and grabbed Mayor Wassail, slamming him against a wall.

A final snowman, wearing a top hat and scarf, glided onto the scene.

"That is enough, Abominable," Frosty told the snowman holding Mayor Wassail.

Abominable dropped the mayor to the ground. Picking himself up, Wassail brushed off his suit.

"Nice to see you, Frosty," Mayor Wassail said. "Your open act of treason will make it very easy to get rid of you."

Frosty ignored the taunt. Paul walked up to the mayor and stuck his gun into the man's stomach.

"If you tell me where my family is, then I won't shoot out your kneecaps," Paul said.

Sirens wailed in the background. Wassail laughed. "You want to assault a political leader, *penguin*, go ahead. It sounds like your friends at NPPD are on their way."

Dozens of police cars skidded into the factory parking lot. Officers jumped out of their cars, pulling snowmen and bodyguards aside as they formed a perimeter around the mayor. Masterson approached.

"Thank goodness you are here, chief" Wassail said. "One of your detectives is becoming insubordinate, and these savages," he pointed to the snowmen, "have all attacked me. I think the Diamond Maker needs a few more residents."

"Yes it does," Masterson said, pulling out a set of handcuffs. He slammed them on the mayor's wrists. "Georg Wassail," the chief said, "you are under arrest for the murder of Santa Claus."

Both Paul and Mayor Wassail stared at the chief in disbelief. Frosty stood beside Masterson and smiled.

"Detective," Masterson said to Paul. "Why don't you take the mayor and throw his worthless butt into a squad car."

Still dumbfounded, Paul led the mayor to a car and shoved him in head-first. The mayor made no attempt to fight back.

"Paul," Masterson said, walking up to the penguin, "your family is okay."

"Are you sure?" Paul asked.

"Yes," Masterson said, "because I have just talked to my wife, who was abducted three days ago. She told me that your family is with her and that they are doing fine."

Paul sank to the ground, hands suddenly shaking. A surge of relief rushed through his body.

"That's … good to hear," he finally said.

Chapter Thirty-Five

Masterson looked tired and almost sad as they walked into the NPPD, even amid the loud cheers that erupted from the entire department. Someone popped a bottle of champagne in the back of the room. Masterson excused himself and went into his office, but before he could lock himself inside, Paul followed.

"I need to ask you something," Paul said.

"I'm sure you do," Masterson said. "You want to know why I suddenly changed sides an hour ago."

"I know it has to do with your family," Paul said, "and that Wassail had them just like he had mine. But …" he trailed off.

"Paul, I have made under-the-table deals with Mayor Wassail for years. Nothing illegal, nothing too shady, just a few I-scratch-your-back-you-scratch-my-back type of arrangements. That is how I got this position. To be honest, that is the way anybody gets my position.

"But that meant that Mayor Wassail considered me to be one of 'his men'. A stooge. So when he concocted this scheme to murder Santa Claus, he inevitably told me about it. In fact, he was counting on me to help him. I was his stooge, after all.

"I was not going to do that. I may be willing to associate with shady people to get ahead, but I was not going to participate in something illegal. Especially not a conspiracy to murder Santa Claus.

"But I knew that if I refused him, Wassail would become desperate and extremely dangerous. Not only did I know his plans, not only did I have the power to arrest him because of that knowledge, but his entire scheme depended on the assumption that I would manipulate the investigation and arrest somebody else. So I pretended to go along with him.

"But when I put you and Iceberg on the case, he realized that I wasn't really going to do what he wanted. So he abducted my family. And I knew that if I made one step out of line, they would be dead.

"I did my best to play both sides of the fence. I goaded you and Iceberg into conducting the investigation regardless of what I assigned you to do. Knowing your partner's personality, I set him up to dissociate from NPPD and do whatever he felt was necessary.

"Though," Masterson said, "breaking Miss Thompson out of prison was, admittedly, a bit of a surprise. I had not known of Wassail's intent to have someone break in and kill her. I assigned you to a minor case that went under the radar but allowed you to investigate the Santa murder at the same time. I hoarded evidence that would incriminate Wassail. But until I could guarantee my family's safety, I would not do anything to overtly cross Mayor Wassail.

"Just over an hour ago, I was able to make that guarantee. Iceberg, without even looking for it, discovered where Wassail was holding your family. Mine was there too. I was able to quietly send in a squad and get them to safety. Once that was done, I went to the factory with as many officers as I could bring to arrest the mayor. But you beat me to the punch. And the rest is history."

Paul sat quietly for a moment after Masterson finished explaining. "So, what's wrong?" Paul finally asked. "You wanted to protect your family, so now you act depressed."

"A little envious, Paul," Masterson said. "Because you and Iceberg, time and time again, demonstrated real courage. You took risks to do what was right. I did not. You and Iceberg have become one kind of man, and I have become another. My reward is position, prestige, and a nice salary. Yours is something different. I don't like to think about it too much, because I know who comes out ahead. And like I said, sometimes I envy you."

"So change," Paul said.

Masterson laughed. "No. I have chosen this life, and for better or for worse, I will live it. If I could go back, maybe I would have chosen a different route—maybe I would have listened to my training officer a bit more. But there's really no going back."

"Just for the record," Paul said, "I've always thought you were a heck of a chief—though these past three days had me wondering."

"And I've always thought you deserve a raise," Masterson said.

"I notice you didn't say that I get one, though," Paul pointed out.

"True," Masterson said. "But just this once I think I *will* give it to you. Now go find Iceberg. Last I saw him he was locked in holding cell three."

Paul sighed. "The case isn't over yet?"

"I have seen the exact same evidence you have. I know the only possible conclusion just as well as you do. Georg Wassail conspired to murder Santa Claus, and he hired Chad Tyler to do it. He framed Susie Thompson and was ready to do the same to Mrs. Claus. I want you and Johnny to tie up all the loose ends. This case *has* to be bulletproof. I don't want an arrest without a conviction."

Masterson smiled. "There won't be any disappearing evidence this time," he assured Paul. "Everything you have done has been cataloged and compiled for your access."

Paul stood up and opened the office door.

"And detective," Masterson said. "I would appreciate it if you didn't tell Iceberg about your raise."

❄   ❄   ❄

"So, now what do we do?" Johnny asked Paul.

They sat in holding cell three, piles of evidence sitting on the table, and no idea where to begin.

Paul blew out a long breath. "I don't know."

"Have you seen Allison yet?" Johnny asked.

"Yeah," Paul said. "Masterson took me to see them right after

241

the fight at the factory."

"You okay?"

"I don't know. I *really* don't like that they got pushed into all this. When I entered the academy, I chose to take the risks. They never chose. They just had them thrown at them without anyone asking.

"There were a few times today that I was sure I wasn't going to see them again. Especially when I went to the factory and saw that I had no chance to get Wassail by myself. I was sure I was going to be killed, and that Allison and the kids would soon follow."

Johnny laughed, breaking the tension. "I still can't believe you took on *fifteen* of Wassail's bodyguards by yourself."

"I didn't even have time to think about it," Paul said. "I was just there, letting Wassail have it, and then suddenly I counted them and there was nothing I could do."

"Thank goodness for the snowmen, huh?" Johnny said.

"And the elves," Paul added.

They both took a deep breath and looked at the evidence on the table again. Neither of them wanted to look through it.

The door of the holding cell opened. Sara, her hair still blonde, walked in and did her best to ignore the two detectives' bewildered stares.

"Blonde?" Johnny asked.

"Do you like it?" Sara asked.

"Uh … it's … great," Johnny said.

"It looks terrible," said Paul.

"I know," Sara sat down. "You don't have to lie, Johnny."

"Okay," Johnny said. "It's hideous."

"It got me something I needed to know," she said. "But first, congratulations to both of you. Thanks to you two we now have no mayor and nobody to run Christmas."

"Right," Johnny said. "I'm sure that Mrs. Claus is just about ready to take over."

"And I think we can last a week or two without a mayor," Paul added. "But we still have to take care of all the holes in the case."

"I thought it was solved," Sara said.

"I can't get past some things," Paul said. "Chad Tyler says that somebody else got to Santa first. I know it's crazy, and I have no reason to believe him, but I can't stop wondering if it's the truth. He has full immunity. Why would he keep on denying that he did it?"

"You should have pressed him harder," Johnny said.

"Wow, Johnny," Paul said sarcastically. "Thanks for the amazing advice. That fixes everything."

"Anytime," Johnny smirked. He became suddenly thoughtful. "How big is this Chad Tyler?"

"Depends on who you're comparing him to," Paul said.

"Compared to Santa," Johnny said.

"Chad's a scrawny little mutt compared to Santa," Paul said. "That's the other thing. I can't completely buy that Chad could physically do it. If Santa had been shot, then fine. But we're supposed to convince a jury that this kid was able to beat Santa to death with a sack of coal?" Paul shook his head. "I don't know. On one hand, I know the case is solved. On the other, something's just not quite right."

"I don't know if this is the right time to bring this up," Sara interrupted, "but Santa's body is missing."

"What?" Johnny and Paul asked at the same time.

"This morning it went missing from the lab. I did this to my hair and bought some ridiculous clothes, posed as Mrs. Claus, and went to the mortuary. It wasn't there. They had records of it in their computer, but no body in the building."

"So … they have a closed casket funeral?" Johnny said.

"I don't know," Sara said. "I don't think anyone has told Mrs. Claus yet."

"I think somebody should probably tell her about this tomorrow," Johnny said.

"Tomorrow's Christmas," Paul said.

"Then the day after."

"That's Boxing Day," Sara said.

"What's Boxing Day?" Paul asked.

"It's … just a Canadian thing," she said. "I was trying to be funny," she explained.

"Oh," Johnny and Paul said together.

"We'll tell her about it the day after Christmas," Sara said. "Unless we can find it before then."

"I bet Wassail knows where it is," Paul said. "We'll add that to the list of things we need to talk to him about."

"So do you believe this kid the mayor hired?" Sara asked, changing the subject.

"I don't know," Paul said.

"The problem is if he really did it, there would have to be some sign of a struggle at the murder scene," Johnny said. "We never got to see the scene. It was messed up when we got there. But we do have three separate accounts that say there was nothing there except a single set of tracks to the body."

"Whose accounts?" Sara asked.

"That's another problem," Johnny said. "Chad's, Mitchell's, and the report from the first officers on the scene. There's not a single one that is really very trustworthy."

Paul suddenly sat straight up, his eyes alert. "We have one other account," he said.

"*The Northern Lights* photo," Sara said.

"What?" Johnny asked.

"Remember that punk photographer I smacked around at the crime scene?" Paul asked. Johnny nodded. "He took a picture of Santa's hat at the scene, maybe a hundred feet from the body."

"There wasn't a hat at the scene," Johnny said.

"The photographer stole it," Paul said, "but that's not the point. The point is the picture shows the exact same thing—nothing around but completely untouched snow."

"Was the photo doctored?" Johnny asked.

"The photographer said it wasn't," Paul said. "I've got the files on my computer, and as far as I can tell he's telling the truth."

"So we have four sources that say the same thing," Johnny said.

Paul groaned. "But now it *really* doesn't make sense. The only people who don't leave footprints are the snowmen, and we know they didn't do it."

"So there's got to be some other explanation," Sara said.

"Like what?" Paul asked, irritated with the ongoing debates. "Did he just fall out of the sky?"

The question hung in the air.

"As if he was flying on a reindeer and fell to the ground," Johnny said.

"If it happened from a great height," Sara added, "it would cause massive bruising, internal hemorrhaging, and multiple fractures."

"And add to that a severe post-mortem thrashing from Chad and his sack of coal," Paul said.

"Do you know what?" Johnny asked. "Everyone I've talked to has told me the exact same thing about Dasher. They don't trust him. He seems to have his own agenda. He's secretive. He keeps running errands that nobody knows about."

"So does anybody know where he was on December twenty-second at four a.m.?" Paul asked.

Chapter Thirty-Six

Mrs. Claus stepped into Susie's hut, where the girl was trying to master the technique of a traditional snowman drum. White-Out, one of the snowmen about her age, was doing his best to teach her, but Susie insisted on doing it her own way. Then she would get frustrated and refuse to try again.

"It takes patience and practice to learn," White-out said.

"Of course it does," Susie said. "Everything about snowmen takes patience and practice."

"It's part of who we are," White-Out said.

"Well, part of being an American," Susie said, "is demanding instant gratification. That's part of who *we* are."

"Of course," White-out said. He looked at his body, which was developing a thin layer of water. "I'm afraid that I must go back outside. There's only so much heat we can take."

Susie nodded. "Bye," she said.

"Bye," the snowman said.

Susie looked at Mrs. Claus, not as a bimbo or a sleazy blonde, but just as a person. A kind person.

"Frosty is back," Mrs. Claus said. "Mayor Wassail has been arrested, and Johnny's been cleared of all charges."

"So we go back now?"

"Yes."

Susie stood up.

"Do you think they'll let me keep the drum?" Susie asked.

"You can ask."

Mrs. Claus led Susie back outside, where Frosty was waiting for them. He stood next to a giant bobsled that sparked with the same odd electric pulse the snowman spears had. Six or seven snowmen were waiting inside.

"So what happens now?" Susie asked.

"The Village Council is conducting another special session," Mrs. Claus said. "They'll reinstate me as Head of Christmas and probably decide on when to hold elections to replace Mayor Wassail."

"What about me?"

"Tonight, Miss Thompson," Frosty said, "you will fly home to Colorado."

"Okay," Susie said. She was somewhat surprised, but she really was okay—okay with what had happened at the North Pole, okay with Santa, okay with her family, and even okay that her sister was gone.

Mrs. Claus lifted Susie up to the bobsled and then climbed in herself. Frosty glided in, and the driver prepared to set off.

Susie suddenly turned to Frosty.

"Why do you keep calling me 'Miss Thompson'? My name is Susie."

"Out of respect," Frosty said. "You see, the rest of the world may pay little attention to you, and it will certainly pay little attention to the North Pole—aside from a few days in December each year, of course.

"But to us, you are very significant. Perhaps the most important person to have ever lived since Nicholas Claus first came and started his Christmas dream. In all the time since then, nearly six hundred years, very little has changed up here. Your letter and your visit have changed everything.

"And for that, we will honor your name forever."

❄ ❄ ❄

Johnny and Paul stood outside the interrogation room, watching Dasher talk to his lawyer, an arctic hare, from behind the one-way mirror.

"Do you really think we can pin this on Dasher?" Paul asked. "We have nothing hard against him. Just a bit of circumstantial evidence and a hunch. We don't even have a decent motive."

"I know," Johnny said. "But it's our only shot right now. We have to act like we have something against him, and we aren't going to back down."

"So why'd he do it?" Paul asked.

"I don't know. Built up resentment for Rudolph and his magic nose."

"I guess," Paul said. "Let's do this."

Paul opened the door and the two of them walked in. Dasher and his lawyer, their faces hard and unreadable, watched the detectives enter. Johnny sat down, and Paul continued to stand.

"All right, Dasher, how are we going to do this?" Johnny asked, "Are you going to tell us anything, or are you just going to hide behind your lawyer?"

"There's no need for personal insults, Mr. Iceberg," the lawyer said.

Johnny ignored him. "Let me just paint a picture for you here, Dasher. You tell me if I'm right or wrong.

"You're the head of the team. The real leader. You're the animals' representative on the Village Council. By all accounts, you may be the most accomplished and respected reindeer in the history of the North Pole, and now you're ready to retire and spend your last years enjoying your legacy.

"Only there is no legacy. Just a giant monument to Rudolph, a freak with a red nose. Only songs about Rudolph, an immature wannabe who commands no respect from his peers. Only notice of Rudolph, a nobody who Santa Claus happened to place at the front of the team one winter because it was foggy.

"You would like to get rid of the strawberry-nosed freak, but you can't. If you make him a martyr, his renown will only eclipse yours all the more.

"Then you get wind of the mayor's plot. He wants to kill Santa and take over, and here's your chance. Because without Santa's support, Rudolph will be gone. Nobody else on the team wants him anyway. Within five years, he'll be a hopeless outcast again—ignored and forgotten by the world for the rest of his life.

"So you do it. You take Santa for a ride, fly high in the air, and drop him. You know all the evidence points to Mayor Wassail, and you let the police follow it right to him. You know Mrs. Claus is sympathetic to Rudolph, so you persuade her to run away. With Mrs. Claus gone and Wassail in prison, there's only one logical person to take over Christmas. You. Frosty would melt down the first chimney, and Morgan couldn't see over the front of the sleigh. You know all the routes forward and backward. So you take over, and your legacy will be, aside from Nicholas Claus, the greatest in North Pole history."

"Is that how it went, Dasher?" Paul asked.

"You don't have to answer that," the lawyer told the reindeer.

"Nobody asked you anything," Paul told the lawyer.

"This is absolutely outrageous," the lawyer said.

"Hold on," Dasher said. "I have nothing to hide."

"Great!" Johnny said. "Bare your soul."

"Give them my medical records," Dasher said.

"You don't have to do that," the lawyer said. "They have nothing on you."

"Give them the records," Dasher said.

The hare pulled a set of papers from Forestview Veterinary Clinic. Paul inspected the papers.

"A pulled hamstring?" Paul asked.

"What?" Johnny asked.

"That's right," Dasher said. "A pulled hammy. I'm not as young as I used to be."

"So what?" Johnny said.

"Oh for crying out loud, Johnny," Paul said. "Will you actually read a report for once in your life? He was hospitalized on the night of the twenty-first. Admitted 9:16 p.m. Discharged 9:15 a.m. the next day."

"Hospitalized for a strained hamstring?" Johnny asked skeptically.

"I'm sorry if I sound rude," Dasher said, "but you have absolutely no idea how hard the Christmas flight is on a reindeer's body. Especially an old one, like me. I needed rest, medication, physical therapy, and constant monitoring. Santa—or Mrs. Claus now—cannot afford to have a reindeer's body fall apart mid-flight. They had to monitor me every half hour for the entire night in order to clear me for the flight.

"I couldn't possibly have been involved," Dasher said.

"I understand there is already a suspect being charged with Santa's murder," the lawyer said. "Why don't you two do some real police work and hope my client doesn't sue you over this frivolous interrogation—"

"Cornelius," Dasher cut off his lawyer, "calm down. It's okay." He turned back to Johnny and Paul. "Listen, detectives. Just like everybody in the North Pole probably has, I have been thinking about nothing but the murder for the past three days. I haven't been able to think of any explanation for what you found at the crime scene. Until now. A fall from the sky fits."

"It's the only thing that fits," Paul said.

"There are only nine individuals who could have done this. We all know who those nine are. Just find a motive that makes sense. Until the murder there was only one thing on any of the reindeer's minds: the change. That's what prompted Mayor Wassail to act. What if it prompted one of the reindeer to act as well?"

"All of you knew about the change?" Paul asked. "Not just you, Dasher, but all nine of the reindeer?"

"Yes," Dasher said. "Like I told your partner yesterday, Santa told the reindeer about it when he first proposed it to the Village Council."

"That's not what Rudolph told me," Paul said. "He said he had heard something about it but didn't really know anything."

"He lied," Dasher said. "Rudolph was the one who was so upset by the idea that he stormed out of the meeting."

"Why?"

"You already explained it when you told me your little story. Without the Christmas flight, Rudolph has nothing. He has no respect among his peers. He's a pathetic little creature, always craving renown, but incapable of achieving it. If Christmas changes, that monument disappears because everyone will learn that it was just a freak genetic mutation that saved Christmas, not him."

Johnny motioned for Paul to meet him outside the room.

"Paul, check up on Dasher's story with the clinic, make sure it's true."

"And if it is?"

"I think we may have called in the wrong reindeer."

CHAPTER THIRTY-SEVEN

FROSTY AND Morgan, from the top of the tower in True North Plaza, went through the procedures to declare themselves a complete quorum. Their only order of business was to reinstate the Claus Monarchy as the rightful proprietor of the Christmas Foundation.

Thousands of humans, elves, snowmen, and animals, all of whom had braved the fog and flurries of an approaching storm, applauded.

Mrs. Claus was brought forth, and Frosty swore her in.

"Amber Claus," Frosty said in a booming voice, "I do hereby declare you Head Claus and overseer of Christmas. May you always discern between Naughty and Nice."

An enormous roar of cheers and applause thundered from the crowd. Mrs. Claus motioned for quiet.

"There will be time for speeches, for memories, and for the future another day," Mrs. Claus said. "For now, I simply wish to say this: you were all kind to my late husband, and he was a good man. You have honored his memory by continuing the preparations for Christmas without him. Thank you.

"And now," she said with an emphatic pause, "we need to get this flight underway."

Cheers rose again, but they quickly died down as the crowd noticed several police officers moving through the crowd and toward the tower. The storm worsened. Mrs. Claus walked out of the bottom of the tower, but the officers stopped her before she reached the sleigh. They said something to her, but nobody could tell what. Mrs. Claus suddenly buried her head into her arms and turned away.

The officers surrounded the sleigh and closed in. The reindeer started mulling around until Rudolph, his nose brightly glowing, was suddenly detached from the sleigh and started running away. He tried to take off, but several officers grabbed his legs and wrestled him to the ground. After cuffing the reindeer's legs, the officers led him to a patrol car and drove away.

All the while, the storm worsened. Soon some people started leaving the plaza, followed by more and more. Finally, as the time for launch had long since passed, the flight security escorted the reindeer back to the training grounds and the last stragglers of the once-exultant crowd disappeared into the fog and ice and snow.

For the first time since Rudolph had become a member of the reindeer team, there would be no Christmas flight.

❆   ❆   ❆

"You know why we're here," Johnny told Rudolph, who was handcuffed and alone in the holding cell. "Care to tell the whole story?"

"There's nothing to tell," Rudolph said. "Santa wanted to change how Christmas operated, and the reindeer team would no longer be a part of it."

"So you killed him?" Paul asked.

"You don't understand. I have nothing without this. *Nothing!* Who am I if not the front of the team? I have no friends, no family, nothing.

"I never wanted to kill him," he continued. "I took him for that flight that night hoping I could just get him to change his mind. But it didn't work. All he could think about was the little girl. He went on and on about what he wanted to accomplish with the change,

253

and I just couldn't stand it anymore. So I bucked him off, and that was it.

"I was just trying to save Christmas. I just … wanted to still be a part of it."

"But you won't," Johnny said.

Rudolph shook his head.

Johnny and Paul walked to the door.

"Goodbye, Rudolph," Johnny said as he opened the door.

"Goodbye," was the weak reply.

Paul and Johnny left the reindeer alone.

"Well," Paul said sadly, "case solved."

"Yeah," said Johnny.

"You know, when I was at the factory earlier today," Paul said, "and the snowmen came and the elves joined in and Masterson finally cuffed Wassail—it was a triumph. We had finally gotten him. The treachery would end, our families would be okay, Christmas would be okay, and it was great. And then when Masterson and I walked in the station, there were cheers."

Paul paused sadly. "But there's none of that now."

"I know," Johnny said. "It's Rudolph. He's not a bad guy. He didn't want a bad thing—just the chance to be a hero a little bit longer. But he did what he did, and all that's left is a very, very sad and pathetic reindeer."

Paul nodded.

"Did you hear they cancelled the flight?" Johnny asked.

"Yeah. It was what—just the third time in the past two hundred years they had to cancel it?"

"Something like that," Johnny said. "They needed him to be a hero tonight."

They silently walked down the hall toward their desks. The station was nearly empty. Except for Paul and Johnny nearly everyone had already taken off for the holiday.

"You have plans for Christmas, Johnny?"

"No," Johnny shrugged his shoulders. "Nothing in particular."

"You're welcome to come over to our place," Paul said. "Allison and the kids always like to see you. And they really owe you one for today," Paul said, remembering who had found them. "There won't be as many toys this year, obviously, but we'll still have a nice dinner."

"I'll have to think about it," Johnny said.

"Okay."

"Paul, would you like to go home now?"

"Today of all days, yes," Paul said. "But I can't. The paperwork on this case is going to be like a novel. We have to charge Rudolph, itemize everything we're prosecuting Wassail for, start the witness protection process for Chad Tyler, though I don't think he'll need it now—"

"Go home, Paul," Johnny cut his partner off. "I'll take care of the paperwork this time."

Paul laughed and rolled his eyes. "Right. Do you even know how to do it?"

"I've done some before," Johnny said, feeling defensive.

"When?"

"Six or seven years ago," he said. "Look, who cares how pretty it is? Once it's off my desk then it's Masterson's problem."

"Are you sure?" Paul asked.

"I'm sure. Merry Christmas, Paul."

"Merry Christmas yourself, Johnny."

CHAPTER THIRTY-EIGHT

JOHNNY STOOD next to Mrs. Claus at the terminal while Steve, as Johnny had promised, had his exclusive interview with Susie.

"Are you going to be okay?" Johnny asked Mrs. Claus.

"It'll be a lonely, disappointing night, but yes," she said. "I'm having my first meeting with Dasher, Frosty, and Morgan the day after Christmas. We'll be going over preliminary plans about what Christmas is going to become and how we're going to get there. I'm looking forward to that."

"When will you start announcing plans?"

"Probably not for several months. Though, I may be willing to let you and your partner in on a secret or two. We all owe you a whole lot."

"We couldn't save this Christmas, though," Johnny said.

"No," Mrs. Claus said, "but there will be many, many others, and they will be very good ones."

Steve stood up from the airport chair and shook Susie's hand. The cameraman packed up his equipment.

"Well, Johnny," Steve said as he left. "You were right about that one: story of the decade. I don't care about anything I've done for you in the past. I owe you for this one. I may owe you for the rest of my life for this one."

"I'll make sure I keep that in mind," Johnny said. Susie stood up from her chair and stood next to Johnny, watching the reporter and cameraman disappear down the concourse. From the gate, the flight attendant announced that the plane was now boarding.

"You have a safe flight home," Johnny said, kneeling down and handing Susie her bag.

"I will, Mr. Iceberg."

"I told you, it's Johnny."

"Of course," Susie smiled. "Thank you. For rescuing me and— and for everything."

"You're welcome."

"Do you know what's funny?" Susie asked. "After everything that happened, I think I believe in Santa Claus again."

She threw her arms around Johnny's neck. After a moment, Johnny realized that maybe he should hug her back. He did.

Susie let go and looked Johnny straight in the eye, a very happy smile on her face.

"Do you remember something you said to me?" she asked.

"I said a lot of things," Johnny said.

"It was right after we broke out of prison and you made me drive the car. You said that 'we were going to be okay.' Well do you know what? You were right. We're going to be okay."

Susie looked up at Mrs. Claus.

"I'm ready to go home now."

Mrs. Claus also knelt down and hugged the girl.

"Thank you for coming, Susie," Mrs. Claus said. "Christmas is going to be better for everyone because you wrote my husband a letter.

"I know we did not start on the best of terms," Mrs. Claus continued, "but you will always be welcome here. I promise to keep the cops out of my home next time."

Susie smiled, "That one's okay though," she said pointing to Johnny.

"One last thing, Susie," Mrs. Claus said. "While I may not be able to deliver presents to children across the world this Christmas Eve, I can at least deliver one to you."

Mrs. Claus reached into her coat and pulled out a paper that was rolled up and tied with a red string.

Susie looked at it curiously. "What's this?"

"It's a scholarship," Mrs. Claus said. "I set it up in honor of my husband. Once you get out of high school, it will pay for all of your schooling, all the way through med school."

"Med school?"

"Or a master's in family therapy, or a masters of social work, or whatever it is you choose to do. And as soon as you're done, there'll be a job waiting for you up here."

"You're really changing Christmas?" Susie said excitedly.

"Yes. It will take time, and we don't really know how it will work yet, but we are going to do it. But don't expect the toys to stop completely."

Susie nodded. "Sometimes a toy is just what a kid needs," she said, remembering the prison guard.

"Exactly," Mrs. Claus said. "I do hope that one day you will come back—and not just to visit. We'll need a lot of smart people to make this new Christmas work. I hope one of them will be you."

Susie stood there for a moment, looking at Mrs. Claus and Johnny.

"Your flight is boarding," Johnny said. "You don't want to miss it."

"No, I don't," Susie said. She walked through the gate, turning once to wave goodbye, and then disappeared through the tunnel.

❋   ❋   ❋

Johnny picked up the phone that sat next to his ugly sofa and began dialing. He was not sure why or what he would say if she picked up, but he continued dialing anyway. The phone began to ring.

"Hello?"

"Hello, Sara?"

"Johnny? Well this is a bit of a surprise."

"Yeah … uh, thanks for everything."

"About the case? You're welcome," Sara paused for a moment.

"So, I guess I'll see you at work next week."

"Wait," Johnny said. "I–I didn't call to say 'see you at work.'"

There was a long silence. "I'm listening," Sara said.

"I was wondering—" Johnny had a hard time actually saying it. "I was wondering what you were doing for Christmas tomorrow."

"Me? Not a whole lot. I'll probably sleep in a bit. Call my mom in Edmonton sometime. How about you?"

"About the same, I guess. Except for calling my mom." Johnny's mouth was uncomfortably dry. "Actually, I was wondering, if you have some time, if you would like—"

"Yes," Sara said. "I would thoroughly enjoy seeing you tomorrow. Your place or mine?"

Johnny looked at his apartment, suddenly very embarrassed. He couldn't think of any way to cover the hole in the wall by tomorrow. Besides, he only had some leftover pizza and a couple corn dogs in his refrigerator.

"Actually," Johnny said, "it would probably be a whole lot better if I came over there."

"You don't even know what it's like over here," Sara said.

"I don't really need to," Johnny said.

"Fine. Come over at one."

"Great. See you then."

Sara hung up the phone. After a moment Johnny did as well. *That wasn't so bad*, he thought.

He pulled out his daughter's phone number from a drawer and started dialing. Before he had finished, though, he set the phone back down. Once again, he did not know what to say after nine years of no contact with her.

He lay down on the couch and pulled the sheet over him. The radio was playing "Stille Nacht." Even though his mind was racing, within a few minutes he was asleep.

DECEMBER 25

CHRISTMAS DAY

CHAPTER THIRTY-NINE

JOHNNY WOKE up with a kink in his neck. *Maybe I should buy real bed*, he thought as he looked at the ugly sofa he had been sleeping on for the past six or seven years.

Susie would be home by now. After everything she had gone through, Johnny felt a bit sad thinking about what she was going home to. Her parents would still be on the brink of divorce, and her sister would still be gone.

But she had seemed happy last night—even knowing her situation at home. Maybe it had been enough to know that she was helping the world become just a bit better. Maybe it was because she believed in Santa Claus again.

As he brewed a pot of coffee, Johnny looked around his apartment. There were no presents. There was no tree. There was still a hole in the drywall.

He shrugged. He was used to it—besides that hole in the wall. But it made him think about kids waking up around the world. They would be discovering the same thing. No presents. Despite everything, he couldn't keep out a nagging sense of failure.

Once the coffee was finished, Johnny sat down and wondered what he was going to do until he went to Sara's house. He couldn't think of anything.

He glanced at his laptop, still sitting on the kitchen table, and something caught his attention. New email.

It was a message from Super Fun Girl 2271. The subject was "*Thank you, Dad.*"

With shaking hands Johnny opened the message:

> *Dad,*
>
> *I've tried writing this email for the past two hours, but I never know quite what to say. It's been so long since I've seen the North Pole, and it's been so long since I've heard from you, but yes, I'll take the plane ticket and come.*
>
> *I've wanted to call you for a long time. Mom has tried to convince me to for even longer, but I couldn't do it. I was afraid that you didn't care anymore.*
>
> *But I guess you do, or else you wouldn't have sent the plane ticket. Mom always told me that you had a hard time connecting with people and with making the first move. I kind of remember that about you, too. So I guess this was hard for you. And I guess I can do hard things too.*
>
> *I'll see you for New Year's. Honestly, I'm so sad neither of us tried to contact each other in all this time, but I'm so excited and kind of nervous that I don't know what to think. But I'll figure it out by the time I get there. And then I'll tell you what's on my mind.*
>
> *Emily*

For the first time in years, tears welled up in his eyes. He had given Emily such a rotten life—*what kind of a father doesn't contact his daughter for nine years?* But she was coming. He couldn't believe it. He was actually going to be able to see and talk to his daughter again. He wondered what she looked like now that she was a grown woman.

But how had this happened? He had certainly never sent any plane tickets. As if prompted by his confusion a second email popped up.

Mr. Iceberg,
Your order #78896332 has been processed. Itinerary for Miss Emily Iceberg:
Flight 677—Departure: Paris, France, December 28, 4:03 PM. Arrival: North Pole December 28, 9:47 PM. Flight 80112—Departure: North Pole January 2, 7:19 AM. Arrival: Paris, France, January 2, 4:20 PM.
Thank you for choosing North Pole Airlines.

Johnny looked up from the computer. According to the message, the tickets had been purchased yesterday, though no method of payment was specified.

Just then a sealed envelope was pushed through his mail slot. *Since when does mail get delivered on Christmas Day?* He hurried to the door and opened it, but there was nobody in the hall. Inside the envelope was a simple note:

You're welcome,

SC

ABOUT THE AUTHOR

JASON TWEDE graduated with his Bachelor's of Arts in Sociology from Weber State University in Ogden, Utah and with his Juris Doctor from Thomas M. Cooley Law School in Lansing, Michigan.